GW01185562

Eagles Hunt Wolves

Eva Molenaar: Wartime Agent Book 5

by

Robert Craven

Cover Design
Robert Craven – image courtesy of Creative Commons ©2019

In memory of Shannon Ware; aka, Xiamara

Friend, author and designer

1962 - 2018

Robert Craven:

The wartime adventures of Eva Molenaar:

Get Lenin

Zinnman

A finger of night

Hollow Point

Steampunk:

The Mandarin Cipher: A Wentworth & Devereux adventure

Holt:

The Road of a Thousand Tigers

My heartfelt thanks to:

Dr. Yossi Elran, the Weizmann Institute of Science, Israel, for answering my enquiries on codes.

Derek Suffling for the impossible task of proofing, suggesting and editing.

Daniel Scott-Davies of The Spitfire Society UK.

"In wartime, truth is so precious that she should always be attended by a bodyguard of lies."

Winston Churchill.

"Wars begin when you will, but they do not end when you please."

Machiavelli.

The U.S.S.R. / 68° 18m N, 161° 38m E

1946

It was a land of ghosts. Three hundred thousand prisoners; Germans, Romanians, Spanish, Italian and Russian Cossacks forced-marched to this desolate hinterland. Those who died from exposure and dysentery were left unburied where they fell. Those who survived were ordered to dig. They tunneled deep with picks, shovels and, at times, their bare hands. Then the engineering divisions arrived with heavy equipment and dynamite. The hard earth morphed into this implausible facility, a thousand miles from the East Siberian Sea and four days travel by aircraft from the 'New Life' collective farms near the town of Anyuysk.

Kommandarm Marko Kravchenko was used to ghosts. His wife Sonja and son Oleg inhabited the nether world of his peripheral vision. He accepted their presence, neither seeking it nor longing for it. They were the albatross around his neck, a fitting punishment from Stalin for his failings as a model Soviet soldier. This far north played tricks with the senses. The mind seemed to over-wind itself to the point where anything and everything appeared real.

Including the ghosts of a wife and son.

Shielding his eyes with a heavy glove, Kravchenko panned the horizon, seeking an image to match the distant drone of engines. An aircraft lumbered towards him. Perhaps it was another arctic mirage.

In the air, Valery Yvetchenko, Commissar first rank of the NKGB dozed, the only passenger in the frigid Lisunov transport plane.

A ream of dossiers on his diplomatic pouch was topped by a scrawled directive in red crayon, from the fist of Stalin himself. Margined with little pen doodles of wolves, it instructed him to take the first available flight to Anyuysk and travel from there. A ministry car had whisked Yvetcheno from his warm, comfortable dacha on the outskirts of Moscow to a freezing airport and a long series of turbulent flights to this desolate backwater where the point of a compass meant nothing.

"Secret protocols, a disinformation stratagem...nothing too complicated, Comrade."

In his sleep deprived state, Yvetchenko cast his mind back over the events that had brought him to this godforsaken place; all the way back to the Berlin of nineteen thirty-nine, a city with the eyes of the world upon it. The neon, the all-night-cabarets and the diplomatic whirl of impending war gave the city an irresistible allure. As an advisor to Marshall Shaponishkov he´d enjoyed a coffee and a potent schnapps along the Tiergartenstrasse. He´d leafed through the typed Cyrillic and leaden German typefaces with the ink barely dried on them. The warm August afternoon sunshine dappled the pages through the verdant shade.

"Keep the variables narrow, to avoid exposure," said Shaponishkov.

"Molotov – Ribbentrop pact?" replied Yvetchenko.

"Stalin has tasked you with forging the salient points on the supporting documents. We will pressure the governments of the Baltic into aligning themselves with the Soviet Union," said Shaponishkov.

A second coffee came accompanied by a fine French cognac.

"You'll be in Lithuania in a fortnight, Comrade Yvetchenko..."

The Berlin Yvetchenko returned to six years later was a necropolis; a smouldering grey moonscape, devoid of any light. Templehof; the flight hub for the new Russian sector, nothing more than an imposing ruin.
The man who met him at the steps of his plane then – Kommandarm Marko Kravchenko – was the same man waiting for him on the frozen steppe today. An armed escort had swept

them both through the devastation to the Reichsbunker where the Hammer and Sickle had replaced the swastika; another red flag for the nation to absorb.

But that was a year ago...

TEXT CORRESPONDENCE / SCIENTIFIC FINDINGS AUGUST 1945:

ARTICLE IV (Continued):

> Under the Reichskanzlerei, seven, forty-kilowatt-generators were discovered; all had been destroyed. The chamber had been booby-trapped. Two sappers were killed defusing the remaining explosives. The walls of the chamber itself are extremely dense; twenty-six feet thick. The metal is of Japanese manufacture; twice as strong as battleship armour.

"*...Secret protocols, disinformation stratagems ...*"

He was snapped out of his reverie by a shout from the cockpit.

"We've only five, possibly six hours of daylight, Commissar. We're putting this thing down – now."

Yvetchenko gathered up the dossier and craned his neck to look through the window as the plane began its final descent. Battered by arctic winds, the aircraft made a gut-wrenching lurch toward the makeshift airstrip scalped from the tundra. Below, an immense fire billowed across the land, casting a long, lingering shadow in the midnight sun.

Rising, Yvetchenko felt his knees grind and his spine untwist. He nodded his thanks to the flight crew and descended the rickety steps where Kravchenko was waiting.

Dressed in heavy winter fatigues, Kravchenko still found it necessary to wear an impressive platter-sized peak cap. He held it firmly down with one hand as it skittered in the Lisunov's downdraft.

"Welcome to our research facility, Comrade Commissar Yvetchenko. I am honoured. Good flight?"

"Delightful, Kommandarm Kravchenko. Simply delightful."

Shouting to be heard over the howling winds, he sensed the first needle pricks of frostbite on his lips. He eyed the sled with its prancing, wrestling snow dogs; he'd hoped for a military half-track with a heater, something less feral.

"It's the best way to traverse this region, Comrade Commissar," said Kravchenko, sensing his unease.

Marko Kravchenko was now Komandarm for the Secretariat for People's Affairs – the MGB. Behind his back, his nickname was *Lazarus*; he had cheated death three times during The Great Patriotic War.

From the icy canvas folds of the sled, Kravchenko produced a heavy reindeer-skin coat and woollen hat. He handed them to Yvetchenko. Once Yvetchenko was bundled up, Kravchenko donned his own thick fur hat. The sled driver, embalmed in native furs, manipulated the team of dogs with a series of whistles and shouts. The sled sluiced across the tundra under the power of their sturdy legs.

The fire that darkened the sky drew closer to them. It was a pyre. Stacks of frozen corpses in flimsy prison fatigues lay in rows as Russian soldiers fed the blaze. The fire spewed thick, meaty smoke across the oblast.

"Disposal team, Commissar," said Kravchenko, "They're using aviation fuel to keep it going."

"And for girding themselves, I see," said Yvetchenko.

Some of the soldiers staggered about in the perpetual arctic daylight. One or two fired occasional shots into the pyre, the memory muscle of their fingers fixed on the triggers of their machine guns.

"Beria was insistent, Comrade Commissar. On completion of the underground facility, the labourers were to be liquidated."

The hiss of flamethrowers and the smell of roasted flesh assailed him. He stared at the sun gliding along the horizon, its baleful, orange glare casting solemn judgement.

The sled passed the pyre and slalomed away towards a small dome that rose from the ground. Behind it in the weak midday sun, the land was dotted with nomad tepees, bivouacs and crudely fashioned reindeer corrals.

"Kagonovich has found something interesting, Comrade Commissar," said Kravchenko.

"Everything Kagonovich finds is interesting," said Yvetchenko.

"This really is, Comrade Commissar," insisted Kravchenko.

"I was to be contacted only when you had *results.*"

"We have results. Trust me, we have results."

Outside the entrance, sheltered in the lee of the doorway, stood a man draped in an oversized fur-collared trench coat. His head sported a crazy shock of black pomaded hair, shaved at the sides, a polar seneschal with a clipboard and earnest blue eyes.

"Comrade Commissar, Yvetchenko, welcome," he said.

"Comrade Scientist Kagonovich," replied Yvetchenko.

"Good flight, I trust? If you will follow me."

Kagonovich walked with the assurance of a man above politics. They descended into the facility.

"The interrogations – have they yielded anything?" asked Yvetchenko.

"Nothing of any importance, Comrade Commissar."

Yvetchenko noted his MGB subordinate was deliberately keeping his voice level.

Kagonovich produced a small packet of cigarettes, Russian front-line weed, an acquired taste. Yvetchenko and Kravchenko took a light from Kagonovich's lighter. It was silver with an eagle and swastika.

"Spoils of war," said the scientist.

Their boots echoed along the warren of sodium lit corridors. Comrade scientist Vasily Kagonovich wasn't one for celebration, but this morning was an exception. Thousands of man hours and round-the-clock toil in hazardous conditions had finally borne fruit. The chamber – embedded under the deep, unforgiving permafrost – had been completed. As an archaeologist assembles a few ancient, strewn bones, Kagonovich's team had re-built the chamber discovered beneath the Berlin bunker.

"We understood the basic shape, it had been a case of just trying to make the pieces fit."
Kagonovich's bulb-like head bobbed between shadow and light. Immense generators several floors below, vibrated through the prediluvian bedrock, giving the metal floor the sensation of a moving ship.

"The barracks are situated at the rear along with the construction billets. The indigenous nomads live above. This section is completely off limits. Top secret," said Kagonovich.

"Under my orders, the Reichsbunker was stripped down and shipped to here, Comrade Commissar, Yevetchenko," said Kravchenko.

"Everything, right down to the fuse wires, Comrade Commissar," echoed Kagonovich.

"And the remains found outside in the pit there?" asked Yvetchenko.

"Rumoured to be Hitler's, we sent them to Moscow," said Kagonovich.
Yvetchenko had heard all the myths. Stalin was obsessed.

"So, Comrade Scientist Kagonovich, Kommandarm Kravchenko – what is so important?" asked Yvetchenko.

"The barometers started to glow two days ago, and haven't diminished since," said Kagonovich. His glasses, fashioned in Western tortoise shell, masked his bloodless lab-rat eyes.
At the end of the corridor, they came to a thick metallic door. Standing sentinel were two armed guards. They saluted and pulled the door aside.
The atmosphere in the room beyond was palpable. Rows of desks and monitoring equipment were manned by grim-faced scientists and technicians, all men. They stared at their equipment is if everything was toxic to the touch.

"The clocks begun whirling like windmills an hour ago," said a technician. The name card on his desk read *Kornilov*. His skin was blanched like the rest of them from bad food, cigarettes and living in a subterranean complex. Another press-ganged minion of the revolution. He lit a cigarette.

At the end of the room was a thick metallic pressure door with a wheel lock. It was open.

"This is really something to behold, Comrades!" said Kagonovich.

Inside stood two of Kagonovich's colleagues with clip boards and two film cameras on tripods.

Yvetchenko looked at the dials and gauges along a paneled workstation. All were twitching out of synch in a St Vitus's dance.

"Did the krauts leave anything by way of paperwork? Notes?"

"No. All burned in the pit," replied Kagonovich.

Yvetchenko removed his calf-skin gloves and ran a thick uneven finger along the control panels.

"That is unfortunate. Have you annotated your theories?" he asked.

"Yes, Comrade Commissar," replied Kagonovich, handing his superior a sealed manila folder.

"Well, that's a start."

Kagonovich walked to the banks of dials and gauges and pointed with a battered wooden clipboard.

"The overhead coils are creating an electro-magnetic wave which is measured on these dials and, here, the compasses are now fixed at a north-north-west direction. They settled on this position early this morning."

"What are those?" asked Yvetchenko. The overhead lights glinted off his wire frame glasses as he peeled them onto his neckless head.

Three levers, each the height of a man, stood at various angles. They were vibrating.

"They're a mystery, we were able to manoeuvre them, but now we cannot," replied Kagonovich.

"A year of construction and no answer? And those?" asked Yvetchenko.

Kravchenko followed his gaze.

"Rail tracks, standard German gauge," replied Kagonovich. "We have re-wired thousands of yards of copper coils to them."

"Was it a power station of some sort – a generator maybe?" suggested Kravchenko.

"Not exactly, but I do have a theory," said Kagonovich. Both men paused and looked at the scientist. Kagonovich, knowing too well that Yvetchenko was a direct line to Stalin, produced his crumpled packet of cigarettes and lit another one. The toxic tobacco drifted around him.

"Escape," he exhaled.

One of the men with the clipboards cleared his throat.

"Be honest, Comrade Scientist Kagonovich, tell them your immediate reaction when you first saw the chamber?"

"And you are?" asked Kravchenko.

"Golikov, Comrade Komandarm," replied the man.

To Kravchenko, the diminutive Golikov looked like a well-fed goat with a pudding bowl haircut.

Vanya Kagonovich swallowed dryly. It could have been an honest request or, in the presence of senior Soviet intelligence officers, a denunciation.

"Well?" prompted Yvetchenko.

"An 'event'," said the scientist. "The krauts could have manipulated matter, altered the wall's atomic structure in some way; shot something through it. Escape."

"An escape vehicle?" asked Yvetchenko.

"For one passenger, maybe?" continued Kravchenko,

"The wrecked generators weren't hooked up to the climatic or electrical functions of the bunker," said Kagonovich. He lit his next cigarette from the butt of the last one.

"Flat out they could have powered those tubes overhead; if we knew what they were for."

Yvetchenko looked around the chamber.

"Your initial report indicated a circle. Eight feet in circumference?" said Yvetchenko.

"Yes. It only appeared on one wall. Carbonised. Moscow stated the results were inconclusive," replied Kagonovich.

The long metal tubes overhead sparked and hissed, long fingers of energy reached from point-to-point and slithered up into the chamber's ceiling.

"That's the end of the tour, Comrades. If you'll excuse me, we must begin our broadcast."

The technician Golikov studied the ceiling in a bovine manner before returning to his camera. With methodical sweeps, he filmed the increasing lightning storm above his head.

Kornilov led Yvetchenko and Kravchenko out of the chamber. The second cameraman gazed at the wheel lock door like a drowning submariner.

The door clanged shut behind them with an ominous finality. Kravchencko felt a strange pang of jealousy as he heard it being sealed from the inside.

Kornilov ushered them into the control room of an immense communications hub. The scientist Kagonovich's voice crackled through the speakers.

"Is Moscow receiving this?" Kravchenko asked Kornilov.

"The signal goes directly to the Ministry of Science HQ."

Kravchenko studied the room, the clocks set to local and Moscow time were now moving at rapid speed in the same direction; counterclockwise.

"Let's hope Comrade Scientist Kagonovich knows what he's doing," he said.

"The man's a fool, Comrade," said Kornilov.

Inside the chamber, Kagonovich studied the dials and gauges. They swung back and forth in near perfect co-ordination. The vibrations increased, and a sudden tremor knocked him and the film crew off their feet. One of the cameras teetered on its tripod, before Golikov found his feet and steadied it. The other cameraman began to take slow steps towards the door. His camera lay fallen and splayed.

"This is incredible, comrades, incredible. The levers are moving independently, it's my assumption that some form of connection is being formed," said Kagonovich. He noticed the microphone was shaking in his hands.

The locomotive-style levers juddered for a second then waved like fingers before settling into fixed positions.

Outside the chamber his voice was lost in a shrill static blast.

"Communications have just gone down. We've lost the link

to Moscow," said Kornilov.
Kravchenko felt the first beads of cold sweat.

"Can that thing there be shut down?" he asked.

"We don't know how to – its Kagonovich's bloody toy," muttered Kornilov. He ran a nicotine-stained hand over his stubbled chin. His eyes were almost pink from lack of sunlight. His unkempt grey hair stood out at jagged angles in places.

"I need a drink. I think we're all fucked. He's killed us all," he said.

"Where´s Comrade Commissar Yvetchenko?" said Kravchenko, looking around.

"Running back to his plane, if he´s got any sense," said Kornilov. "He´ll die of exposure out there. Still, it´s got to be worth the risk ..."

Kravchenko turned, but Kornilov was gone.

The only sound in the room now was the humming of the clocks. Kravchenko ran to the pressure door of the chamber. It was sealed from the inside. He began pounding on it.

"Marko," said a voice.

He closed his eyes and pressed his head against the cold metal door. The wraith hung close, her breath in his ear.

His Sonja.

He turned to look at her. Her smile was warm, inviting.

"Marko," she whispered.

She was as cold as the metal against his forehead.

"Come home, Marko. Come home to us," she breathed.

Chairs overturned inside the chamber as the technicians made to flee. But there was nowhere to go.

Despite the chaos around him Kagonovich continued to jot things down on his clipboard. Golikov unclipped the film reels and the two cameramen placed everything into a heavy leaden box. They heaved open a chute a few feet away from the pressure door and slid the heavy box in. Reinforced, the chute was the length and width of a coffin. They closed the chute and locked it. The men found a corner and wedged themselves into it.

They waited.

One moment, the chamber was a vibrating drum, the sonic

shrieks deafening. Bolts of electrical energy skipped across every part of the chamber, creating an uneven web of light.
The next moment, an artillery shell, several metres long appeared between the glowing railway sleepers. On the far wall appeared a perfect black carbon circle.

"Jesus Christ," said Kagonovich.

The artillery shell detonated.
The blast plumed up through the stratosphere, hurtling metal, earth and rock. A great swathe of land churned and evaporated. Gradually, with silent grace, the molten debris succumbed to gravity, scattering soil, metal and incinerated pieces of flesh for miles around.
And became silent.

PART ONE

AN APPOINTMENT IN BERLIN

March 1946 – Zürich

Anyone walking along the riverside of the Limmat might have picked her out; a pretty girl of about twenty, whose maroon-looking lipstick accentuated her wan complexion. Her arm, bent at the elbow and carried at an awkward angle, might have given pause for thought; her fist, balled up into a permanent clench, was concealed between the buttons of her expensively cut overcoat. An attentive eye might even have noticed the small spattering of blood in her wake; tiny droplets that pooled from the crooked elbow before dripping to the ground.

But it was a busy rush-hour Monday; the trams rattled by, buses and bicycles fought with cars as busy citizens dashed to some urgent appointment or pressing matter at their places of employment.

If someone had seen the girl stumble and steady herself with her free arm, they would have put it down to her high heels; black crocodile skin with a buckle and peep toe; a dress shoe rather than a practical one on the unforgiving pavement. Watching her pause, leaning against the river wall, a casual observer might have thought she´d forgotten something, or had stopped to admire the unseasonably azure March sky.

But the pretty girl with the maroon lipstick was badly injured. Satisfied that no one was paying her any special attention, she dropped her purse into the river. She watched it float away, gradually slipping into the depths.

Pushing away from the wall, she resumed her dash to Zürich Hauptbahnhof Railway Station, urgently mingling with the pedestrians as a funereal black Mercedes Benz turned onto the strasse. Glancing back, the girl increased her pace, her deep brown eyes glittering, a strand of blonde hair coming loose beneath her stylish felt hat. A fine glaze of sweat betrayed her fear.

She reached the main doors of the station and lurched toward the train timetables in the main concourse. She had to stem the flow of blood; she was beginning to feel light-headed – but first she had to make the rendezvous.

Taking up position in front of the timetables, she looked up and down the destinations – the railways from Zürich could take you anywhere in Europe. She suddenly longed for her small brass bed. The pretty girl swayed on her heels and buried her fist deep into her overcoat pocket. Her exertions had made the blood flow more freely; she could feel it pooling around her tailor-made leather glove. Her blouse felt glued to her arm.

"I believe the waterfall at Rhine-Falls is the source of the River Rhine itself, Fraulein?" said a man's voice; it was the correct code.

"Does it go all the way to the ocean?" she replied.

She turned to the man. He was middle-aged with florid razor burn, dressed in garish tweeds. His hat had a jaunty feather in its band.

"No, only to Berlin," he replied. His moustache was as white as the snow on the alps and waxed up to two fine needle points. Message received and understood.

"I think you will find this map useful then, sir," she replied.

Reaching into the folds of her coat, she handed him a map. An observant passer-by might have noticed its title; *The Canton of Zürich* in bold type. Inside it was a microfilm.

The man, in return, handed her a rail ticket.

"Thank you, Fraulein. Your train is the 10:15 to Bern. A representative will meet you there."

She glanced up at the departure board, her train wasn´t advertised yet.

It was 9:05.

"Thank you. I must fix myself up a bit first though; best look presentable."

Her maroon lips drew a thin, sere smile.

Her handler, Swiss Desk Section Head Douglas Gageby, paused.

"I'm quite alright, sir; no need to worry," she said.

Tipping his trilby hat, Gageby turned on his highly polished tan Oxfords and strode out of the station, a beige raincoat draped nonchalantly over his arm, concealing the map and its contents.

The girl glanced around and spied the ladies' toilet.

Paying the attendant an extra franc, she murmured,

"Unwanted attention. Need a moment."

The attendant grinned, a gold tooth winked mischievously, she whistled as she mopped the tiled floor.

The girl found a vacant cubicle, fastened the latch and peeled off the overcoat and bloody blouse beneath. She hung them on the hook and carefully placed her fashionable felt hat on top. The knife wound was deep, she thought the tendons in her shoulder might be severed. Every movement resulted in a bolt of white-hot pain.

Removing the gloves revealed lesser nicks and cuts; one ran deep beneath her right thumb. Holding the gloves between her teeth, she tasted the coppery blood and felt her tongue drying out. She needed a cold drink of water.

Pulling wads of toilet paper, she made a crude gauze. She fashioned a bandage with strips of her blouse, winding it around her shoulder with her free hand. Her breath was coming in muffled rasps. She could smell her sweat in the antiseptic-smelling toilets. The cubicle swam in her vision; she eased herself onto the toilet seat. She closed her eyes.

She thought of her little wrought-iron balcony. On it she had a little table, a folding chair and a delicate china vase she'd purchased in a market in Montmartre; she loved to place little bunches of flowers in it. On Sunday mornings she liked to doodle fashion designs along the margins of the newspapers, the sounds of the American big bands drifting up from a café in the street below.

Her head rocked back and struck the cistern pipe; snapping her back to the present. The gloves had fallen from her mouth and lay splayed on the toilet floor. Strangely, she felt the urge to cry.

The attendant's whistling had stopped. The girl rose and stuffed the blouse behind the toilet. She gingerly pulled on her overcoat and reached for the gloves. Then, with difficulty, she tilted her hat, shadowing her eyes.

She needed a hospital and a sympathetic doctor – and knew both were just a train ride away in Bern. For a second, she debated flushing the ticket, but thinking about the comforts of a train stopped her.

Opening the door, the girl saw in the mirror a statuesque blonde applying lipstick. Carefully placing a handkerchief between her lips, she dabbed off the excess gloss.

Her eyes were ice-cold blue.

The injured girl opened the door and stepped out into the toilet. Too late she noticed the attendant lying on the floor, just out of view of the dwindling rush-hour crowds. Blood was pooling around the attendant's head, the mop casually tossed on top of her.

The woman at the mirror spun suddenly, striking the injured girl full force in the face. The girl staggered and collapsed, landing on her injured shoulder. Her head struck the tiles and she could feel her wound opening again, blood bursting through the bandage.

"Where is it?" asked the woman. Her accent was German, not Swiss.

"I'm not sure what you're talking about, Madame," replied the girl.

She knew then she was going to die right there on the toilet floor.

"Not sure? Allow me to help." She delivered a ferocious kick to the girl's face. Blood flowed from the girl's ruptured nose. With her free arm, she feebly tried to wave away the next incoming blow.

The blonde crouched down and ran her fingers all over the girl. Thorough and precise, no area was out of bounds. Hunting through the cubicles she found the sodden blouse. Shaking it out and finding nothing she expressed her rage with a single stamp of her foot. It echoed around the walls.

"Who did you give it to?" she hissed.

"Not sure..."

The bloodied girl was growing faint; consciousness was slipping away.

The blonde motioned to two back-suited men in identical hats who were loitering just outside the toilet door. One came in and hauled the lifeless attendant into the nearest cubicle. The other stood over the girl, produced a syringe from a small leather pouch and tapped its lazy, lethal contents.

"A ticket to Bern," announced the blonde, holding the ticket up to him like a trophy.

"Then let's send a message to Bern," he replied. His voice was cultured; it was laced with the cadences of an aesthete.

"Yes, let's," said the woman.

The man who had moved the attendant now stood sentinel at the toilet entrance; a long tapering blade lay sheathed along his arm. His pock-marked complexion twitched with a stressful tic.

"It will dissipate in a few hours, a new recipe from our old friends in Romania," said the man with the cultured voice. He handed the blonde woman the syringe.

She plunged it into the girl's jugular, just below her hairline. The girl's eyelids fluttered for a second and her left leg juddered in a spasm, then with a slow exhale, the pretty girl died. The tall blonde wiped the blood from the girl's face and rolled small balls of tissue paper, forcing them into the girl's nostrils. Taking her compact, with a few dabs, she powdered out the bruising.

"She'll do," said the cultured man.

"Did you see her talking to anyone?" asked the woman.

"Could have been anyone here," replied the man.

The rush hour was almost over. The shunting of rolling stock, blasts of steam and whistles announced departures and arrivals. The men hoisted the girl and draped her arms over their shoulders; a silly young debutant wasted on casino champagne. Led by the tall, voluptuous blonde they smiled apologetically at the porters and the conductor, flashing the ticket before placing the girl in her empty compartment on the Bern train.

Seeing them alight laughing and shouting "Au revoir, mon cheri," a casual observer might have clucked their tongue at the hedonistic antics of these Sunday night revelers.

And anyone glancing into the compartment or looking at her pale face pressed against the glass would have thought the pretty girl with the maroon lipstick was simply taking a nap.

Outside the station the cultured man motioned discreetly to the driver of the black Mercedes waiting obediently where they´d left him. The trio climbed inside, and the gleaming black sedan accelerated smoothly over the bridge, blending seamlessly with the traffic.

***

Gageby doubled back and boarded, through the course of the morning, two trams heading in different directions. The jaunty feather in his trilby was now deflated and he buried the travel guide deeper into his pocket. Alighting and walking briskly along the Talstrasse, he crumpled up the hat and stuffed it into his raincoat. From the other pocket he pulled out a tweed flat cap and dipped it low over his eyes. He spotted the hotel where the drop had to be made. His stride took on a greater purpose. Once in the lobby, he handed the guidebook to the courier, another young woman. She looked a studious type as serene and as non-descript as a nun. She casually finished her coffee and folded the guide into her newspaper. He watched her leave through the lobby doors; a sudden downpour drove pedestrians to the awnings of the cafes and shops.

Gageby couldn't shake the feeling that suddenly, everything was out of control. His years in Hong Kong before the war had honed his instincts; something was off, didn't smell quite right. He had the sudden overwhelming urge to hear an English voice. He found a booth and fed it with coins. It was well positioned in the lobby; he could see who was coming in and out of the reception. He dialed the number to the Bern desk.

It rang. It kept on ringing.

The operator came on speaking high German.

"I'm sorry?" said Gageby.

"There is no reply," crackled the telephone exchange operator in guttural English.

"Please try again," said Gageby.

The number kept ringing.

"There is no reply," said the operator.

The coins ran out, the line went dead. Turning to reach into his pockets, Gageby failed to notice the tall woman and the two men enter the lobby. A coin slipped from his fingers and started to roll between his feet. It was then he realised that in a city of uniform black, bureaucratic Swiss shoes, a pair of spit-shine tan Oxfords would stand out.

He dialed another number, checking the digits he'd jotted along the banner of a local newspaper folded in his pocket. The number rang. He thought it had picked up; he whispered hurriedly into the receiver.

"There is no reply," said the operator`s voice. Her voice jarred alarmingly.

Cursing under his breath, he reached down for the coin, it had come to rest just out of reach. With a lunge, he gripped it and jammed it into the slot.

He tried the number again.

Gageby felt only a slight prick to the nape of his neck and before his death, all he could hear was the interminable ringing of the telephone.

2

Fawkeston Gyre, Southern England

The man was in the garden when the telephone rang. He let it ring; he refused to answer the phone when he was working in the grounds. He swept the dry leaves, pulled up the dead plants to make room for the new.

The train to Honiton clattered across the Devonshire countryside, a thick plume of smoke streaming like a bilious pennant. He shaded his eyes in the bright spring glare. Sunlight splintered off the carriage windows.

The telephone rang again. Insistent.

Kneading his tired back muscles through the heavy knitted jumper, he walked through his brutally pruned rose bushes to the simple antique telephone stand just inside his imposing front door.

As he reached it, it stopped ringing. After a beat, it started again.

"Hello?" he said.

"Halidane, Edgar Aloys Halidane?"

He didn't recognise the voice.

"Speaking."

"Edgar Halidane?"

"Yes."

"Edgar Halidane of Elm Wood, Honiton?"

"How did you get this number may I ask?"

"She's dead."

The voice sounded cold, formal, and bureaucratic; a male voice of indeterminate age; it had the trace of a foreign accent; bohemian.

"Who's dead?"

"Ann Chambrel."

"Ann Chambrel is dead?" said Halidane.

"Yes. Dead."

"I see," said Halidane.

"Natural causes. Heart failure. It's in the Swiss morning papers," said the voice.

"I avoid reading newspapers," said Halidane.

"I will post you a copy."

"Please don't – save the postage," replied Halidane.

"She may have managed to get sensitive information to foreign interests."

"Foreign interests?" said Halidane.

"Intelligence services, MI6, O.S.S.," said the voice.

Edgar Halidane's heart tightened in his chest.

"That is most unfortunate, most unfortunate. I was led to believe that this situation was under control?" said Halidane.

"It is." came the reply.

The voice carried a seed of doubt. The coolness faltered.

The caller hung up.

Edgar Halidane wasn't used to being cut off. Beside his phone was a large box-shaped device, metal with a series of switches. He flicked a switch, he listened through the hiss of the atmosphere as the phone dialled the number back.

He steadied himself, and then stared at the phone, willing the return call to be answered.

It wasn't.

A ticker tape spat out the number including Swiss prefix. He committed it to memory; numbers were his passion; his 'bread and butter' he would joke when he was in the mood. Reaching into his breeches he produced a creased matchbook and looked at the cover. It read '*Prestige Au Lac*'; the last time he had seen Ann Chambrel was on the dance floor of this hotel. After several shaky attempts, he struck a matchband and lit the ticker tape. Dangling from his forefinger and thumb, it blazed like the holy

fire.
He dialled up his offices in Zürich, and repeated the number to the secretary there,

"Please ensure this time, it is handled discreetly. A fact-finding mission only, for now," he said.

He repeated it three times for emphasis.

Edgar Halidane strode through the low-ceiling rooms, past his tidy desk and tall shelves of crowded leather-bound books. In the living room, he reached for a crystal decanter and poured a generous measure of vermouth.

"Dead," he whispered.

He lowered himself into his leather sofa.

He began to sip the smoky alcohol slowly. The plan would have to be expedited.

Rising, glass in hand, he walked through the large, dusty living room, past the empty mantelpiece with its unlit hearth and ornate cornices to the cool kitchen. His footfall echoed across the chequered tiles and he opened the half-door that overlooked a newly swept patio and quilted wicker chair. At the doorway, he checked the three wall-mounted brass barometers hanging side-by-side. The glass was pulsing a faint green, the mercury separating and lolling around in small globules. Under a fading arboretum of holly, he walked to the greenhouse.

The greenhouse was a sprawling white Edwardian affair. The panes hung perilously from tendrils of ornate iron, the ancient glass shimmering in the early evening light pulsed a deep vermillion.

Edgar Halidane walked through the ferns and exotic orchids that he prized so dearly to a cluttered worktable at the centre of the conservatory. He finished his vermouth in a gulp. His hands had lost some of their tremor. He pressed down on a foot pedal. The table slid quietly aside, revealing a stairwell. Along a smooth, recently completed tunnel, he came to a metal pressure door. Spinning the wheel lock anti-clockwise he pulled it open. Using a battery torch, he found a line of switches and pushed them. The banks of underground generators hummed into life. The overhead lights flickered, lighting up the metal underfoot.

It was a chamber more than a room. Hexagonal in shape, every bolted panel was perfectly symmetrical. A high vaulted ceiling with enormous coils of copper wiring attached to long hanging metal shafts; stalactites of menacing proportions hanging from the bolt-plated arches.

At the far metallic wall, the hands of three clocks were spinning wildly in counterclockwise directions. They whirred like bees in their brass casings. He stood over the three nautical compasses spinning on their gyros. Edgar Halidane paused; this wasn't supposed to be happening. With a supreme effort, he pushed the three floor-mounted levers into an upright neutral position. Wiping his brow with his silk cravat, Halidane reached a conclusion; someone had discovered another chamber. Not only that, they were actually trying to use it.
Overhead, the long tapering metallic couplings began to spark and spit; it was only a matter of time before a full connection was made.
He would have to act quickly.
He went to a panel and opened it. Inside was a cryptograph device, a German Lorenz cipher machine. He thought for a moment, then looked around his chamber which was beginning to slowly thrum to atmospheric forces.
He input a short message to his offices in Switzerland.
After a pause, the ULTRA device's gears flashed back the following message

**** RUSSIA CURIOUS / CONNECTION SEVERED – PERMANENTLY. EXPECT RESPONSE ****

Edgar Halidane folded his arms in quiet contemplation. A decision had been taken without his knowledge or consultation; and that was unacceptable.
Halidane made a concious effort to quell his rising anger by focusing on the step-by-step process of deactivating the chamber. As the table slid back to conceal the stairwelll once more, he paused to contemplate his precious orchids and stood

for a long moment looking out through the mottled panes of glass, for all the world a suburban homeowner enjoying the peace and tranquility of his carefully tended garden.

3
Zürich

The tall blonde, Hannah Wolfe, sat back in the plush seating of the black Mercedes Benz. Her companions, Kahn and Pfeifer, sat in stony silence at the front. As Hannah twisted a cigarette into a long onyx holder, she quietly cursed to herself; how had this operation gone so wrong? Neither of the agents - the girl or the buffoon in tweeds - had the microfilm.

She lit the cigarette and rolled down the back-seat window. There would be some explaining to do.

Beside the lake, the Mercedes glided past a boat house and marina where yachts, pleasure steamers and expensive motorboats ploughed the waters. Along the tree-lined Strasse towards a modest-looking lakeside building, discretely fronted by trees and a high stone wall where a highly polished brass plate read; HALIDANE CORP.

Beneath the banner was an embossed image of a globe, it had the equator, tropics and poles jutting in elegant relief. Equidistant on the outside were twelve lightning bolts, positioned like the minutes of the clock and at each of the poles, was a large squat *H* and *C*.

Skirting manicured lawns and smoothed gravel driveways, the Mercedes was directed by a braided doorman to an underground car park. It slewed past luxury and high-performance cars, Rolls Royce, Mercedes and top-of-the-range American marques.

The trio were escorted by an armed security guard to a marble and gold elevator, the mirrors reflecting their set expressions in a kaleidoscope of black, white and red.

At the top floor, they were met by a pretty secretary in a crisp blouse and pencil skirt, who ushered them into an office with a breath-taking view of the lake. Sitting at the desk with his back to the view was Herman Malleus, European Director of the Ausland

Organisation, A.O., the former Reich's Foreign Intelligence Service.
Malleus, like Hannah, was one of life's survivors.

"Sit please," he motioned to the three.

Hannah noticed her chair was closer to the desk than the other two.

"The microfilm?" he asked.

"No," said Hannah.

She held his gaze evenly.

"What happened?" asked Malleus.

"The girl was more robust than we expected," said Kahn, the knifeman. Without his hat, his forehead was a sweeping dome with uneven ears, the pockmarks along his jowls, the only relief on his features. Below his chin, along his neck, a series of scratches stood painfully out.

"She put up a fight," said Kahn.

"Allow your senior officer to speak, please, Herr Kahn," said Malleus.

"The girl is dead," said Hannah.

"Did she achieve her objective?" asked Malleus.

"Yes. It would appear so, Herr Director," said Hannah

"Unfortunate. The contact?"

"Eliminated too," she replied.

She twisted another cigarette into her holder. She held it out to Malleus, as much of a challenge as a request.

Malleus lit the cigarette with his service lighter, an eagle with a twist of garlands in its talons.

"But no microfilm?" he said.

"It wasn't on either of them. We checked," said Pfeiffer. He was an accomplished poisoner, a skill perfected in the human vivisection wings of the Eastern European death camps. His cadences were cultured and soft.

"Thank you, Doctor Pfeiffer," said Malleus.

He turned his attention to the papers on his desk, allowing an uncomfortable silence to brew. Hannah smoked. A few years ago, in Berlin, she had almost doomed Malleus to follow his boss, Admiral Canaris, to the concentration camp and an appointment with a meat hook. But the wily Malleus had thrown himself on Himmler's mercy, knowing that Himmler loved to dispense it where he saw fit.

"Not going to offer us coffee, Herr Director?" she asked.

"No, Miss Wolfe. I have a busy schedule," replied Malleus.

"Is Herr Halidane here, then?" she asked.

Malleus eyed her ample curves, long legs and narrow waist. Her clothes, hair and make-up were expensive and her powers of seduction irresistible. She had rebuffed Malleus many times in Berlin.

"Herr Halidane isn't here today, Miss Wolfe."

He allowed himself a smile,

"For a field agent of your capabilities, letting this microfilm fall into enemy hands, is not just disappointing. It is frankly, Miss Wolfe, unacceptable."

"We were working against the clock, Herr Director, the details were late coming to us," replied Hannah.

"Then the directive will have to be accelerated. I'll be contacting the Reichsleiter today. He will also find this ... disappointing. 'Casa Rosa'?"

Hannah afforded herself a smile.

"Ready, Herr Malleus," she said. "We await the Reichsleiter's orders."

Malleus looked up. His sharp suit, pencil-thin tie and pomaded hair gave him a vulpine demeanour. He looked every inch the urbane banker, at home amid the veiled transactions and cold secrecy of Switzerland. He had secured almost all the Reich's international assets and now wanted to fulfil the Führer's dying wish.

"No more mistakes, Miss Wolfe. This was a simple retrieval of information that failed. If it falls into the wrong hands, the sacrifice of our glorious forces during the defence of Berlin will count for nothing. Nothing. Remain on stand-by while I review the potential damage. That will be all. Good day, Kahn. Pfeifer. I need you to remain here, Wolfe."

Hannah pushed her chair out. Kahn and Pfeiffer skulked out into the reception. She stood for a moment, staring at Malleus.

"I still out-rank you, Herr Malleus," she said.

"The war is over, Miss Wolfe, there are no ranks anymore."

"That is where you are mistaken, Herr Director," said Hannah.

"Still at the Hotel Storchen here in Zürich?" asked Malleus.

"Yes. You know that already?" she replied.

"Herr Halidane has requested someone follow up on a call he received. I immediately thought of you. This is near your address."

Malleus handed her a number neatly typed out.

"Appears to be a government department in the city. The person didn't identify themselves. Herr Halidane has expressed an immediate check be made."

"Are you serious?" said Hannah

"Your employer, Edgar Halidane is very, very serious."

"Hauptsturmführer Wolfe, Herr Director."

"Good hunting, Wolfe, and please avoid any further unnecessary casualties."

She left a furious wake of Chanel behind her.

4

Berlin

Wendell H. Keyburn watched the ruins of the city flash by from the back seat of the British Embassy car. The upholstery was plush, the engine no more than a whisper.

"What's that camp there?" he asked the driver.

"That's the Tiergarten, sir. They're refugees, sir. German civilians, sir," said the British driver, a solid man of limited conversation. They turned from the Victory column and meandered around Allied checkpoints and armoured vehicles.

The woodland was totally denuded. Stark slashes of destruction and rubble interspersed with army vehicles and military outriders flowed past the car windows. The gutted Reichschancellry and the battered Brandenburg Gate appeared and disappeared in a haze of still-burning fires.

The driver pulled up outside Charlottenburg Palace, Union Jacks now swaying where scarlet swastikas once hung. A dapper-looking bureaucrat was waiting by the battered kerbside. He opened the door smartly,

"Good morning, sir. I trust you had a pleasant flight?" he said. Wendell H. Keyburn was a short man who nevertheless managed to occupy a lot of space. His flat nose and lipless mouth gave him a pugilist's mien,

"Let's get this over with...?"

"Hopkins, sir," replied the bureaucrat, "British Intelligence liaison, Berlin sector."

His hands were remarkably clean.

They strode into the new Headquarters of the British Zone; once a hub of Prussian power, now reduced to an English civil service outpost. Keyburn's patent leather shoes, paisley bow tie and perfectly fitted Garfinkel double-breasted suit clashed with the subdued surroundings. Everyone stood to attention; Keyburn was here on President Truman's direct orders.

With Roosevelt dead, Churchill chucked out of power and a potentially communist-backed Atlee government in London, Hopkins extended the royal treatment for the nation that had dropped two atomic bombs.

"What do we know about this guy?" asked Keyburn. His Missouri cadences bounced around the hushed corridors.

"Only gives his name, rank and serial number, sir," said Hopkins.

They came to a stairwell leading to cellars below. In one smooth movement, the file under Hopkins arm was handed to Keyburn.

"Hopkins, I've hop-scotched non-stop from St. Joseph, Missouri, to Nova Scotia, to Greenland, Iceland, Scotland and Paris to be here, it had better be damn good," said Keyburn. He leafed through the file as they walked. His hands were soft and smooth, a haberdasher's hands, thought Hopkins. He noted Keyburn pronounced his state 'Muzoorah'.

They descended another flight of steps to the cellar.

"He was released by the Russians a few days ago in exchange for another asset they wanted. This one is interesting, though," said Hopkins.

Keyburn stopped and turned towards Hopkins. Pulling on a pair of thick black framed glasses, he stared up at the liaison, thinned out by army rations,

"Why?"

"The Russians found him shot and injured outside a U-bahn station, dressed in a Russian army uniform. He was shipped off as a POW to Buryrka Prison; then press-ganged onto a construction crew building a new prison wing in the Lubyanka in Moscow."

"So, he's a spy?" asked Keyburn. "Ours or theirs?"

"Neither, I'm afraid. Though one can't rule out either possibility."

"No, one can't. I haul-ass across the Atlantic Ocean on the orders of the President of the U-S-A, for a meeting with a kraut soldier who's been shot in Berlin?" said Keyburn.

Hopkins, who was used to peppery American personalities from the O.S.S. since the armistice, calibrated his smile and tone to be as disarming as possible.

"Here, it gets interesting; our boy in the cells below turns out to be a mountaineer – AOK Norwegen, going by his rank and number. One of the Politburo's scions took a little Nikkita up a mountain and promptly got himself into a spot of bother. Your kraut private, as you call him, put together a climbing team and rescued them. Earned himself better prison conditions."

"Better conditions?"

"Less whippings and a cell that didn't have a layer of ice on the walls. Here we are."

A burly MP saluted them. He took their identity papers and cross-checked them methodically. He handed back their papers and opened the cellar door with an impressive looking key.

"Cell three, Gentlemen," he said

"After you, sir," said Hopkins to Keyburn.

"We better not be boiling the ocean here, Hopkins," said

Keyburn.
The huge wine cellars had been converted into holding cells. The corridor smelled of wet cement and mould. At the door of the third holding cell, Hopkins produced a heavy looking key on a chain, and turned the lock.

Inside, sitting at a modest table facing two empty chairs was an emaciated man. His head was shaved. Lines were etched into his skin, the cheekbones angled into deep shadows beneath the naked light bulb. But his blue eyes snapped between Keyburn and Hopkins with quick intelligence.
Keyburn pulled his chair as far away from the table as possible.

"I don't have lice," the prisoner said, "...currently."
As he spoke, he reached to the back of his shaved head and idly picked away at some old and irritating bite.

Keyburn patted his own buzz-cut. Swinging the chair about face, he straddled it like a rodeo rider,

Hopkins eased his slender frame onto the remaining chair and tucked it tightly under the table. He straightened the dossier Keyburn had tossed there and took out a packet of cigarettes and the lighter.

"Your English is excellent," he said to the emaciated man.

"I'm fluent in Russian too," the man replied.

Hopkins offered the cigarette, the emaciated man declined. The three sat in silence. Somewhere above, another door clanged shut with a titanic boom. The three men stared up.

"This gentleman here is Wendell H. Keyburn of the O.S.S.," said Hopkins.
He lit a cigarette with deliberate movements, "He's flown all the way from St Joseph, Missouri."

"That is a long way," said the man.

"You know America, son?" asked Keyburn.

"A little," said the man, "Cowboys – bang-bang."
He pointed his two forefingers at Hopkins as he spoke.

"In America, son, we wouldn't be sitting at a table politely requesting information from you," said Keyburn.
The man scratched idly at his crotch beneath the table. The dungarees were Russian prison issue; fumigated and washed. No

point in dressing him in anything else if they were going to throw him back into the gulag system, thought Hopkins.

"What were you doing outside Stadmitte U-Bahn station in a Russian army uniform?" asked Hopkins. As he spoke, he leaned forward over the desk in a kindly manner.

"My details are all there, gentlemen," said the man. Despite looking down on his luck and close to an unmarked grave, his voice still carried self-assurance. He looked like the kind of man who, when all the smoke had cleared, would still be standing. In the naked light, his forehead shone with a light fever.

"Answer the question," said Keyburn. His voice ricocheted around the brickwork.

The man stared at Keyburn. He remained silent.

"You were found shot in a Russian army uniform outside U-Bahn Stadmitte and we caught three high-ranking Nazis fleeing from the Reichsbunker," said Hopkins.

Keyburn abandonded his seat and stood with his hands on his hips.

"Look, here's the deal, either you start talking, or we throw you back into the Russian fish tank we found you in. Simple as that, Bub." Keyburn's tone was hardening.

The man remained silent.

"Who were you driving?" asked Hopkins.

"Who said I was driving?" asked the man

"Your uniform and insignia. What happened to your vehicle?" replied Hopkins

"Vehicle?" said the man.

"There was a breakout from the bunker; a few of your High Command were spotted at Kaiserhof U-bahn – the station before Stadmitte - who were you arranging to meet?" asked Keyburn.

The man stared silently ahead. He spread his hands out on the table. They were strong and calloused.

"You have my name, rank and serial number," he said. "If being stripped naked, beaten, held down on a table while being whipped didn't get an answer in Moscow, you two have no chance."

Keyburn's expression darkened. In the naked light, his eyes

seemed to sink into the recesses of his skull.

"You claim to have information. I'm waiting for that. You were found near Hitler's bunker in an Allied uniform, a Russian driver's uniform. Who were you driving?"

Silence.

"Who shot you?" asked Hopkins, his words were soft.

"I was lucky; it was a bullet graze. Upper shoulder," replied the man.

Keyburn approached the table and picked up the service dossier. He took a slow walk around the prisoner, his eyes darting between the file and the man himself. No doubt about it, he was an officer and had seen combat. His other shoulder had a much harsher scar; a through-on-through with an ugly weal of an exit wound that had slowly healed. On his upper arm was a scarred tattoo; some kind of fish.

The man began to smile.

"What's so funny?" asked Keyburn.

"Nothing. You seem fascinated by me."

Keyburn leaned into the man, speaking directly into his ear.

"You mounted a rescue mission in Russia. Whose kid did you rescue?"

"I can't answer that.

"Beria?" asked Keyburn

"No," replied the man.

"Molotov?"

"I'm afraid I can't answer that – it was a tricky climb; I lost three men on the descent."

Silence. Then it dawned on Keyburn and Hopkins simultaneously, Stalin. The only way a German POW had any hope of a reprieve.

"Of course, they weren't buried. They were left to the buzzards," said the man.

He found a new scab on his head to scratch at.

He reached for a cigarette; "May I?"

Hopkins pulled three, shared them out and lit them.

"Thank you," the man exhaled.

He turned the cigarette around and admired it as if it was a fine liqueur.

"I'll only talk to one man – Henry Chainbridge."

Hopkins and Keyburn stared at the man.

"Tell Henry Chainbridge I need to talk to him. I'm an active member of Int. 7. And I have information. Vital information. Chainbridge, H-e-n-r-y Chainbridge," said the man.

Keyburn leaned forward, his fists were balled,

"Who the hell is Henry Chainbridge?"

5
Oxfordshire, England

His hair was as absent-minded as his cardigan. The gallery, a modest faux-Tudor building on the main street of Little Shotton, had the polished brass plate *Fine prints & antiquities a speciality* mounted at eye level. It had been retrieved from the bombed-out rubble of its previous premises in London. Anticipating what was to come, the man in the cardigan had shipped the contents for storage in Scotland. Now unpacked and dusted down, they hung proudly on display. Unlike its owner, the gallery exuded an organised feel, each gilt frame perfectly level, each old publication standing neatly to attention on polished oak shelves. Delicate pamphlets and prints were displayed under glass. The shop itself gave off the distinctive aroma of beeswax.

"This exquisite miniature is a fine example of the Restoration Court era," said the man in the cardigan. His features, though a little sunken, had a hawk-like profile.

The couple stood uncertainly staring at the piece. The man, taller and older than the woman, idly filled a pipe while waiting for the woman to decide.

"I'm afraid tobacco smoke wouldn´t be conducive for any of the pieces hanging here," said the man in the cardigan. Its elbows had patches of different material.

"Put that thing away, Geoffrey."

The woman, pretty in a Cotswolds-fete sort of way, leaned in close to the miniature.

"How did you come by this?" she asked.

"I acquired it recently from a stately home struggling to make ends meet," the man in the cardigan replied. "The artist was Gibson."

"Richard Gibson - a dwarf, I believe?" said the girl. Her voice had a musical quality.

"Yes, he was of that nature, but it certainly didn't impact on his gifts."

The man with the idle pipe glanced at his watch. Like their clothes, it was expensive.

"Ruth, we are a little pressed for time."

His voice had a reedy, nasal quality. He was at least twenty years her senior.

"Gibson took a wife of the same stature, and they had a lavish court wedding," said the man in the cardigan.

"How divine," breathed Ruth. He could see by the way she set her jaw a decision had been made. No turning back. The man in the cardigan wondered if Geoffrey knew what he had let himself in for when he said, 'I do.'

She stood straight and gave a satisfactory click of her tongue.

"For that alone, we shall have it. Do you like it Geoffrey?"

"If you love it darling, then yes, I love it."

A man of action, thought the man in the cardigan. He smiled at Ruth,

"An excellent choice. I'll arrange the provenance and necessary paperwork. Is it a gift?"

"An anniversary gift," replied Geoffrey.

"We're a year married today," chimed Ruth from the back of the shop.

"Congratulations to both of you."

Geoffrey strode to the counter and pocketed his unlit pipe.

"Cash?"

"Always welcome, sir. If I could have some details?"

"My office will handle the necessaries," said Geoffrey.

He produced a pocketbook and counted out the notes.

"The young lady was very taken by it. There's a clarity and

honesty in the work, don't you agree?"

"Everything she's *taken by* costs me money," muttered Geoffrey.

Turning around, he seemed suddenly alert to Ruth admiring another picture.

"Darling, our train..." he called out.

She raised a delicate gloved hand in a shooing fashion without breaking her stare.

He turned back and pulled out a business card.

"Still, it keeps her quiet, eh?"

"A woman's touch, I feel, brings elegance to every endeavour."

Geoffrey Harvey, *Overseas and Foreign Office Procurement Department, London* read the card. London: *the city of kites and crows*, thought the man.

"Now we really must leave – Ruth?"

Ruth came to the counter reluctantly.

"I promise we will come back. Thank you Mr...?"

"Chainbridge, Henry Chainbridge."

"Thank you, Mr. Chainbridge. May I say, I love your accent – Scottish?"

Ruth's smile lit up this dark and dusty world, momentarily banishing the faint waft of decay.

"Northern Irish – Belfast, and I grew up in Liverpool."

"Good day," said Geoffrey.

In a burst of jingling door chimes, the Harveys left. In the bright sunshine, framed by the shop window, they climbed into the waiting taxi. They seemed oblivious to the privations of rationing. Petrol was in short supply; the fare would cost a small fortune. Geoffrey and Ruth Harvey certainly weren't *mend-and-make-do* like the rest of the country.

It had been a good morning – the Richard Gibson miniature and an Augustus John portrait had been sold.

Henry Chainbridge tapped his fingers along the counter. In another time, such success would have been celebrated with a fine Turkish cigarette and a large whiskey.

6

Seville, Spain

Thousands of brightly lit paper lanterns adorned the tent city beneath the swaying shade of cooling stretched canvas. The colours blended in a kaleidoscope of hues with hot bolts of late afternoon sun seeking gaps in the gaily adorned fabric. Loud cheers from the *Plaza de Toros de Maestranza* told the revellers the first of the bull fights had already begun.

Eva Molenaar adjusted the aperture of her Leica to its widest setting and smiled. The two beautiful young Spanish girls, in traditional flamenco dress, smiled back; dappled in the shadows. Eva captured them at just the right moment. The girls flounced into the nearest caseta, where thrumming guitars and rhythmic claves blended with the songs and chants of the festival goers. Eva was dressed in a white blouse nipped into long pleated corduroys and incongruous-looking combat boots. She carried a knapsack with more cameras, a notebook and journalist's permit, stamped by the local police chief. Parked just outside the Real de la Feria was her motorcycle; a fire-engine red Moto Guzzi which had taken time to master. The panniers contained cameras, rolls of film, maps and a change of clothes; she had an appointment in a café later that evening. Eva moved through the crowd like a ghost. Her lush russet tresses were bound up with clips and a black velvet ribbon. She wasn't wearing make-up or jewellery, yet her grey, green-flecked eyes glinted beneath her lashes. She watched a group of children, nut brown and stripped to the waist, sprint off chattering to dive into the cooling Rio Guadalquivir. She recalled the little heartbeat she had carried for a few weeks before miscarrying. Its father, the man she lost in the depths of the Rhône in the city of Lyon. She was still young, there was time enough yet.

As she rolled her film on, calculating how many shots were left, Eva looked up to study the light. The warm breeze, the smells and sounds of life being lived at full tilt all around, made her close her eyes and breathe in, giving her pause. She planned to return here after her rendezvous to dance and drink until dawn with the Feria de Abril revelers. She walked the length of the tent city, stopping to sip from cups dipped into buckets of wine. She relished the flesh of oranges, iced gazpacho and spicy chorizo gladly proffered by vendors. Eva accepted a light from a dashing young man in a tight black bolero jacket who was leading a breath-taking grey horse to the parade. They both stood proudly for their photograph. A loud roar rose from the bull ring, followed by a reverential silence; the first *toro bravo* had been slain. The bells from the cathedral tolled matins as Eva circled back for her motorcycle.

Under the gaze of two teenagers idly smoking cigarettes, Eva retrieved a heavy black embroidered wrap and a black lace veil from the Guzzi's panniers. It was hard to tell which the young men lusted after more; her or the bike. She tossed them a few pesetas to keep an eye on it; the prospect of pleasing her might just keep them from stealing it themselves, she thought.

The searing heat of the stone streets forced her to seek the shade of the trees and late afternoon shadows, their coolness, a summer shower.

Stooping slightly and pulling the wrap about her veiled head, Eva entered the café where she was to meet a former comrade - *nom de guerre* 'Spassky'.

At one table sat four men playing cards. Other men leaned or sat against the wall, smoking. She was the only woman in the café and they brazenly sized her up in her misshapen weeds. On the walls, beneath the pulsing fans, hung black and white photographs of matadors, some with signatures dashed across them. Peppered between the pictures were bull-fighting posters. Over the bar, the stuffed head of a bull glowered glassily out at the clientele. Beneath it, a hunchback bartender in a vibrant silk shirt cleaned a beer glass absently. A radio blared out what Eva assumed to be the bull fight. Two men at the bar hissed and tore up chits. They handed cash to the hunchback; his grin was a gnarled, gold-flecked maw. With his eyes he directed Eva to a separate room at the far end of the bar.

Sunlight slashed through a high window across the table and floor. A thin, middle-aged woman sat at the end of the table. She had let her hair go grey and wore it pinned severely back. Her left eye was covered by an ornate eye patch. Eva had never known her real name. They had travelled from France into Spain during the civil war to settle old scores.

Eva sat down and settled her wrap about her shoulders. A waiter came in with a young boy in tow. He waited for his cue.

"Dos cafes con leche y lo del siempre," said the woman.

They bowed and left.

"Still have that stiletto the French whore gave you?" she asked.

"Lost it in Argentina," replied Eva.

"Given up killing krauts?"

"Only the rapists. We're at peace now."

"The war isn't over, child," Spassky replied.

The waiter and the boy returned. The waiter was carrying a tray with a bottle of brandy and a long-handled coffee pot. The boy carried the milk and a bowl of olives. They set them down and with a bow, left.

"Hernandez, the hunch-back, is a good guy, he's loyal to the party; we can talk freely."

"Thank you for contacting me," said Eva.

Spassky lit a cheroot. The heat of the room, the smoke and the smell of the brandy made Eva remove her veil and shawl. She loosened a button on her blouse.

"You look a little sadder, child?" said Spassky.

Eva sipped the coffee and poured the liqueur into it.

"I'm luckier than most."

"It wasn't easy, your request. I have a contact with the French Communist Party. The person you are looking for was hard to find."

"I just need to know if he's dead," replied Eva.

"He was alive when the Resistance pulled him out of the river in Lyon. But when they found out he was German, they handed him over to the local communists."

Eva stared ahead intently. For some reason, she didn't

want Spassky to see her cry.

Spassky tapped her ash into the saucer deliberately.

"He was swapped for a French prisoner and sent to Moscow."

Spassky's English acquired a Russian burr on the vowels.

"He's as good as dead then."

Spassky leaned forward.

"He's alive as far as my contact knows. A year ago, the Central Committee in Moscow emptied their prisons of German POWs. Some big project. Very hush-hush. Most came out of The Butyrka prison. If he's alive, he's either there or on the move."

Eva sat frozen for a moment, her thoughts a myriad of images – bullets, shouting, spotlights, her lover falling into the river. He was alive. Without any contact for nearly three years, she had hardened her heart to him being dead.

It complicated things.

"Thank you," she said.

Eva produced a small folded envelope. She handed it to the woman.

Spassky opened the envelope on her lap. Inside were two uncut diamonds.

"I cannot accept this, child."

"Please. Please take them," urged Eva.

Spassky sighed. Then nodded.

"Speaking of krauts, I've jotted down these directions. You might want to let your British contacts know there are three U-Boats moored on the far side of Huelva, in the Gulf. Arrived a few days ago – they're code-named The Nina, The Pinta and the Santa Maria. German officers, German crews, blabbing to the local *putas*."

Yvette, the French *puta*, had once said: *"they open their mouths as well as their flies for a pretty face."* No medals for these girls nowadays, only a brutal shearing in public, thought Eva.

Spassky passed her a folded sheet of paper.

"I watched you at the feria today, you have a camera."

"You followed me?"

"I had to be sure you were who you said you were. Franco

is hunting us down and killing us like dogs. Spain is crawling with his former comrades-in-arms. Those U-Boats are probably German. They're up to something."

Eva looked at the penciled directions, a two-hour journey away.

"Maybe Franco bought them?"

"Possibly. We must be careful who we contact, a wrong word to the wrong person and it's a one-way ticket to the garrotte. Have you your journalist's permit?"

"Signed and stamped," said Eva.

Her thoughts turned to Henry Chainbridge, her former section chief, now just a fading memory. Three years; a long time.

"I'll need petrol," she said.

"I've already arranged it," said Spassky.

"Pictures?"

"Drop the film to Hernandez, he'll arrange everything else."

"Do it through the Jesuits, send it to Señor Miles Curran in London," said Eva.

Curran, the man who had sneered at her injuries in Argentina; a hard man to forget. A man as cold as his daily baths; a former Jesuit himself.

Eva rose, no need for the widow's weeds, she thought. The waiter´s eyes turned the size of saucers when he saw her without them.

She shook Spassky's hand.

"Be careful, child. There are no rules now," said Spassky, appraising Eva's figure admiringly,

"I know. May I ask, what is your name?" asked Eva.

"Seeing as you saved my life in Cordoba, I owe you that – Margarita."

Eva walked over and planted a soft kiss on Margarita's cheek.

"Muchas gracias, Margarita," she said.

Margarita waved a thin, scarred hand,

"Muchas de nadas," she replied.

Eva left the room. At the doorway of the café stood Hernandez. The hunchback held up a hand and the room stopped. He turned his head awkwardly back toward the crack in the door. Two men at the bar, recently left penniless, stood up and produced pistols;

they let them hang loose about their fingers.
There was a pause. The sound of jackboots passed from the local militia and Hernandez mimed the shawl. Eva donned her veil and wrap and stooped. Hernandez stepped out onto the pavement; his white shirt enveloped by the blinding early evening light. He stepped back in and waved her through.

"Go. Go now," he rasped.

Eva looked up and down the street and slipped across to the shade of the trees.
Her Guzzi was where she had left it. One of the young men was pouring the last drops of fuel into the tank from a military-sized jerry can. The other made a toothy mime of polishing the machine. Eva handed them the black weeds and the last of her folded pesetas. They smiled and disappeared into the tented carnival, merging with the throng in an instant. Eva pulled her hair up, winding it under the padded leather pilot's helmet and looked back at the festival. The music and lights suggested the possibility of escape, of losing herself.
She pulled on her thick goggles, climbed aboard the bike and gunned the engine into life, heading for the Gulf of Cadiz.

7

Oxfordshire

Chainbridge stepped into the small office-cum-kitchen and sat down on a spacious leather chair; the one indulgence he allowed himself. He turned up the large radio tuned to the BBC World Service; old habits die hard, he thought.
The shop bell tolled.

"Another sale, Carson - we're on a roll," said Chainbridge.

Carson, a tawny stray cat that had recently taken up residence in the shop, sat up in a storage box lined with newspaper. His eyes closed and his ears twitched; he purred for no apparent reason. Chainbridge walked back to the counter. The man standing opposite was tall, dressed in Harris tweeds and matching raincoat. The lean complexion, broken blood vessels and underlying sneer were instantly familiar, though Chainbridge hadn't seen the man in nearly three years.

"Curran," he said.

"Chainbridge," replied the man. Each syllable seemed to roll around for a moment before being slowly uttered. Miles Curran had the demeanour of an unfulfilled curate.

"Enjoying retirement?"

"It has its compensations."

Curran glanced around the shop and turned slowly back,

"The last time we spoke was in Tehran?"

"You accepted my resignation."

"Things have changed, Henry."

Curran had never called him Henry before.

"I'm closing for lunch; we'll have some privacy."

Just as Chainbridge reached the door Carson darted out, neatly side-stepping Curran. Chainbridge locked the door and slowly turned the CLOSED sign. By the kerb was an official looking car.

"Yours, Curran?"

"Bracken's."

Brendan Bracken, once Churchill's minister without portfolio. Another echo from 1943, thought Chainbridge

"Very ostentatious – drawing some attention, I might add. We can chat in the back room. Tea?"

"Black, with lemon, thank you," replied Curran. He had already gone around the counter.

"Lemons haven't quite made it to Little Shotton, I´m afraid. Rationing," said Chainbridge, "But I do have some splendid Assam."

Chainbridge lit the little gas hob and filled the kettle. Curran already had his tan leather briefcase open, a stack of papers and a Manilla folder out on the table. He pushed a sheet over to Chainbridge with a pen on top. From the depths of his cardigan Chainbridge produced a pair of glasses,

"Official Secrets Act? I'm retired, remember?"

"Churchill accepted your resignation with regret, not Atlee. The new PM's quite paranoid about such matters," said Curran. Chainbridge looked at the heavy silver fountain pen, the nib gleaming in the dim light of the office. From such pens, wars were declared, nations divided, and people's lives altered forever. He reached over and scratched his signature on the sheet.

"The Swiss desk, Bern, lost an operative," said Curran.

Chainbridge turned off the radio. The shop was silent. On the other side of the plate glass, Little Shotton went about its daily business. Everyone was either walking or cycling, enjoying the fine weather; a young mother, pushing a pram, moved at a leisurely pace. Chainbridge sat down opposite Curran, suddenly feeling every day of his six decades.

Curran produced a photograph from the folder. It was of a very pretty girl, her head leaning against a train window.

"Anna Chambrel; a severe knife wound to the shoulder, several lesser lacerations, a broken nose and also, we believe, poisoned."

"How old was she?" asked Chainbridge.

"That's immaterial."

"In Bern?"

"No. Zürich. She was discovered in Bern where the contact was to meet her. To her credit, the girl kept her head; managed to dress the shoulder wound."

"A message?"

"Appears so."

"From whom?" Chainbridge asked.

His first instinct was the Russians; but they would have butchered her and dumped her after breaking her.

"We don't know," admitted Curran. A slight note of uncertainty clouded his voice, "A new threat."

The kettle boiled. Chainbridge rose and filled an ornate china pot. He rummaged around and located a shortbread biscuit. He put it on a saucer and placed it beside Curran.

"Must be causing a diplomatic stink, Currran?"

"FO had to step on a lot of toes to get her out," replied

Curran.

"Who was her case officer?"

"Gageby, Douglas Gageby."

"That explains a lot." Chainbridge poured tea into two pewter mugs. He sipped from the chipped one.

"As a caveat in your resignation, you insisted he be moved from London *out of harm's way* – your words?"

"And you moved him to Switzerland?"

"Yes."

Chainbridge felt the first stirrings of rage. Anna Chambrel probably thought she was on a little adventure – it would have been phrased that way, an off-hand remark. Instead she walked into a snake pit. Bloody Douglas Gageby.

"Anna was killed for what, exactly?" he asked.

"Microfilm. Miss Chambrel did manage to pass it on to Gageby who in turn, handed it over to MI6. Bern Office decrypted it. They took one look at it and sent it on to Int.7."

"So, Gageby found something and went off on his own. Flawed tradecraft if you ask me. I thought Int.7. had been mothballed once Bracken moved to the Admiralty," said Chainbridge.

"For all intents and purposes, it was - until last week when Int.7. popped up in Berlin. Charlottenburg, British sector, has an individual in its cells claiming he's Int.7. He wishes to speak with you personally."

Chainbridge longed for a cigarette; something to fire up his synapses, but his lungs were operating at forty-per cent capacity and the local doctor insisted he quit. She left a bag of her home-made shortbread in his shop every Saturday morning to sweeten the pill. Her biscuits had a knack of surviving for several days.

"Berlin?" he asked.

Curran slid a photograph over. It was a profile and frontal shot of a man. Chainbridge gave a start.

"Brandt? Alive?"

"Swapped for another asset. Gulag system for nearly two years. Found shot outside Stadmitte U-Bahn dressed in a Russian officer's uniform in May 1945."

"His identity has been confirmed?"

Looking at the image, Brandt seemed thinner, more lined, but the eyes gazed out cold and steady.

"Name, rank and serial number all match," replied Curran. He idly dipped Doctor Esther Galloway's shortbread into his tea.

"You have to confirm this *facie-ad-faciem*, Chainbridge."

"I'm retired, Curran. I'm satisfied the man in the photograph is Captain Nicklaus Brandt, AOK Norwegen Korps, part of SOE foreign auxiliaries."

"Bracken is keen to investigate this one, Chainbridge. MI6 are tied up like everyone else with the atomic bomb and Soviet moles. This is strictly off-the-books, as Miss Chambrel's death and Brandt's reappearance may have a connection."

"Connection?"

"Edgar Halidane," replied Curran.

"Should I know him?"

"Halidane Corp. Very powerful, very rich. Miss Chambrel acquired the microfilm during a soiree at his organisation."

Chainbridge leafed through the dossiers. He placed the two photographs side by side; a pretty girl and the gnarled features of Brandt, now resurrected in Berlin.

"So, the Swiss desk sent her in for...?"

"Irregular banking, Henry. Halidane's office in Zürich is of interest to them; it transferred a substantial amount of money and gold into the Basler Handelsbank in Zürich; reputedly Martin Bormann's private bank. Now that Gageby has cocked things up royally, Halidane will be on the look-out for British Intelligence."

"Chopin?" asked Chainbridge.

"La Grande Horizontale? Incognito. We think she's in Spain, looking for her precious Captain Brandt," replied Curran. He rolled the words sourly in his mouth.

"You never seem to approve of her methods; shades of the iniquities of Eve, Curran?" said Chainbridge.

He slid the chair out and refilled the kettle. The water spat and choked its way out of the tap.

"She doesn't appear to have a moral core."

"Ernst Röhm's SA saw to that, Curran."

Chainbridge placed both his palms on the hob as he watched the kettle. On his right middle finger, the nail was missing, and the tip had folded in on itself; the result of a shrapnel wound in Murmansk in 1920.

"De Witte?"

"He's in Lisbon. Still hunting renegade Nazis." Curran swilled the dregs of his tea as he spoke.

"And he's aware of Zürich and Berlin?" asked Chainbridge.

"Yes. We´d best press on now, Chainbridge, the clock is ticking."

"I'm afraid I run a business now. Can't just up sticks and leave."

"Bracken insists you return with me today. You will be compensated handsomely."

"I've a good stipend from the last mission. I can refuse you know, Curran."

With reverential moves Curran placed all his paperwork back as if it were a chalice being placed into the tabernacle.

"The Americans are involved now, Henry. We really don't have a choice."

"The Americans? Well, that makes it all right then," replied Chainbridge.

He looked around his small office and neat little gallery. Ruth and Geoffrey Harvey seemed a lifetime ago.

Brandt had two paths waiting for him if his information proved worthless; one led to the gallows as a spy, the other back to the gulags. Chainbridge owed him his life.

"I have some paperwork to finish up, Curran. Then we will go to Berlin. Berlin, only, Curran – no more adventures. Just a visual confirmation."

"Do the necessaries. I'll wait," replied Curran.

A thought occurred to Chainbridge,

"Bracken wants to send in Chopin?" he asked.

"Yes. She'll listen to you - if we can find her."

Chainbridge stacked the draining board, emptied the tea pot and made a few phone calls to locals who could watch the shop. His last call was to Doctor Galloway; she was unable to take his call and the receptionist took a message.

"Eva doesn't know Brandt is alive then?" he asked.

"No. Codename *Chopin* doesn't know Brandt is alive," replied Curran.

Where on earth *was* she? thought Chainbridge.

8

Gulf of Cadiz, Spain

Eva panned her binoculars across the sweep of the bay. The motorcycle lay on its side, the panniers supporting its weight on the scrub. The cove was a tight half-moon with sheer cliffs meeting at a dull-looking shale beach. The sea was like glass and the clouds were beginning to shade it in the early evening light. Side-by-side, sheltered in the cove, lay three U-boats at anchor. Their clean lines and narrow aspect didn't offer up any identification. Eva pressed herself down onto the scrub. Lank grasses swayed in the breeze, the coast wind considerably cooler. She'd have to get closer. Leaning up on one elbow, she looked around; the road she had come down was deserted. The isolated area near the cove rustled with the wind and the occasional shriek of a seabird. The Moto Guzzi was a hardy model and handled the coarse terrain better than she had expected. From her knapsack, she pulled the road map she'd used to get to Seville. Taking her pocket compass and Spassky's directions, she populated the top corner with notes. On her left wrist was a pilot's watch; it had thick numbers, hands and a luminous dial. The casing was scratched, the winder unreliable and the crystal lined with a webbing of cracks. But its timekeeping was impeccable. The one keepsake from her lover; she hoped to return it when she found him.

Eva folded the map away. She planted her foot firmly onto the engine frame and used it as a fulcrum to haul the motorcycle upright. Steadying it on its stand, she re-attached the panniers and pulled out her second camera. It was a tough Leica with a Russian lens adapted to allow as much light in as possible. She wished it had a zoom. The light was fading, the day's heat evaporating quickly. Zipping up her fur-lined jacket and donning her helmet and goggles, she cranked the engine into life and slid downhill in a low gear.

Searching for somewhere to hide the bike, she idled the machine towards the beach. Once she had it leaning against a lichen stained outcrop, she crunched along the shale. The U-Boats seemed more menacing up close; pristine and lethal, they were also huge, riding high on the waves. She took several carefully composed shots and then photographed repeatedly, using up the film. Experience told her one developed image would probably suffice.

It was then she heard the engines. Banking overhead, a seaplane dived towards the water. Moments later it appeared at the mouth of the cove. It was silver and white, without any visible markings. It idled the propellers of its four engines as it cruised towards the U-boats. Then a door slid aside on its fuselage. A small boat was lowered from it and five men jumped in, rowing strongly toward the submarines.

They were dressed in Kreigsmarine uniforms; no question they were German. No question too, Eva had been spotted. A glass turret at the top of the seaplane turned and the mechanical popping of machine gun fire sent splinters of rock jumping around her. Shouts were coming from the rowboat and Eva felt a bullet whistle past her ear. Clawing, scrambling, sprawling, Eva made it to the motorcycle. To get to the road, she would have to pass the few yards of open space in the aircraft´s gunsights. She had no choice. Mounting the Moto Guzzi, she opened the throttle and skewed through the hail of bullets. She felt the back tyre kick out and then recovered control, feeling the earth juddering up through the heel of her combat boot. The back wheel was shedding spokes, but she was fully committed; she opened the throttle up further. She flattened her sinuous figure against the contours of the bike, using it as a shield. Bullets pinged off metal then fell short, kicking up shale and dust.

Two hours later Eva arrived at the outskirts of Seville and the glistening Rio Guadalquivir. It was getting dark, the bright lights and sounds of the Feria de Abril drifted across the river. She was alone. The Moto Guzzi was dented, battered. The gearbox was a mess and the back wheel badly deformed. She checked the cameras, both intact, her binoculars shattered, the map with an impressive bullet hole in the middle of the Gulf. She took one pannier and placed everything inside, then pushed the motorcycle into the river. Gracelessly, it splashed into the depths. Goggles, helmet and gloves followed. Crossing by the iron bridge, Eva plunged back into the all-consuming fiesta. The festivities had, if anything, intensified and she gave silent thanks that she, like her lover Brandt, was still alive. Clutching the pannier close to her body she made her way directly to the café and the safe hands of Hernandez, whose Jesuit contact had pledged to get her intel to London.

9

Huelva, Spain.

Martin Bormann wasn't a man for sentiment. The former Reichsleiter listened in sullen silence as his right-hand man, Heinrich Müeller reviewed the report from the flying boat. The U-boats were fully crewed; provisions and weaponry would be complete by end-of-week. But they had been spotted. They believed the observer had been hit, but they wouldn't be able to search for the body until daybreak.

"I thought we weren't trying to draw attention?" said Bormann.

"The gunner thought he saw a camera," replied Müeller.

It was inevitable, thought Bormann. Two of the vessels were state-of-the-art, designed to transport him and several others, including Müeller, to Argentina. They were wanted men. The third had been specially adapted – she had the best captain, the best crew.

The hotel was quiet, located off a side-street in Huelva away from the cafes and bars. Four SS bodyguards occupied the room on the opposite side of the corridor. Bormann and Müeller were immune to distractions; they had to finalise their departure.

"Casa Rosa?" asked Bormann. Once smooth-shaven and stone-like, he now had a full moustache, neatly trimmed. He was thinner.

"Ready," replied Müeller.

Müeller too was thinner, giving his face the gaunt expression of a cadaver. He handed over the sheaves of communiques and Bormann immersed himself in the decrypted files. Malleus had been thorough in his financial dealings, he noted; the banking transfers had all been completed successfully.

"The Orkneys?" asked Bormann.

Once accessible from Norway by seaplane, reaching the Orkney Islands now implied a hazardous voyage for the U-Boat that would take weeks, skirting British waters and her navy.

"SS-Obergruppenführer Hoeberichts is on standby. Herr Halidane, though, is very unhappy about the unsanctioned launch," murmured Müeller.

"Halidane is already surplus to requirements," said Bormann.

Halidane was all *ma-and-pa American apple-pie*, thought Bormann. He would've preferred to deal with the Russians; at least they stab you in the front, grinning.

"That'll be all, Müeller."

"Herr Reichsleiter."

To salute in shabby hand-me-downs would have looked ridiculous.

Bormann lowered the lights in his room and looked out at the street below. He loosened his shoulder holster and placed his Mauser pistol on the modest table. He poured another shot of Armenian brandy and prepared himself for another sleepless night. As he dozed, the same thoughts kept recurring, Hitler's little study in the bunker. The faint whiff of bitter almonds recycled through the air vents; the last will and testament of the Third Reich.

"Perhaps I wasn't demanding enough?" whispered Hitler. Bormann ignored the nervous tics, the palsy shaking of the left fist.

"Perhaps I was too kind, Bormann?"

The voice that had commanded legions was lost amid the thump of Russian artillery fifty feet above and less than a mile away.

"Take the treasure, bury it. When the time is right, use it. You know what to do," said Hitler.

Bormann broke the seal on the directive. He scanned it and nodded.

"Good. Good – deny them the fruits of victory, Bormann. Even the abandoned cities must burn."

They had been Hitler´s last words to him.

At least the Fuhrer had tested the cyanide on his dog before offering it as a wedding gift to his bride. The image of Eva Braun's dainty silk slippers flashed through Bormann's mind, small feet sticking out from her robe, now just ash.

Bormann and Müeller had stalked along the maze of corridors, past the communications room where Goebbels was still declaring final victory speeches. As the Soviets raped and rampaged through the city, the civilian cries for help were muted and forgotten, the dial turned down until the screams went silent. So much for heroic last stands by the glorious legions, thought Bormann.

The rats had abandoned the bunker one-by-one; Herr *artistic genius*, Speer was nowhere to be found, Goering was no longer responding to communications. Martin Bormann wasn't going to stick around to be shipped to the gulag or the torture chamber. He knew too much.

Down the three levels of the bunker Bormann and Müeller, dressed in identical three-quarter length leather coats, had skulked. They inched their way along the wooden planks thrown over the flooded Kannenberg Allee; the rancid flood water spilled over their combat boots; the one thing that would make them stand out from the terrified civilians.

Through the labyrinthine passages, lit by the generator's dying pulses, they arrived at the shattered windows overlooking

Wilhelmstrasse. They paused. Opening their mouths slightly, they listened intently to the sounds outside. Sporadic gunfire and explosions echoed in through the window. Distant. Not close. Their breaths, long trailing finger-like gasps, lingered about them. Bormann nodded. Tapping out the glass fragments around the pane with his pistol butt, he forced his ungainly build through the window.

Müller followed lithely.

They loped along the shadows to Kaiserhof U-Bahn, stopping whenever a loud explosion rang out. Dust and smoke rose into the dawn; the city of Berlin was now in its death throes.

Bormann stood for the last time on the streets of the capital, then dashed down the station steps.

Below, huddled on the platforms, the population stared out in silent resignation. Bormann tilted his hat a little lower over his face and the two men dropped onto the train tracks. Probing and fumbling their way along, each step one closer to liberation, they came to Stadtmitte Station.

Here they would separate.

"Good luck, sir," said Müeller.

Ascending the station steps, Bormann paused and looked around. Satisfied there was no-one watching, he removed the coat. Underneath, he wore the uniform of a Russian General. From the coat's deep pocket, he produced a movie prop from Goebbels' film studios; a cloth cap which, when pulled down, appeared to be bandages covering a severe head wound. Even the dried blood appeared authentic; an off-colour brown.

He gave a low, clear whistle out through the station entrance.

He repeated it twice.

A single whistle came back.

Martin Bormann walked out of the station entrance.

At the kerb amid the ruins, was a Russian car, a Gaz-61. He had purchased it, fuelled it and hidden it in one of his secret bunkers. The two soldiers dressed in Russian army uniforms were German, both fluent Russian speakers.

"Your gun," Bormann said to one of them.

The soldier was tall, lean and in his mid-thirties. He had strong, sinewy hands. He handed the Reichsleiter his Maschinenpistole 38.

Bormann sprayed the Gaz with bullets, avoiding the engine block. He fired two bursts into the back-seat windows.

He turned to address the soldiers.

"You, I know," he nodded to the shorter of the two.

"You, I don't."

The tall man froze as Bormann turned the weapon on him. But the normally reliable MP-38 jammed. The trusted soldier spun to strike the tall man who deftly dodged his rifle butt, but not the shot from Bormann's pistol, pulled from a pocket.

Clutching his shoulder, the man collapsed. Before the coup de grace, a Russian artillery shell landed close by, showering everything in cloying dust. Bormann and his driver leapt into the Gaz, leaving the injured soldier bleeding in the street.

Bormann's Gaz-61 sped through the Soviet roadblocks. At the sight of an injured Russian officer, the vehicle was ushered on by Soviet signallers. At a secret airstrip at Charlottenburger Chaussee, held by a full SS division, a British Lancaster Bomber was waiting for him. Amid the Heinkels and immense Junkers, it stood out like a sore thumb.

It flew out under a scratch fighter escort along with other evacuating German forces, but instead of heading to the fall-back at Obersalzburg, the Lancaster banked towards neutral Spain; loaded with bullion instead of bombs.

Bormann could not stop thinking about that injured driver; the reds had probably killed him, but it was a loose thread, and Martin Bormann hated loose threads. They had a habit of unravelling.

To kill the nagging doubt, he poured himself another generous measure of cognac and waited for the dawn.

10

Oxford

At midnight, the GWR locomotive pulled into the station. Behind the riveted glistening bunker was a single carriage, heavily armored, with large metallic slats angled over the windows. It rolled squat along the tracks. *South Central Pullman* was stenciled incongruously along its metal flanks.

Chainbridge and Curran watched the train slow in a titanic pulse of steam and smoke. The station was deserted, there was no announcement, no porters and no station master. At the rear of the carriage a door slid open and a tall man with owl-like glasses stepped onto the platform. The pomaded red hair and unusually full lips were unmistakable; it was Brendan Bracken.

"Chainbridge, Curran, excellent. Like old times," he said.

They stepped aboard into a world of unparalleled luxury. Deep rich wooden panelling, lush carpets and leather settees lined the carriage. Tables were set with Irish linen, Mappin & Webb silverware and Royal Doulton porcelain. A liveried naval attendant took coats, hats and umbrellas and stashed them away neatly. In the corner sat an old familiar figure; a quilted dressing gown draped over the paunchy waistcoat and heavy watch chain, half-rim glasses and a cigar being slowly chomped – Winston Churchill.

"We have about two hours before we reach Paddington," said Bracken. "Then you'll be flying out on my personal Avro York to Berlin. Your liaison is Hopkins in Charlottenburg."

Churchill, the old defeated lion, stared over the piles of dossiers stacked against his hip. Red ribboned despatch boxes lay open at his feet.

"I take it Prime Minister Atlee doesn't know you're in the country?" asked Chainbridge.

Churchill shifted his weight on the settee like a corpulent Maharaja. The smoke from his cigar hung about him like a conjuror´s trick. A large crystal decanter of whiskey sat between his slippered feet on the floor, he refilled his glass heftily. He gave the slightest of nods.

"This is Winston's private carriage, quite a piece of workmanship," said Bracken.

"I call it *The Marlborough*," growled Churchill.

"The rift between you and Mr. Bracken here?" asked Chainbridge.

"Propaganda," said Churchill.

"We've fed a story through the AP wires that Winston is in America," said Bracken.

"Resting for a few weeks, influenza, or some such thing," said Churchill.

Once they took their seats, Bracken pulled down a plain white screen. As the locomotive lurched forward, he dimmed the lights. A sequence of photographs was projected onto the fabric. The naval attendant fed the slides with slow deliberation.

"Latest developments from the foul-up in Zürich; Douglas Gageby, found dead in the lobby of the Hotel Bahnhof," intoned Bracken.

Chainbridge stared at the screen. Gageby's skin looked flaccid in the harsh black and white still; as if his soul had been sucked straight out of his chest.

"Bern office has most likely been compromised. Gageby made two calls from the hotel phone booth; one was to the office, the other, Zürich Polytechnic," said Bracken.

"How did he die?" asked Chainbridge.

"Natural causes, apparently. Poisoning most likely," said Bracken.

"Why the polytechnic?"

"We're exploring theories, Chainbridge," replied Bracken.

Another slide. This time it was a grainy shot taken at hip level between two bodies, their mass formed a V that went to the bottom of the photograph. In the middle of the V stood a man in a white coat with a shock of wild hair.

"Dr. Vassily Kagonovich; Moscow Institute of Sciences, good political connections, his star is on the rise within Soviet circles, popped up in Berlin in August of last year," said Bracken.

Another slide, another mass of bodies. Kagonovich talking to two

Soviet commissars.

"These photographs were smuggled out from the Reichschancellery, which has been on lock-down. A packet of Lucky Strikes to a Russian guard would´ve got you a personal guided tour of Hitler's bunker a year ago. Now, there's a Russian armed division all over it."

Another slide, a wide angled shot of trucks and armoured cars lined up with a cordon of heavily armed soldiers.

"Not your usual gang of looting, raping peasant yahoos, but a crack combat unit. They'd obviously found something. Flights were leaving Templehof almost hourly. Stalin had even sanctioned the use of his armoured train, supported by a full armoured division," said Bracken.

"Any idea as to why?" asked Curran.

"No," replied Bracken.

"Can you go back to the commissars, please?" asked Chainbridge.

The slides ground slowly back; each click sounded like a gunshot. Chainbridge stood up and examined the image.

"Valery Yvetchenko. I dealt with him during the war when he was with the Stavka. The other one, I met in 1941 in Helsinki, his name is Kravchenko; then, a Colonel in the NKVD. We tried to recruit him, but alas, he's a loyal Soviet citizen. I heard he died in the Crimea three years ago."

Chainbridge leaned in closer. The quality of the photograph, though poor, had an urgency about it. The body language exuded unease.

Returning to the big leather chair, Chainbridge caught Churchill´s eye. His features, submerged behind the glasses, glowered back.

The next slide was a series of papers with distinctive cursive handwriting consisting of figures, formulae and a partial schematic of an architectural cut-away.

"Decrypts from the microfilm; Halidane Corp," said Bracken.

"Edgar Halidane is an American born, naturalised British citizen; lived in Berlin in the 1930's and was smuggled out of Marseilles through Varian Fry's rescue committee in 1941. Ore and commodities broker, a self-made man who calls himself an 'electrical innovator'. His businesses are almost certainly a cloak for the former Third Reich, siphoning substantial financial transactions through the Basler Handelsbank and Schweizerische Kreditanstalt in Zürich. Martin Bormann has his fingerprints all over this one. This is a picture of Halidane from a few years back."

The next slide was of a paunchy, balding man, smartly dressed, staring heroically off into the middle distance. He looked as assured as the commissars were uneasy, thought Chainbridge. An untouchable, well-connected, smartly groomed man, this Edgar Halidane.

"Properties in New York, London, Zürich, Stockholm and a huge private estate, Fawkeston Gyre, in Devon. Secretive, unmarried, but has a penchant for young women; the younger the better apparently," added Bracken.

The train glided smoothly along the tracks. The liveried attendant supplied coffee, cigars, brandy and thick steak sandwiches. The men stopped to eat. Champagne, whiskey and soda water were poured into German crystal.

Chainbridge rose and stretched. Burying his hands in his cardigan, he stared at the images on the screen, the formulae, transactions. Two people had died already. Edgar Halidane – who the hell was he, really?

Beneath an image of hand-written banking transactions was a small torn strip of paper. The writing was fluid, smooth - it read:

X I J O -T B X = 5 9 D w 5 7 M n + 2 D Z Z M w.

Chainbridge tilted his head. Using his tortoiseshell glasses, he hovered over the image.

"That's a code," he said.

Bracken, Curran and Churchill glanced up.

"Pretty sure it's a cryptarithm. Looks complete, not cut off by the camera lens; it looks as if it was accidentally caught in the photograph."

"It must have been overlooked," said Curran. He rose and

stood beside Chainbridge, "Who took the photograph?"

"Miss Chambrel," replied Curran.

She was a smart girl, thought Chainbridge.

"Has Bletchley seen it?" he asked.

"MI6 have passed this one over, Chainbridge. Bletchley has been wound down and the remaining code breakers have moved to the Russian Analysis Department. That's why we're here. It's INT.7's now," said Bracken.

"Looks straightforward; do we have anyone available?" asked Chainbridge.

"No. This is it I'm afraid; well - if you include Brandt and Miss Molenaar," said Bracken.

"If it *is* Brandt, Mr. Bracken. De Witte?" said Chainbridge.

"We've sent a copy over to his offices in Lisbon, but as Brandt's appearance has added a degree of urgency, it's on our desk," said Bracken.

"It's our boy, alright, Chainbridge – Brandt fought with the Freies Deutschland Brigade against Himmler's divisions after D-Day and was sent in to assassinate a top Nazi. Got himself caught by the Russians for a second time," said Curran.

"Was he successful?" asked Churchill. He had lowered his papers. Until he spoke the only sign of life seemed to be the flashes of red at the tip of his cigar.

"He won't say," replied Bracken.

Is this what had brought Churchill out of the wilderness and back into the shadows? thought Chainbridge. The old Prime Minister now held his gaze squarely at Bracken.

"I ordered the elimination of Martin Bormann. We lost contact with the SOE unit at the start of May 1945. Brandt was in command of the unit on my orders. As Bormann hasn't surfaced, I surmised they had been successful," he added.

"O.S.S. want to throw Brandt back into the swamp," said Curran. He leafed through the reams of intelligence slowly, deliberately. "Should we let them?"

"Not yet," said Chainbridge.

Brandt may well end up dead, he thought, but still had a slim chance if he could get there in time.

He looked back at the code. His years working for British Intelligence during the 1930s had broken several Nazi and communist cells. Several of the men caught - and subsequently jailed - were geniuses, and one name struck him.

"How far are we from London?" he asked.

"Forty minutes," said Curran.

"Mr Churchill, we need to turn this train around," said Chainbridge.

The grizzled old warlord rose with remarkable ease and pulled on a cord above his head. The liveried attendant entered.

"Where to, Chainbridge? Where shall I direct *The Marlborough?*" A glint had come into his eyes.

"Newcastle, Mr. Churchill, I know someone who might be able to decrypt that code in a few hours."

Curran leaned over to a large radio-telephone and dialled.

"I'll put that plane on hold for now."

11

Newcastle-on-Tyne

Alastaire Findlay studied the boy in front of him; McGhee, a thin kid with a glassy stare, already beaten down. Beaten down by his father and most of his classmates in the yard.

"Do you know what time it is, McGhee?"

McGhee blinked, he fidgeted and looked out of the early house windows. Dockers and day-shift crews loitered around the quays, a heavy fog billowed in and clouded the Tyne, the Dutch called it a *Haar*. It could last for days.

Findlay glanced up at the old pendulum clock above the bar; five-thirty am. He checked his watch; it was a minute faster than the old school clock; the story of his life.

"Alcohol, substance – what is it, dear McGhee?" said Findlay.

Along the wharf-side taverns, just about every vice could be

bought and sold; two tired looking streetwalkers hunched over pints of porter at the table opposite.
McGhee shrugged his slender shoulders, his hair looked greasy in the dimmed light. Findlay knew McGhee's father; number three at the end of the bar; a bear of a man in a Donkey jacket who could belt out a mean *Old Man River*.
Findlay counted them out every morning as he tapped his cigarette ash into the half-drained glasses around the bar; four men who had cash for beer and horses every day. McGhee senior would regularly fall off the stool or get abusive before clocking on at the docks, or sometimes shout over 'If I had to teach feckin' eejits like my dummy bairn, I'd be a pish-head too!'
Findlay knew *pater* McGhee well; knew his type; hardened on the banks of the Clyde.

"It's affecting your schoolwork, son," said Findlay.

"You're not my father," muttered McGhee.

He still wouldn't make eye contact.

"No, but I'm your form master; I have a duty of care,"

"I don't care," replied McGhee. He stared back suddenly; the repressed fury in his eye; shades of his father.

"I can give you the name of a man to talk to. He's a priest, a good man, hates the demon drink."

"A name?"

McGhee began to work a hangnail between his yellowed teeth nervously.

"A lifeline, son..."

"I don't need your help. Bugger off," said McGhee.

Findlay could smell the booze floating over on McGhee's breath. Another teacher told him young McGhee had pissed his pants in class. They had laughed it off as they had both 'done it on a night themselves.'
How old was this boy? Eleven, twelve?
Findlay looked up at the clock again; it would be hours before the school opened.

"A life-line," repeated Findlay. He touched the soiled Legion of Mary pin on his lapel.

"Are you finished, sir?" said McGhee.

"Yes, McGhee, you can go back to your dad now."
Findlay slid over a hand. He wanted to connect with the boy in some way.

"FUCK off, you-filthy-old-man!" roared McGhee, his voice suddenly shrill.

Pater Findlay leaned back along the bar to see the sudden commotion. A thick low forehead ringed with pomaded curls reminded Findlay of a very old, very vicious circus bear.

McGhee sidled over to his father.

Findlay offered to buy a round for numbers one through four and the vile brat he tried to help. Pints were poured, but none for him.

"Findlay," said a voice.

Findlay turned slowly to the man. He smiled in twisted recognition.

"Henry-bloody-Chainbridge," he said.

"It took a while to find you, Findlay," said Chainbridge.

"I have no desire to be found, Chainbridge. Drowning my sorrows and all that ... still hanging around with that blind bastard, de Witte?"

"I hear you've a teaching post? Well done, Findlay," said Chainbridge.

He nodded to the barman; two fingers of whiskey appeared on the counter.

"It pays the bills, Chainbridge; needs must and all that; now, what the fuck do you want?" Findlay's eyes were rheumy, but slightly, and unfocused beneath unkempt salt and pepper brows. His Scottish accent melded uneasily with the gruff north east cadences.

He downed the whiskey in one gulp and eyed Chainbridge's shot with the slow lick of his lip.

"Help yourself, Findlay,"

"Don't mind if I do. Chin, chin!"

The nails on his left hand were yellowed with grime and nicotine, his cuffs and collar were seedy and stained. His frayed striped bow tie clung to his shirt heroically like a wilted corsage.

Chainbridge looked at the bar, his gaze slowly took in the mass of soiled donkey jackets and cigarette smoke. He heard young McGhee's wheedling voice before it was silenced with a slap.

"Alcoholic parents and their children, Findlay?"

"Not like you to display a conscience, Chainbridge – what brings you to these salubrious surroundings at five-thirty in the morning?"

"You."

"Me? I'm honoured."

"You were given every opportunity to come clean, to explain yourself, Findlay," said Chainbridge.

"He died, you know, Yuri," said Findlay.

"Who?"

"My Yuri, Chainbridge, my consolation prize. Died at his majesty's pleasure – pneumonia."

"I'm sorry."

"My Yuri. Twenty-one."

"Sorry, Findlay."

"No. No, you are not, Chainbridge. No. Get to the point, old bean, get to the bloody point!"

The twilight denizens of the bar began to turn toward them.

"I need your help," said Chainbridge

"Piss off."

"Okay, your government - the country you betrayed - needs your help."

"Well they can just fuck right off then, can't they?"

Findlay gestured to the empty glasses and jerked a dirty thumb back at Chainbridge.

The barman obliged.

"They can pay you," said Chainbridge.

"I've paid my debt to society, Chainbridge, you and that blind Dutch rat of yours made sure of that," snorted Findlay into the glass.

"They pay your teacher's salary, that can go if they want," said Chainbridge. "I thought I'd start nicely, but it's down to this now."

Chainbridge looked at this watch. It was five-thirty gone. Four old men wide awake when they should be at rest; three sitting in an armoured train from another era, trying to dragoon the ghost of a spymaster's past glories. Chainbridge longed for his shop, his tea and the uncomplicated companionship of a cat.

"Meenagh?" asked Findlay.

Chainbridge was quietly taken aback, his wife had always been a closely guarded secret because of her caste.

"Dead. Luftwaffe raid," said Chainbridge.

"Spared her the agony of seeing dear old blighty on its knees then," Findlay bellowed.

The drinkers ignored him, wrapped up in their private miseries.

"Not that dear old blighty treated her well, her nationality ´n´ all?" said Findlay.

"Just like you and thousands of others; a casualty," said Chainbridge.

"Spare me your mock righteousness. Now be a good fellow and fuck-right-off back to the rock from under which you crawled. Go on, chop, chop, toddle off then," said Findlay.

"One for the road?" said Chainbridge.

Chainbridge put a few crowns on the bar; the barman poured a hefty shot.

"Rule Britannia," said Findlay.

He swallowed the liquor and wiped his mouth with a sleeve.

"Yuri and Meenagh, their war is over now, Findlay, ours continues. I need your help; I need a few hours of your time; I will pay you."

Findlay fished a battered tweed hat and overcoat off the floor. He shook the cigarette ash and dust off them vigorously.

"Little bairns need their education, Chainbridge – thanks for breakfast."

"It's a little more complicated than that, Findlay. As well as selling secrets to the Russians, both you and Yuri indulged in ... inappropriate behaviour. Behaviour I can appraise your school management about. As well as your consolation prize, there were other men."

"Only men, Chainbridge. Men. Not boys, not ever. All consensual," replied Findlay.

"Still against the laws of the land, Findlay; consensual or

not."

"Done my time, Chainbridge. My criminal record speaks for itself. Luckily for me, Adolf - f'ckin' - Hitler thinned out enough educators to allow me back into the bottom of the barrel, pardon the pun."

Findlay swept his arm around, the master of all he surveyed.

"Unfortunately, that complaint is about to be lodged," said Chainbridge.

Findlay paused, he looked at Chainbridge, head inclined like a bird. Findlay's eyes at that moment seemed unaligned, as if one had come loose and was rolling around his skull independently of the other one.

A cheer had gone up from the far end of the bar. Young McGhee had vomited up his whiskey onto the bar and floor. He grinned queasily up at his father before another beating began.

"Never face-to-face, Chainbridge; always bloody cloak and dagger?"

"Wash your face and hands, comb your hair and try to look presentable. I'll be waiting outside in the car. You have five minutes, there's a good chap. Chop chop."

***

The Marlborough thundered through the early hours towards London. A splash of cologne and brilliantine had improved Findlay somewhat, but the rank undertow of unwashed clothes still made Curran's nose twitch.

"I want it noted, I'm signing this under duress," said Findlay.

"Sign the bloody thing, sir. Sign it," said Churchill. He thrust the Official Secrets Act at Findlay like an epée.

"I never voted for you, Churchill," replied Findlay.

Churchill poured another whiskey into Findlay's glass.

"Join the bloody queue, sir," he replied.

Curran and Bracken glanced from the disheveled newcomer to Chainbridge.

"His mind is like a steel trap, our Findlay," said Chainbridge, "though how he oils it is a matter of some concern."

"Bottoms up," said Findlay. He quaffed the alcohol down.

"Mr. Findlay, the cauldron of Europe is bubbling ever closer to the surface of the morass. It is a rubbish heap, a charnel house, a breeding ground of pestilence and hate. Kindly place your signature where it is required, and do your duty, sir," said Churchill.

"Well seeing as you've put it that way, why the hell not. I want my criminal record purged too."

"I'll look into it, Mr. Findlay," said Churchill.

With a scrawled dash, Findlay eventually obliged.

"Now, where's this f'king encryption?" he asked.

X I J O-T B X = 5 9 D w 5 7 M n + 2 D Z Z M w.

Findlay leaned over the table. From his inside pocket, he fished out his glasses and wound them around his ears. He splayed his hands out either side of the page. He drummed each finger deliberately as if practicing piano scales.

"I'd like a cup of tae. Strong," he said.

The attendant arrived with a delicate china service. He poured in the tea and milk; Findlay added the last of his whiskey.

"Well?" asked Chainbridge.

"I'll need a little time; I'd like to be undisturbed," said Findlay

"Anything else?" asked Chainbridge

"Pencil, paper, silence."

Churchill pulled back the heavy Turkish woven drapes that hung mid-way along the carriage. Behind them were folded accordion doors. Along with the attendant, Churchill pulled across folded oak doors that bisected the carriage. Locking the door, they watched Findlay at the desk. Hunched over and sipping from the cup and saucer as a dog would lap a bowl of water, he tapped a muffled tattoo with the pencil on the desk.

"First in maths at Oxford, glittering academic career ahead of him, one of the few to have met Albert Einstein personally as a peer," said Chainbridge.

Curran studied the Scotsman with barely concealed distain.

"Sold state secrets to the Soviet Union, though didn't he?" said Curran.

"He fell in love," replied Chainbridge.

"Can he crack this code quickly?" asked Bracken.

"Since we're against the clock and thin on personnel, he's the best shot I'm afraid," said Chainbridge.

"True enough, gentlemen," said Bracken.

Churchill returned to his leather sedan, his blanket, his robe, his cigars and his despatch boxes. Chainbridge thought, for an instant, that the old imperialist was smiling.

***

The Marlborough was close to London, a murky dawn filtered through the metallic slats and greasy carriage windows. The points and junctions clattered beneath the superstructure, muffled by Persian rugs.

"I don't like Mr. Findlay being here," said Curran, "Official Secrets Act notwithstanding."

"I have a dossier on him the size of a bible. He'll play along," replied Chainbridge.

Findlay sat back, laced his thick fingers behind his head and met the gaze of the table.

"It's a code that needs to be solved quickly, a code-on-the run, so to speak. If that's the case, without encryption notes and one-time pads, it's a 'true' code that can be produced anywhere; in a newspaper, periodical, written down or broadcast on the wireless."

"True code?" asked Chainbridge.

"The results are straight – six letters equal the result," replied Findlay, "Where did you get it?"

"Edgar Halidane," replied Chainbridge.

He slid a photograph across the table, cleared of its finery, now replaced with ashtrays and coffee cups.

"Edgar Halidane. Met him once, in Zürich. American. An absolute fucking genius. Grilled Einstein as I recall."

"Zürich Polytechnic?" asked Curran

"1908 or '09, possibly," muttered Findlay.

"Gageby's second call was a message?" said Chainbridge.

"A breadcrumb to follow," replied Curran.

"This Halidane - we'd never heard of him until a few days ago," said Chainbridge.

Curran's stare bored through Chainbridge, he glanced at Findlay and back to Chainbridge.

"What a stroke of luck – you met Halidane? Our very Edgar Halidane? In person?" said Currran.

"Your very own Edgar Halidane was the Betty-fucking-Grable of mathematics. Small community at his level. Sorry, I didn't catch your name?"

Suddenly he was the schoolmaster facing down an unruly pupil.

"Curran."

"Edgar Halidane, Mr. Curran, is another level of science altogether; theoretical mathematics and physics – pure bloody alchemy, sir."

Findlay stood up. To his delight, behind maps and aerial reconnaissance photographs from the past, he'd uncovered a dusty blackboard on the carriage wall. Clicking his tongue, he rummaged around and found a box of chalk. With a flourish, he wiped a corner of the blackboard & wrote out:

X I J O-T B X = 5 9 D w 5 7 M n + 2 D Z Z M w.

"The first part I assume, would be a sliding code, like Caesar's Gaul codes. If we assume that, the letter in the code is either the letter preceding it or, the letter after it."

Findlay's chalk creaked and threw a fine powder as he wrote below the code.

X I J O-T B X

He then wrote:

Y J K P - U C Y

"Assuming the A is preceded by the Z as a circle," said Findlay.

"Doesn't make sense," said Chainbridge.

"No, it doesn't, Chainbridge. But if we go to the *right* of each letter, we get..."

W H I P-S A W.

The letters stood out on the board.

"At least it is a word," said Chainbridge.

"So, gentlemen, let´s assume this algorithm is true. If it *is* a code on-the-hoof, and assuming a possible military application, the next part gives co-ordinates. Z is a zero, D a degree, M a minute and the numbers equal this Whip-Saw location."

Findlay leaned back against the board, the old assurance, for a moment, returned.

"Whip-Saw – whatever it is, is located at these co-ordinates," he said.

Leaning forward, he tapped the board with the chalk stump.

"59 degrees west, 57 minutes north, 2 degrees, 00 minutes west. If Edgar Halidane created it, then these are most likely English Ordinance Survey co-ordinates. Gentlemen, we need a map of The British Isles."

"What on earth is Whip-Saw?" asked Bracken

"I've de-crypted your message, the rest is up to you," said Findlay,

"I'm afraid, it's not that easy, Mr. Findlay," said Churchill.

Findlay unwound his glasses and produced a tired looking handkerchief to polish the lenses.

"What do you mean, Churchill?" he asked.

The old man stared at them over his glasses,

"You're now part of the team Mr. Findlay. Get some sleep, there's work to do tomorrow. You'll be accompanying Chainbridge and Curran to Berlin."

"What makes you think that's going to happen, Churchill?"

"You're fluent in Russian from your involvement in the Aberdeen Soviet and these gentlemen are going to need a translator."

"...and if I refuse?" said Findlay.

"I'll ensure, personally, you will never hold a teaching post anywhere here or in the commonwealth," said Churchill.

"Christ all-fucking-mighty," muttered Findlay. He slumped

into a leather settee.
The train thundered through the suburbs and points of London and through Paddington Station without stopping. Churchill's armoured train accelerated toward the Southern counties of England.
A washed-out dawn crept across the countryside swirling about the clouds.

12

Berlin/Charlottenburg

The future, it appeared to Nicklaus Brandt, was short and brutally unpromising. He stared up at the ceiling of his cell; he had been confined in one way or another for nearly three years, but the passage of time eluded him. From damp cellars in France to a huge prison in the Soviet Union, he seemed to be looking at the same four walls.
His persecutors in Moscow told him; "Jesus Christ suffered, but he'd never been to Russia."
And suffer Brandt did. Men died every day, in every possible violent way, pitiful lives ended on the cold prison floor.
Eva haunted him, appeared in his thoughts and his dreams when least expected. She couldn't be beaten out of him; she was always there - always. Whether he had been knocked unconscious, vomiting and shitting onto the floor, she was a beacon in the blood-stained, blacked-out night. During his darker moments, he saw her married with a family, assuming he was dead; he was only a breath away from the grave at any time. He thought of his big, heavy cast wristwatch and the defiant way she wore it.
Brandt's luck changed suddenly. One day his jailers washed him, shaved him, de-loused him. Then the commissar arrived. A pockmarked, scarred, shaved meathead of a man, squeezed into

a uniform, he instructed Brandt to find men willing to undertake a tough climb.

"What will you need?" asked Commissar Belov.

"A map," replied Brandt.

Belov bellowed for a map. One was found. The Altai mountains; three days by train from Moscow. Belov was in a low-key phase of panic.

"Rescue or retrieval?" asked Brandt.

"Classified," said Belov.

It was late November; they would be ascending to just over four thousand feet, judging by the smeared red crayon circling the target. The map was poor quality; Brandt had to assume they would encounter sheer escarpments.

"Yak grease," said Brandt.

Belov's porcine eyes blinked in quick succession.

"Tibetan, preferably. Also, provisions; meat, cheese, black bread. Coffee thermos, vodka. Short length skis – that looks like a glacier there. Boots with crampons. Compass, torch – ropes – heavy and light. Chalk or talcum powder. Have you good quality pitons?"

"Pitons?" replied Belov.

"Don't the Red Army have mountain divisions?" asked Brandt.

This brought a wheezing laugh from the commissar,

"All Red Army in Berlin!" he roared, "All Red Army in Germany! Why do you think we need you?"

"Give me some paper – it'd be easier to write it down," said Brandt.

Belov didn't like Brandt's tone; he slapped Brandt hard across the face.

"I will get paper," said Belov.

In simple Russian, supplemented by crudely drawn pictures, Brandt made out his list.

He worked his way through the German POWs. He sought out the names Kant, Kramer and Hauptmann but no-one had heard of them. Some of the prisoners recognised him, some sneered at him; already three-quarters of the way to the grave. He found two; a Luftwaffe officer named Meyer and a Wehrmacht private named Koch. Koch was in particularly bad shape but claimed to have ascended the Teufelsturm; that was enough. Brandt demanded an improvement of diet; he got a beating, black bread and sausage.

It was a start.

Eight men in the end; five Russians including Belov, three Germans. Brandt, Meyer and Koch were chained up in the goods wagon of the train. It took two days to get to the nearest town of Barnaul. Then Belov requisitioned local guides and mules at gun point. The Russians had guns, the Germans didn't; but Brandt had managed to ensure he and his men had ice-axes; they could be effective weapons. The caravan made its way to the base of the mountain, and a small camp was built. The guides refused to go any further, eyeing the climbers as if they were fools.

On the morning of the ascent Brandt instructed the men to strip naked and smear the foul-smelling yak grease onto their bodies; he hoped it would act as an extra layer of insulation, especially for the prisoners, who were not kitted out nearly as well as the Russians.

The thrill of the ascent, the wind, the biting cold, all energised Brandt. Every muscle drew on memory, as his fingers and feet sought crevices and cracks to ascend. His scratch team were hardy, as were their Soviet counterparts. Belov kept up with them, proving himself tough and fearless. More importantly, he began to listen to Brandt. Like everyone else, he wanted to live to see the next day.

At three thousand feet on a flat steppe, they found the wrecked aircraft, twisted and shattered. Belov cursed under his breath. Then the eight climbers found a sad-looking campfire and the man huddled drunk, staring into the guttering flames. Beside him lay a revolver and a shot-up pack radio.

"Comrade, Major General Dzgugashvili," saluted Belov.

"The girl is dead," slurred Vasily Dzgugashvili, "she's in the plane."

To Brandt, the resemblance was unmistakable; all the man needed was a pipe; Stalin.

"You all smell like animals," said Vasily Dzhugashvili Stalin.

"Yak fat, Comrade Major General," replied Belov.

The young Stalin clawed up his revolver and made shooing motions with it.

"Move away, you disgust me," he said.

The Russians, to a man, stepped reverentially back several paces.

Brandt walked over to the wreckage. Over the nose of the aircraft, thick splashes of dried blood spread in cloying rivulets.

He spotted a shock of blonde hair sticking through the shattered cockpit.

As gently as possible, Brandt dragged the girl out of the plane.

Broken neck, no bullet wounds.

Brandt, Meyer and Koch buried the girl in a shallow grave, using their ice axes. They found a few rocks and piled them over her reverentially.

Belov was pouring his thermos of coffee into Stalin´s son.

"You should save that for yourself, Commissar Belov," said Brandt.

Belov glowered up from under his Reindeer skin hat.

"Shut up," he said.

"Weather's about to break, Brandt," said Meyer, nodding toward the in-rushing thunder clouds.

"Storm," said Brandt.

"We are to return him to Moscow immediately," said Belov.

The Russians released the safety catches on their automatic weapons.

Brandt inhaled the mountain breezes; the wildness of the air and thought it was a better place to die than in some frozen, fetid subterranean cell.

"Your funeral, Belov," said Brandt.

Stalin had to be helped up. He stank of alcohol and vomit.

"Can you climb down?" asked Brandt.

Stalin blinked; his thick shock of hair sprang up from under the blanket he wore like a babushka.

"Possibly," he replied.

"Right answer," said Brandt.

The storm hit with an expected ferocity half an hour into the

descent.
Brandt rolled over in his cot. The thin prison issue blanket offered little protection from the cold and the fever running through him.
He slept.
He dreamed.
Belov´s ghost was sitting on the edge of the cot. The corporeal Belov now lay at the bottom of a ravine, food for the buzzards. Meyer and another Russian lay broken up beside him; their screams as they fell, swallowed by the storm.

"We should have bundled up that little bastard, knocked him out and carried him down like a Persian carpet," said Brandt.
The wraith Belov just nodded.

"Sorry," whispered Brandt.
The ghost shrugged.
It was a very Russian one.
The fever took hold, Brandt's teeth chattered, and he floundered around for a comfortable position. Belov moved closer to the shadows, his features slowly became the faces of friends he had lost, Meyer too, though Koch had surprised everyone. Brandt thought the wily, ferret-like private would survive the gulag system. He was hard-wired for survival.
Brandt snapped awake. He stared up at the ceiling, he had lost all sense of time. He coughed uncontrollably and, staggering from his cot, heaved up phlegm into his slop bucket. Turning back, he saw his father lying in the cot; the brilliant sportsman rendered a paraplegic by a French shell at Verdun in 1917. A man who held court in the veteran's ward, a man who had defied the odds much longer than expected,

"Be like a shark, Nick," he whispered, "Never stop. If you stop, you die."
Brandt ran his finger along the tattoo on his arm. It was a shark, the flesh around it scarred from a Polish soldier's bayonet and now his insurance policy – expertly sewn into it was a microdot. Encoded into the dot was information for Henry Chainbridge. Kallerhoff, the scientist, the man he had shared a frozen cell with for a week, had stitched it into the scar tissue before being dragged off for another interrogation.

"They like you, Brandt. I hear you're getting out of this frozen slice of paradise for a week," he'd whispered through shattered molars. "You're like them, you see? That's why they like you. Me, they hate."

Brandt had hardly felt the cut, made with a sliver of metal, or the stitching afterwards.

Kallerhoff never returned from interrogation.

Brandt urinated painfully into the bucket and looking back, saw his cot happily free of ghosts. He climbed into the bed as if it was a life raft in a storm and slipped into a fitful hour's sleep.

He dreamt of climbing out of cell, up through the ceiling and into the highest alps of Switzerland.

13

Barcelona

Eva lit the candles in front of the Virgin. About her, the air hung heavy with incense and penitence. The shadows of the church cooled the worshippers and the stained-glass windows burned a spectrum across the tiled nave and altar. She stepped back and glanced up at the statue. The Virgin's eyes stared heavenward; a serene smile carved on her mouth. It made Eva think of her holy communion in Krakow, a simple white dress and the warm calloused hand of her grandfather, Henk.

"*Selig sind die sanftmütigen,*" said a voice behind her,

"*Denn sie werden das Erdreich besitzen,*" replied Eva.

It was the correct codeword.

"And the meek shall truly inherit the earth, Miss Chopin," said the man. He was tall, tanned and dressed in a business suit that poorly concealed his paunch. He held his hat delicately in his hands. They were small and neat; a pen-pusher, she thought. He had a small tan leather satchel draped over one shoulder, which, along with his wide hips, made him appear oddly effeminate.

Eva spied a vacant pew as benediction began. The rustle of clothes, the faint clatter of rosary beads and the call-repeat chants of the faithful echoed around the stone. They made their way to it a few paces apart. She took her seat; she was a long way from genuflection now.

"Pay attention, Miss Chopin," whispered the pen pusher. "You are now officially a UNRRA nurse."

Glancing around, he slipped off the satchel and placed it between her feet.

"Passport, travel permits – all stamped for the British military sector in Berlin."

His voice had a nasal quality and the words seemed to emanate from the back of his throat. It was an English accent with Iberian inflections.

"The information?" she whispered.

"Well done. Whatever you sent; it appears to be very important. Int. 7. scrambled as soon as it was de-coded. The aircraft that fired on you was identified as a Japanese H8K flying boat."

"When do I leave?" she whispered.

Eva bent her head forward and placed it on the pew in front of her. The wood felt cool on her brow. Her heart was beginning to race; the adrenalin was flowing.

"Tomorrow morning. Have you somewhere to stay tonight?"

"Yes," she replied.

Uncut diamonds bought transport, comfortable beds and no questions in a bankrupt country.

"There's a Beretta automatic and twenty rounds in there too. I take it you know how to use one?" he said.

"Yes."

"The Russians aren't very gentlemanly towards women in Berlin, so please be careful."

He stared at her with uncomfortable concern.

"I can look after myself," she smiled.

"Good luck then, Miss Chopin. Hasta mañana," said the man.

He slid out from the pew. In a moment, his awkward bulk was lost in the dim light.

"Mañana," whispered Eva.

She knelt. The crucifix, high above the altar, was backed by a blood-red cloth, a vermillion reminder of senseless sacrifice, bloodshed and pain. Christ hung there, framed in gold and carved white marble, dappled in sunlight, shadowing his burnished stigmata. Moments like this gave her pause; to some, she had lived a wicked life, but she had no regrets. She had killed and she had loved, and all had been deserving. She was lucky; she was still alive, while millions of people were dead before their time. Eva believed in ghosts. And now, as the priest turned back from the altar for a final blessing, amid the swirling dust motes, sunlight and incense, she saw Jonas Zamoyski. It was a trick of the light; god's sleight of hand, that brought her dead fiancé, Jonas, there and then to the altar. Her lover kicked and beaten to death before her very eyes by a Nazi crowd, thirteen years ago; the night Goebbels burned every book in Berlin.

The sunlight shifted its direction, and, in a breath, the resemblance passed; the priest became anonymous again. Bowing, Eva opened the satchel discreetly – wrapped up in oil cloth was the blunt-nosed Beretta. It glinted with oily intent. Eva pulled her headscarf up and, head bowed, left the church through a side entrance.

***

The Spanish Airforce Junkers J-52 landed on a makeshift strip. It had been an uncomfortable journey; Eva sat sandwiched between crates of medicines, blankets and clothing which bounced dangerously around her during the flight. After two gut-churning sweeps of the airstrip, the pilots finally put the plane down. A sudden squall drove sheets of rain across the airstrip as Eva stepped down the rickety steps. Pulling her blue raincoat above her head, she peered out at the murk. A red cross ambulance pulled up and under a wind-strangled umbrella, Henry Chainbridge stepped out.

Eva sprinted across the sodden grass to him.

A crew offloaded the relief packages and hurled her suitcase in the opposite direction. It landed with a hefty thud.

"Welcome to Berlin, Eva," said Chainbridge, "Let's hope there's nothing fragile in that case."

Eva glanced into the driver's seat. A thin, bald man stared back.

"Hopkins," said Chainbridge. "Formal introductions later." He strode towards her case.

Aircraft of every kind taxied along the strip. The drone of in-coming engines filled the grey skies. Trucks and ambulances collected or deposited equipment, people, containers. The skies were a mosaic of aircraft.

Chainbridge came back with the case, it was stained and muddy. He wore heavy hob-nailed boots, the hem of his trousers appeared drenched.

Eva stood in front of him.

"Brandt?" she asked.

Chainbridge took a deep breath and held her gaze,

"Alive. But barely."

"That's enough for me," said Eva.

***

Somehow the tree had survived, its thick, solid bark climbed up towards the sky, like something from a fairy tale. As the turbaned Doctor sliced into his arm, Brandt took in every branch, every shoot, every leaf. He couldn't keep eye-contact with Eva. He felt dirty, ashamed. His bed was in the second room of a large, airy, high-ceilinged, 'L' shaped apartment. Like the tree, the building itself had somehow emerged unscathed from the final Allied assault. There had been no suicidal last stands here.

Past the tree, lives continued. Kettles boiled, kitchens were swept, clothes lines fluttered, families gathered. Individuals stared blankly out, framed by shattered glass or obscured by boards and scraps of newspaper.

"Here you go, sir," said the doctor, holding the tiny piece

of film in a pair of tweezers.
A set of magnifiers clipped onto his glasses lent his hazel-brown eyes an unsettling amphibian stare. He dropped the comma-sized mocro-dot into a petri dish and sealed it.

"There's a micro-dot processing facility in Charlottenburg HQ," said Chainbridge.

"On its way, Mr. Chainbridge," said the doctor. He removed his glasses and packed away his bag. His face was broad and handsome. He stood up and heaved on a heavy military coat,

"This man needs complete rest. I mean, *complete* rest, sir. You can advise Mr. Bracken that there's an enormous shortage of medicines for the civilian population, let alone this gentleman here. Try to get some food into him. I've left some army rations in the kitchen."

"Thank you, Doctor Pannu. Please ensure you hand that directly to Mr. Hopkins, liaison-office, no-one else. This is eyes-only level," replied Chainbridge.

"Must be important?"

"Very," replied Chainbridge.

"That explains the man riding shotgun on the way over," said Pannu.

"Doctor, this address is eyes-only also; discretion is paramount."
The doctor brushed out his lavish, oiled beard over the coat´s lapels and saluted. His silk dastaar topped off an already imposing build.

"No need for salutes, Doctor. Please exercise the utmost caution."

"Don´t worry. I seem to scare the Russians away, for some reason," grinned Pannu. "But thanks for the advice".
In his turban and heavy coat, Doctor Charan Pannu occupied an impressive amount of space; his beard was positively satanic. He produced a Webley revolver.

"I shall guard it with my life, Mr. Chainbridge."

"Trust no-one, Doctor. Berlin is a snake pit."
Chainbridge eased himself up and put on his own heavy duffle

coat over his knitted jumper. The building had no heating, light or running water. A standpipe in the main street below issued grimy water from time to time. In the apartment's tiny kitchen, a small kerosene stove heated a coffee pot; its aroma wafted in under the door.

Chainbridge stamped his feet to kick-start his circulation.

"I'll leave you two alone," he said.

Eva had said nothing, watching from the back of the room. She had helped Brandt from the car and up the four flights of steps to the safe house. He seemed entirely reduced to bone and gristle. Her fingers had once mapped his body in tingling pleasure; now they shied away from contact.

An inner voice told her he was dying, and she wanted no part of it. She resented the moment, resented herself.

"Three years, Brandt. I thought you were dead."

She slid the chair over and held his hand, cold like stone.

Brandt returned her gaze. She was even more beautiful to him now than the day he'd first seen her, in the wilds of Russia. He drank in her hair, her eyes, he lingered on her lips, their shape,

"What happened in Lyon?" he asked.

"Two weeks in a railway siding before we got over the border. You?"

"Your friends in the resistance handed me over to the communists. Kant? Hauptmann? Kramer?"

"We separated at the border. I haven't heard from them since," said Eva. "I'm sorry, Brandt."

"Don't Eva. Don't."

Each breath from his chest burned up through his windpipe,

"Mrs. Hauptmann? The pension?"

"Both fine, Brandt. I've kept it going on a retainer."

"Thank you," he whispered.

Brandt had used a stipend to keep a pension in Zürich. Only he, Eva and Chainbridge knew its exact location. He also had a shepherd's lodge in the Swiss Alps. He needed to go there, he needed to breathe. Live.

Eva wanted to spill out her secrets, her indiscretions, but the sick bed made her think twice.

"No one could find you. No one knew where you were. I kept searching, I tried..."

"But you got tired, you were lonely?" Brandt replied. He was smiling. It was real, not forced, accepting.

"Yes," she replied.

From her wrist, she removed his heavy watch. With great care, she slipped it onto his arm.

"It was my lucky charm, Brandt."

"It's fine, Eva, its fine. Things happened to me. I thought I was dead. You owe me nothing, I made that clear from the start. It's okay, it really is, Molenaar."

"Brandt."

He paused. Eva was trembling. It ran though the nerves in his hand, coursed through his veins and danced around his chest,

"Eva?"

"I was pregnant. It didn't work out. It was ours..."

Eva wiped a tear with the heel of her hand. "Maybe it was for the best."

"Maybe," murmured Brandt.

The silence between them then was a gulf. So they sat, gazing at the tree.

14

Fawkeston Gyre, Devon

"'To eat, to love, to sing and to digest; in truth, these are the four acts in this opéra bouffe that we call life, and which vanish like bubbles in a bottle of champagne' – wise words indeed, gentlemen, from the great Rossini," said Edgar Halidane.

He smiled like an old vaudevillian and bowed to the polite applause from his guests. The dining hall of Fawkeston Gyre was lit by six enormous crystal chandeliers. Its interior, an Anglo-Saxon hall; high vaulted stone arches with heavy hanging Turkish carpets; their ancient weave glowing in the light. The floorboards were old Norse oak, worn thin by many generations of

supplicants. The windows of frosted aged glass were held in place with fine fingers of lead.
Halidane sat in pride of place at the banqueting table, a sprawling ebony affair, ornately carved and polished to a sheen. To his immediate right sat his close confidant and friend, Doctor Kaspar Bellowes. Halidane sipped the fine vintage from the same chipped tin mug that had been sitting on the table of his subterranean chamber.
It caught the Doctor's eye.

"I found it amid a pile of detritus, a garbage heap, Bellowes," said Halidane. "It changed my life completely."

"It looks like it's been through both world wars," said the Doctor, his Adam´s apple pronounced as he spoke. His white tie and black tails hung about him like curtains. His diamond-studded cufflinks rattled off the starch when he moved. He toyed with his food; the local game consommé didn't appeal. He rotated his crystal champagne flute in slow, measured turns. This evening´s Herrenabend wasn't to the old Belgian's taste.

"Nineteen thirty-one, Bellowes; a frozen winter spent queueing on the soup lines of Chicago. I was wandering around Grant Park, scrounging for food. I found a half-chewed cigar and this tin mug. The mug was the answer to my formula, the cigar the taste of things to come," said Halidane. "The solution to my problem."
He drained the last of his champagne and stared into the mug; it was a daily reminder to him of the Wall Street crash and Great Depression, the loss of his position, his research and, above all, his prestige. He dwelt for a moment on the futile, cold nights in the flop house; five men to a room with no heat but a naked lightbulb. He´d drunk from that cup, lathered soap to shave from it; the one constant in his life; a constant that enabled him to build an empire. It was dented, the handle skewed and the bottom charred.
"A lucky little tin cup," thought Halidane.
The servants, all male, young and well-groomed, cleared the first course. Bellowes' dish remained untouched. The next course of *Foie gras* and *Entrée d'Abats,* drew a raised eyebrow from the

dour physician. He sipped from a fresh glass of dry champagne. Halidane surveyed the invited guests; ten men, captains of industry, banking, commodities, precious metals, chemistry and armaments. Six on each side, seated in high-backed ebony chairs with each plush armrest carved in the profile of an eagle. All starched and stiff in full dinner attire. The ten guests had flown from Switzerland into a private airfield – a deserted former RAF base – and were collected in a fleet of Halidane's high-performance cars. The chauffeurs were all well-armed. As their distinguished passengers dined, they formed a loose perimeter around the grounds of the high-walled estate; private contractors dredged from the demobbed British army.

The diners´ place cards were gold rimmed, embossed with symbols from the periodic table. They addressed each other as such; Au, Ti, Cr, H, Ag, Pt, Zr, Hg, Zn, and Fe. The silver service knives were etched along the blade with the motif *Blut und Ehre* – blood and honour. The high-backed seats were inlaid in ivory; a six-pointed star with a key at its centre. The star was surrounded by a snake whose head and tail met at the apex of a reversed swastika. Each chair had a different symbol above the swastika. Twelve diners, twelve symbols, ten elements.

"We have successfully built a working relationship with a number of American firms using pre-war patent agreements. We should see the benefits of them later this year," said Au, alias Mr Gold.

The group of elements listened intently.

"As requested, we have transferred several million dollars of Reichsgold into your accounts in Switzerland. The recent incident in Zürich, involving the British secret service, has been buried. MI6 and the O.S.S. aren't interested," said Ag.

The personified fusion of copper, silver and gold, Ag was sleek and urbane.

"They used the term *far-fetched."*

This was met with laughter and polite applause.

"The Vichy facility in Senegal?" asked Halidane,

"The final shipment arrived in Buenos Aires two days ago. The facility is empty now. It has been destroyed," said Ag.

"I'll advise Herr Bormann. Thank you, Mr. Ag," replied Halidane.

"Halidane Corps' board of directors advises that we now have three hundred and eighty companies, factories, mines and power installations around the world under your control," said Hg. We recently acquired several operations in Argentina, including the Casa Rosa site, near Buenos Aires. We are almost at the end of the cycle of aggressive acquisitions."

Like mercury, this man was hard to pin down, thought Halidane. Casa Rosa was unofficially the final redoubt of the Reich. Element Hg wouldn't figure in the scheme of things for much longer; it was his briefcase that Anna Chambrel had photographed and escaped with.

"Casa Rosa will be the start of the fight back, gentlemen," announced Halidane. "We now have the financial base secured. Please accept tonight's feast with Reichsleiter Bormann's heartfelt thanks."

The ten elements applauded loudly. But element Cr, the armaments representative, cleared his throat and spoke up,

"There was an incident in the Gulf of Cadiz, Herr Halidane," he said.

"Continue, Mr. Chromium," said Halidane

Cr was tall, with Latino matinee idol looks. "The three U-boats were discovered along with a Halidane Corps flying boat. We believe the observer was neutralised."

"Has this been confirmed?" asked Halidane,

"No. not yet," replied Cr.

"Thank you, Mr. Cr," said Halidane.

A shadow of doubt flashed across Cr's features. He´d been bracing himself for the famed Halidane temper. He took his seat. Elements Pt, Zr and Fe gave their individual fiscal reports. By the end, it was clear to Halidane that a substantial portion of the defeated Third Reich's fortunes was now consolidated in one operation: his.

"The first stage of acquisition and security of funds has been completed. This really is most excellent news, gentlemen," said Halidane. "Tonight is also a celebration of stage two; a toast

to Whip-Saw!"
Glasses were raised and tinkled. Fine expensive vintage spilled onto the bees-waxed table.

"To success, gentlemen," said Halidane. "We are the last bulwark against the Bolshevik menace enveloping Europe. And you, gentlemen, with your drive, imagination and ambition have brought this project to its fruition."
On the underside of his setting was a button. He pressed it. The blaze of the chandeliers dimmed. Over the fireplace, a large Gainsborough portrait of two sisters rotated and a sliver screen appeared. Projected onto it was footage of an island.

"Gentlemen, may I present to you the Whip-Saw site. Three hundred years ago, a storm so severe raged across the British Isles that it created whole new islands in the North Sea. I give you one of them, situated hundreds of miles north of Scotland's Orkney Islands. It's virtually unknown, too small to map, surrounded by hostile seas. It took considerable resources to locate and build on it."
The island appeared to be nothing more than a promontory pointing out of the sea; a jagged, dark index finger. The film then jump-cut to an interior shot of a chamber, identical to the one under Halidane's greenhouse.

"The Führer and the armaments section arranged untermensch labour to excavate and develop this site. Working non-stop, they built the Halidane chamber under my personal supervision."
There was polite applause. A course of rhubarb and lemon sorbets appeared. The condensation along the crystal flutes glistened like droplets of rain on a spider's web. The next course had been recommended to Halidane personally by Bellowes, on the understanding that palates should first be cleansed.

"As of yesterday, this site is fully operational and ready to fulfil the Führer's last Nero Directive."
Edgar Halidane reclined; his fingers made a spire. The cuffs and links chafed on his wrists and the sere skin about them turned red.
An image cross-faded, a panning shot of the north of the Whip-

Saw island. The image drew the viewer into a neat u-shaped cove, a metallic jetty and the shark-like outline of a U-Boat.

"Just before the collapse of Berlin, I took delivery of a copper-head artillery shell, capable of wiping out an enemy division. Under my strict instructions, it was modified for a test."

The next shot was of an immense artillery shell towed on a carriage by a jeep. It was lowered into the depths of the island by a group of men using ropes.

The room fell silent.

"The test I might add, was a success," said Halidane. "Another U-boat will arrive in the next few weeks with another copper-head shell, the last of its kind. Its codenamed *Fenrir*. By launching it we are going to make an example of Marshal Stalin and set him at President Truman's throat," said Halidane.

The ten men stood and applauded. Bellowes didn't rise. He arched a withered eyebrow at Halidane and downed the champagne; Halidane had played it cool about the unsanctioned launch. Perhaps he knew?

The chandeliers blazed back into life and the Gainsborough painting revolved back into position above the carved marble mantelpiece.

The main course was served, bottles of *vin gris* were placed in the centre of the table.

"Cold roast rabbit, marinated in pig's blood and wine, served on a bed of lettuce," announced Halidane. "Doctor's orders!"

Bellowes finally found his appetite.

"Did you read my results?" he asked.

Halidane paused. He had read the report through, carefully underlining several of Bellowes' observations,

"Yes. That's why I created this evening's menu. Dessert, though, I promise you, will be exceptional."

None of the human test subjects from Bellowes' Criminal Biological unit in Berlin during the war had survived. Halidane and another scientist, Friedrich Kallerhoff, had requested more inmates, but they were needed elsewhere for the war effort. The best that Bellowes and his superiors could come up with thereafter were Roma and Gypsies. The war had turned once Hitler hurled his forces into Russia. Bellowes' results and recommendations had drawn the same conclusion. The tin cup, though, had opened other possibilities.

Halidane watched Bellowes slaver over the plate as he devoured his meal. Halidane's eyes swept the table; he was looking for discomfort, unease, some tell-tale sign from the assembled guests that his knowledge, his secrets, had fallen into the wrong hands. His gaze fell back on Bellowes.

Folded neatly in Halidane's dinner jacket was a communiqué from one of his contacts in Moscow; disaster had struck a research facility in Siberia; a facility rumoured to be experimenting with electromagnetic fields. Someone here, in this room, had sold the secrets of his life's work.

Fine cheeses and slivers of saltines and breads were accompanied by bottles of port, vodka and more chilled champagne. The cadre of elements stood at the table, faced Halidane and raised their glasses. Flushed by the evening's excesses, they lit fine cigars from Halidane's collection of Havanas, and flopped back onto their carved seats.

"Now gentlemen, as it's the wee small hours of the morning, I suggest we retire; the flight in the morning will be leaving very early. The weather report for the channel is poor and it would be a shame to jettison this splendid feast!"

The tables were cleared. Back-pounding handshakes were followed by staggering hugs up to the bedrooms. The chandeliers were dimmed.

Halidane stared up at the priceless Gainsborough canvas; the old roue had fashioned his daughters lasciviously with linseed oil, crushed colours and intimate strokes.

"Her blood?" he asked, "Anna Chambrel's blood? Your final analysis?"

"Alas, not as pure," said Bellowes.

"Diet? Hygiene?" said Halidane,

"Won't make any difference. There's no such purity these days, I'm afraid," said Bellowes.

"Pity,'" said Halidane. "In Berlin, before the war, it was

plentiful. Goering and I loved to visit the clubs. Such pretty girls. Now, we have disruptive confluences and no viable solution. The gods are working against us, Doctor, in this respect; we must be smarter and work harder to appease them. Blood and circulation are the problems with these experiments. Leave things as they are for now."

"There's also the other matter?" said Bellowes,

"Matter?" asked Halidane,

"Element *Hg*," said Bellowes

"Bormann wants Mr. Mercury eliminated," replied Halidane.

"What about the rest of the elements?"

"Planes crash all the time, Doctor, pilots are nickle-and-dime these days. They've served their purpose."

"Mr. Chromium was suspicious," said Bellowes.

"The phones are redirected to the main switchboard here. And, besides, all the upper floors are wired with microphones," said Halidane.

He looked at his watch,

"Now, my good Doctor, a light dessert as promised."

Halidane eased himself off his chair and pulled the bell rope. A servant opened the huge oak dining room door.

"Is Olivia ready?" asked Halidane.

The servant nodded. His name was Mercier. Halidane felt his swept back grey hair and quiet demeanor gave the estate a monastic air.

"Send her in, Mercier," said Halidane.

Halidane resumed his place at the table.

"There was a club that Hitler, Goering, Goebbels and I frequented – *Sündig und Süss* – a speciality venue, as they were known. What I have prepared is not only sweet and sinful, but almost eighty-per-cent pure too. I found her amongst my typing pool in London. Only child, both parents killed in an air raid. A lost little orphan," said Halidane.

Olivia entered. She was dressed in a loose silk kimono with pyjama pants. Her arms were folded across her breasts. Her hair was tied up with a simple ribbon.

Halidane smiled in welcome,

"Come in, come in. How are you tonight, my dear? Are you pure?" asked Halidane.

Oliva nodded with a smooth motion; she slid the kimono down at the back.

"Turn around, my dear. Turn," said Halidane.

With a smile, Olivia turned. From her shoulder, surrounded by surgical dressing was a platinum spigot tap. At various points on her back, small scars were visible in the dim light of the crystal chandeliers.

Halidane turned the handle on the tap and a thick stream of her blood began to flow.

"So very, very pure," said Halidane as he offered his mouth to the tap in Olivia's shoulder,

"I'm feeling very pure, Mr. Halidane," said Olivia. Her eyes appeared a little glassy.

"You are pure," said Halidane with a smile, "so very pure indeed."

Halidane and Bellowes suckled on Olivia's blood until Bellowes announced "Enough. Enough, Halidane – the girl."

Olivia staggered away and lurched toward once of the carved chairs. Once seated she waved away any assistance,

"I'll be fine; I just need a moment, thank you," she said.

With a wince, she eased the kimono over her shoulders and wrapped the soft silk about her.

"She needs time to replenish," said Bellowes. He stood above her checking her pulse.

"Replenish," replied Halidane. He dabbed his mouth with a cotton napkin,

"So very pure indeed. Thank you, my dear."

Halidane leaned back and looked at Bellowes,

"The gods require a sacrifice, Dr Bellowes,"

"A sacrifice?"

"A sacrifice, Doctor. If our work and research here and at Whip-Saw is to continue, we must prepare an offering. *Fenrir* needs to be consecrated."

"I'll make every arrangement."

"Virgin's blood, my good Doctor, virgin's blood," said

Halidane.
Bellowes rose. Halidane noticed the Doctor's gait had more spring in it.
"Blood and vigour," whispered Halidane.
He smacked his lips, savouring the last drops of Olivia.
"Blood and vigour," echoed Bellowes.
Halidane pulled the servants´ bell and Mercier assisted Olivia to her room.
There was a job of work to do.

***

Kaspar Bellowes ascended the old stone staircase, worn smooth over the centuries. At the top of the corridor, the old physician thought of seeking Olivia's room. After a pause, he resumed his shuffling journey to his own quarters. The corridors were well-lit with electric light and at one mullioned window, he peered out into the night. The magnificently tended gardens were lit from the house. The high stone walls surrounding the estate appeared and disappeared into the shadows. Fawkeston Gyre felt like a prison. Below the window two armed sentries dressed in warm fatigues idled over a cigarette.
In his room, Bellowes removed his clothes and stored them neatly in a portmanteau. He donned a silk cowl and robes before pulling out a thick canvas holder from a nearby compartment. As he´d requested, four candles sat ready on the dresser. After lighting each one in turn he rolled out the sheet from the canvas carrier. It was an enormous chart. Heavy candle sticks placed at each corner prevented it rolling back up. It was his Navamansh; an Indian astrologer´s chart. The chart was plotted with concentric circles, days and months of the year. Across the circles Bellowes had plotted the cycles of the moon, sun and planets. He had noted the twelve signs of the zodiac and the positions of the twenty-seven stars influencing the destiny of the earth.
Pulling several cushions from the wardrobe, the old physician placed them on the exotic carpet and sat cross-legged on them. His old spine creaked in protest as he eased his old hips down. His buttocks felt hard against the floor.

He began charting the next weapon launch – the *Fenrir*. The U-Boat would have to make better time. Charting Olivia's birthday, the date of the previous launch and today's date, Kaspar Bellowes calculated the most auspicious moment would be fourteen days from now. *Fenrir's* launch through the Whip-Saw chamber would have to take place at 11pm exactly.
He checked and re-checked, carefully running an old, dirty fingernail across his carefully drawn lines.

"*A most auspicious star, whose influence if I court not, but omit, my fortunes will ever after droop*," he murmured as he re-checked his alignments and calculations.
Edgar Halidane was suspicious, the test launch had been decreed in the heavens and the heavens had been right. Perhaps giving Halidane a deadline this time would improve Bellowes' standing in the eyes of the man.
With great difficulty, the old physician stood up and ambled to the ornate phone beside the dresser. He first tried Halidane's extension, then Mercier's, without success. He retired to bed and slept fitfully, nervous about the dawn.

15

Zürich

Hannah Wolfe took the tram from the main train station to the city's civic offices. As a precaution she changed at two stops and walked the final quarter mile. She was dressed in a formal jacket, mauve pill-box hat, tweed skirt and flat shoes. She took a moment to swap them for black leather peep-toed stilettos, accentuating her intimidating stature. Stylish sunglasses kept the strong spring sunshine at bay.
She leafed through her big leather bag with deliberate intent as she approached the government office building.
A dour, matronly woman, seemingly hewn from the same grey marble as the foyer floor, stood sentinel at the reception desk.

"My employer, Mr Halidane, requested an appointment," said Hannah.

The receptionist placed a silver pince-nez onto her hooked nose; an unsavoury Semitic profile in Hannah´s eyes.

"I have his telegram and business card here," said the receptionist. "How may I help you?"

"Mr Halidane has a private correspondence for the head of this department, Herr Clarke. He received a phone call a few days ago from the Hotel Adler. I've been asked to speak with him directly on behalf of Mr. Halidane."

"I'm afraid Herr Clarke isn't receiving visitors," replied the receptionist, her demeanor escalating from grim to implacable.

"That is most unfortunate," said Hannah.

Removing the hat pin from her pill-box hat, Hannah jabbed it hard into the receptionist's thin, bony hand. The toxin acted almost immediately. The victim gave a gasp and slumped onto the desk, spilling an inkwell over her leather blotting pad. Thick black ink pooled around her, dripping onto her skirt.

Glancing around, Hannah stepped deftly behind the desk. She took the telegram and business card. Running a finger along the vellum desk diary, she found the department extension matching the slip of paper. Jefferson Clarke; Sciences – Room 101.

Hannah checked the receptionist's pulse; it was slowing down. The woman was old; it would look as if she'd suffered a heart attack. Hannah placed the hat pin back in place. With her scent trailing along the grim, non-descript corridor, she checked the breech of her Luger.

Jefferson Clarke was drafting a report when the stunning woman marched in. The room was well lit from six large windows as well as strong overhead lighting. The uniform benches, replete with state-of-the-art scientific paraphernalia, were unoccupied.

Clarke´s desk was neatly laid out. A leather-bound notebook with gold leaf pages acted as an impromptu coffee coaster.

"How may I help you, Frau...?"

"Jefferson Clarke?" demanded Hannah. She removed her hat. Her features were a flawless alabaster, but he noticed her eyes seemed dead – glassy like his daughter's toy dolls.

"Yes. And you are?"

"I represent Edgar Halidane. He sent you a correspondence. You failed to reply."

Jefferson Clarke was a small man, round with a soft, bureaucratic appearance. His bowtie was expensive red silk, his hands stained with the chemicals of his profession. He reached for the telephone.

"I'm afraid this is an area for authorised personnel only Miss.? I'll have a caretaker escort you back to reception."

"That won´t be necessary, Herr Clarke."

Hannah leaned over Clarke´s desk, her impressive hour-glass form instantly overwhelming him. She shrugged off her bolero, and Clarke took in her full bust, straining against expensive silk.

"Herr Halidane simply requires a few details. For example, you received an urgent call from the Hotel Adler a few days ago. Who called you and why? And how did you get Herr Halidane´s home telephone number?"

Clarke's eyes darted briefly to the stack of leather journals. Perched on the top of them, his coffee was going cold. Suddenly the silence of a building he´d always valued as a cloistered haven, now felt cloying. He began to sweat.

"I have no idea..."

With one swift movement, Hannah swung her snub-nosed Luger like a hammer, cracking its butt across Clarke's knuckles. The pain ricocheted around his brain. The slap of a kid glove across the face forced him to focus. The cold muzzle of the luger barrel pressed into his good hand.

"Name. Details."

"Please... don't... there was a call. I wasn't here. It was directed to reception."

The hammer of the gun clicked.

"Not according to Herr Halidane."

Hannah placed a strip of paper on the desk.

"This confirms you lifted the receiver."

The sight of the gun paralyzed him. Somewhere in the back of his mind a voice was telling him it was half-an-hour from lunch. Hannah threw her handbag onto the desk and from its depths, produced a silencer. With deliberate twists, she fastened it to the barrel.

"Details," she said.

Clarke blinked from her to the sheet of paper. He saw a sequence of digits, including his extension number and the word – 'connected'. The number for Falkeston Gyre was the last thing on it.

"The line, it went dead," said Clarke.

Before he could speak, the click of the gun´s breech sent hot waves of agony into the knuckles of his left hand.

"One last time, Herr Clarke. My employer is not a patient man."

The hot rim of the silencer seared into the scientist's brow. He could smell the cordite, her perfume and his blood. He wanted to pass out.

Cold dregs of coffee were hurled into his face.

"Gageby, Douglas Gageby – said he had something."

"What exactly?" said Hannah.

"He was cut off; I swear to you. I heard only that he had something. He told me to tell Halidane that a Miss Anna Chambrel was dead. Then the line went dead. Please, Miss, tell your employer that's all I know."

"Why did Gageby want to talk to you?"

"I don't know," said Clarke. He fought the urge to vomit.

"Why did he call you?"

"I have no idea, honestly."

"There were no other details? Please be clear."

"Please, please – I don't know. Maybe he was mistaken?"

"Why did he call your number?"

Hannah stepped slightly back, holding the Luger between gloved fingers.

"I have no idea."

"You knew Ann Chambrel?"

"Yes."

"How?"

"The hotel. The hotel Prestige au Lac."

Hannah paused. The hotel was nearby, popular with foreign bankers and their staff for socialising. Hannah knew female agents were more cunning, subtle, and efficient. The girl killed in the train station fitted the profile.

"You were there? You met her?"

"Yes, then I saw her face in the morning papers. I reacted. I was scared."

"Who gave you Herr Halidane's number?"

The point of course was moot. Halidane had now changed all his contact details.

"I found it here, on my desk. That's all I know. He thought I was someone else."

Clarke's voice was becoming reedy, whining. "He told me there were to be no more mistakes. I think he thought I was someone else."

Clarke's smile was desperate, it danced about his face.

"Maybe he did. But that's immaterial now, Herr Clarke."

Hannah fired three times into Clarke's forehead, just to make sure.

Looking around the room, she walked over to the open windows. Closing them one by one, she checked there were no bystanders. The grounds were deserted. She returned to Clarke's desk. She nudged his body off its chair. It splayed with a dull thud onto the polished herringbone floor. Hannah took one of the journals from the stack of leather notebooks. Fanning the pages, a matchbook fell onto the desk. Hannah picked it up.

It read: Hotel Prestige au Lac.

Halidane was due in Zürich shortly; the hotel was a place he was rumoured to frequent for relaxing and dancing. If British Intelligence were to try again, this would be the place. She placed the books in her bag. It was then she looked at the blackboard – spots of blood were splashed across the chalk formulae. Across the top of the board, Clarke had written and underlined,

Einheitliche Feld Theorie – UFT

"Unified field theory," she murmured.

She found a duster and cleaned off the board, smearing the spots of blood.
Her eyes swept the room one more time, then Hannah closed the door and strode back through reception.
The only sound to break the silence was the staccato clip of high heels on the polished marble.

16

Faro, Portugal

The blind man arrived every day at precisely the same time. His taxi pulled up at the same point at the kerb. The driver, always the same one, diligently assisted him out. The passenger was smartly attired in one of his two light summer suits; today the cream one, with a crumpled but clean blue shirt. He used a simple bamboo cane to tap the way. The café hissed and spat with coffee machines and the clatter of lives taking pause, watching the rolling ocean from their tables before going about their daily business.
The bartender, spotting the blind man's straw fedora at the doorway, sugared his cafe solo and crossed the room to seat him. He wiped the table and laid out the setting with the precision of an architect.

"Thank you, Dinis."

"You're welcome, Mr. de Witte."

Peter de Witte placed his cane against the wall and removed his hat. His hair, now fully grey, was swept back and neatly trimmed. He wore smart sunglasses that concealed the scarring around his eyes and sealed lids. He had been blinded in Russia fighting the Bolsheviks; now, a quarter of a century later, he found himself fighting them again. With communist parties taking hold of Italy, Greece and France, Stalin's sights were now set on the Mediterranean and the English Channel.
The blind man savoured his coffee and waited. Inside his wallet

was a folded strip of Braille.
An American big band came on the radio. Dinis raised the volume. De Witte tapped out the beat on the table gently with his fingertips.
The man he was meeting arrived five minutes later.

"Peter," he said.

"Father Francis," replied de Witte.

The Jesuit´s summer suit had seen better days, his black shirt worn open, without the collar. From his jacket pocket, the priest produced a small ivory inlaid travel chess set and opened it out. He set the pieces out; he was white, de Witte was black. It was their daily ritual, a comfortable routine.

De Witte motioned for coffee.

"Thank you for the information," said de Witte.

"We don't have many friends here," said Father Francis, "but those we have are very loyal. White, pawn, e 4," he said.

Father Francis´ opening move was as de Witte expected; reckless, without much thought. The priest must be preoccupied, he thought.

"The Jesuits have sent word to the British and Americans, not through the regular channels, but directly through Int.7.," said Father Francis. "Three German U-boats left the coast of Spain forty-eight hours ago; now no-one can locate them."
De Witte could visualize the chessboard's layout in his mind's eye. Francis' spoken moves gave away his strategy. A bold opening, high-risk.

"Black, Knight, f. 6," he said.

De Witte swiftly calculated the game. After three moves, he took a knight; exposing the queen. The game was going to be short.

"Definitely German?" he asked.

"New generation of them. One is rumoured to have Martin Bormann on board."

"He's dead; killed on the Weidendammer Bridge - escaping," replied de Witte.

"The Russians aren't convinced," said the priest.

"They aren't convinced Hitler is dead either," said de Witte.
Checkmate was suddenly two moves away and he toyed with his

beard as he pondered his next move.

"Stalin thinks Bormann is moving all the Reich's remaining finances into Switzerland, out of his reach."

"Stalin's fantasies have a habit of becoming realpolitik," said de Witte.

"This one may have some substance; Bormann was spotted in the Spanish port of Huelva, or at least someone matching his last known description. If it´s true, the assassination attempt failed."

"Then we'll have to try again," said de Witte.

The fragment of Braille lay coiled like a serpent in his jacket pocket. De Witte imagined it writhing, twisting, gnawing through the material.

"Chasing ghosts is getting to be a preoccupation, Peter," said Francis.

"The guns never fall silent, Father," replied de Witte.

Father Francis switched to a new tack, trying to claw back advantage.

He took a rook with a flourish, but it was a pyrrhic victory. In less than ten minutes he was defeated.

De Wittte paused, his head angled toward the breeze coming in through the doorway.

"*Chopin* discovered the U-Boats?" he asked.

"She did. She delivered her intelligence to the Jesuit mission in Barcelona and they sent it on to London."

Eva, thought de Witte. It had been years now since he´d held her, smelled her, tasted her. A long-hidden pain, long thought healed, rose in his chest.

"Where is she now?" he asked.

"Berlin. Arrived a few days ago," said Francis.

The cries of the gulls wheeling overhead, a warm breeze and the sounds and smells of a seaside café reminded de Witte of Den Helder, the Dutch town where he grew up. He taught at a school there and had joined up in the market square to sail to Russia and fight Bolshevism. Severely injured from grenade wounds, another volunteer, Henry Chainbridge had saved him and befriended him.

If Eva was active again Chainbridge would be too.

"Berlin?" asked de Witte.

"Berlin. A dangerous city, even for a man in the fullness of health," replied the priest.

"... let alone a blind one?" concluded de Witte.

A faint smile creased his handsome features.

"I'm not completely helpless you know."

Father Francis cautiously turned the chess board around. Sliding out a hidden drawer, he removed a piece of folded cigarette paper and placed it in de Witte's hands. As the blind man fed the freshly imprinted braille through his fingers, the priest slid the drawer closed.

"She's at an Int.7., safe house – address and details enclosed."

Berlin. De Witte paused. He had been captured and delivered into the hands of the Abwehr there. He recalled the imaginative ways he had been tortured. As a blind man, he'd presented a challenge, but his tormentors had more than risen to it. Henry Chainbridge and Nicklaus Brandt had rescued him.

And he had lost Eva, forever.

"Brandt?" asked de Witte.

"Who?" replied Francis

"Never mind."

Francis, now playing black, won a game. It was the Jesuit who now sensed his opponent's mind was distracted. It had been too easy; de Witte was usually ruthless.

"Best of three?" asked Francis.

"Yes. Best of three,"

"One other thing; came in from a different wire; the Russians are working on a huge project. They've diverted a lot of forced labour out of Moscow."

"Any ideas?" asked de Witte.

"Alternative energy. Possibly. Weapon, probably."

De Witte paused. From his inside pocket, he produced a slim cigarette case, silver, unadorned. He removed two cheroots and lit them both with a steady hand. Father Francis never stopped marveling at this trick. The flame would never miss. De Witte handed one to Francis. The priest enjoyed the smoke.

"Alternative energy?" said de Witte.

"The Red Army stumbled onto something in Berlin last year. Beria's Ministry of State Security has now taken over the project."

De Witte won the game. Barely a minute later Dinis delivered the customary crepes. Returning to the bar, he phoned for the taxi.

"Guess I'm paying for the crepes again?" said Father Francis.

"I won't be here tomorrow Father. But I'll make sure your chess set is returned."

"On the move then, de Witte?"

"Berlin. If my old comrades-in-arms are gathering there..."

"Bring the chess set with you. You can hand it back on your return. You know Peter, we're both too old for adventures, you should enjoy your retirement. Here you have the sun, the sea and immensely inferior opposition. What more could you ask? Besides, you have a wonderful wife at home. Let the past go. Enjoy your life with Martha."

De Witte, smiled ruefully,

"In China, crisis has the same meaning as opportunity. Now that the dust has settled, all the pieces have come back into play. Bormann, if he's alive, is making his gambit."

He tapped the chess box, "For what, we don't know."

The taxi arrived.

"Take care, my friend," said Father Francis.

"I will," replied de Witte.

"I wish I could believe that," growled the priest as he gently guided his friend into the back seat of the waiting car.

"Light a candle for me then, you old shaman," grinned de Witte.

Martha was waiting. From the taxi, she took her husband´s arm and guided him into the house. She had noticed his recent distraction and a silent tension had seeped into their marriage; the same kind of tension that had made her leave him once before.

"There's a new correspondence," said de Witte.

Martha took the chess set from him and popped open the hidden drawer. Unfolding the cigarette paper, she fingered the correspondence. While he was recovering from his injuries, she had nursed him, loved him and taught him braille.

"DG dead. Berlin. Chopin there. Int.7. Re-activated - an address too?" she said.

De Witte slumped into a chair,

"I'm going to Berlin, Martha. Henry's there."

"She's there, Peter. I thought she was dead?"

"Evidently not, Martha. She's not the reason."

"She is, Peter. She always is."

Martha lit the strip of paper with a match and washed the ashes down the kitchen sink. She glanced through the window to the carefully cultivated back garden they had lavished so much time on. It had been the happiest time in their marriage. This modest lodge surrounded by orange groves, olive trees and fields had been their home for three years.

"The war is over, Peter," she said.

"Henry is there."

Martha de Witte squeezed her eyes shut. Tighter than a child fearing the dark.

"So, you said - I'm not deaf."

"I have contacts, I can be useful," he said.

"So is Eva, Peter – she's there too,"

"That´s not the reason – I have my uses, Martha,"

Martha slammed her fist on the sink. The stacked crockery juddered.

"I need you here, Peter. The work you are doing here is more important. You can assist them better from here. Berlin is suicide."

"I have a friend, Martha, a Doctor. He's a Sikh, Calcutta Office I authorised him to assist Chainbridge."

"Pannu?"

"Yes."

She turned around and saw her husband staring away from her voice. His fists were clenched too.

"Do what you want then," she said.

Martha de Witte donned a headscarf and strode out into the garden. As she toiled in the borders, Peter's voice drifted to her through the open window. He was talking into the long-wave radio, his intonation crisp and precise.

17

Berlin

Found upended in the garden, the table was an old wooden tea chest with rusted edges and the words *'India & Ceylon'* stenciled on its sides. On the rough cloth thrown over it, was a bottle of vodka and the opened contents of an army ration pack; luncheon meat, cheese and tough, stale biscuits that tasted of salt. With the few small pieces of chicken that Eva had procured and cooked, to Brandt, it was a feast.

The courtyard had been swept clean of detritus, piled into a corner by the women of the building. Leaning back on the battered, worn old chair, Brandt stared up at the tree. The first shoots had appeared on the gnarled bark, but no birds had appeared. The drone of distant aircraft broke the early afternoon silence.

"I can't understand a word you are saying," said Brandt.

"Russian, then?" asked Findlay. He was dressed in a Russian uniform of a plain olive tunic and breeches. His hair was pomaded flat, the sideburns jutted at odd angles.

A crumpled forage cap with a plain red star lay on the table alongside the opened American ration pack.

"Who are you again?" asked Brandt.

"Findlay, Alastaire Findlay, Captain Brandt. I specialise in Cryptorithms, Algorithms – codes if you will, dragged into this; not here by choice."

He proffered a lumpy looking hand,

"None of us are. Your Russian is excellent. We'd better

whisper, then, Herr Findlay, or is it comrade?" replied Brandt.

"Findlay will do, Brandt - the news, I'm afraid, isn't good."

Findlay handed Brandt an official looking form,

"She's listed as dead. I'm sorry."

Brandt scanned the report. Düsseldorf had been reduced to ash. His mother lived there or had.

"How did you get this?" he asked.

"Chainbridge," said Findlay, "Fire brigade report. Pretty accurate. RAF raid."

There on the casualty lists was her name; Brandt, Maria Dorothy - at least it was confirmed. Brandt felt hollowed out; he didn't recognise the face in the mirror every morning as if a piece had been left out after he had pulled himself together. Sometimes, when he was shaving, he contemplated the blade and then he'd remember Eva.

It was just another death he had to process, without any time to mourn.

"Gravestone? Cemetery?" asked Brandt.

"Doubt it. Reisholtz was wiped off the planet. Do you need a moment?" asked Findlay.

He touched Brandt's arm. He squeezed it with genuine warmth.

Brandt took the bottle of vodka and quaffed a few huge slugs.

"No. No I don't, Findlay. Thank you."

The sun began to light up the tiled roofs above them. A bright orange triangle spread across the far buildings of the courtyard, breathing life into the old stones. The shadows retreated further.

Findlay reached across and removed the ration pack of cigarettes. He lit one, pocketed three. His uneven eyes glowered at the bottle.

"Medicinal purposes," he said.

Brandt nodded.

Wiping the rim of the bottle with a sleeve, Findlay downed several shots.

"F'king Berlin. It's a f'king mess is w'ht it-is," said Findlay quietly.

"You can finish it," said Brandt.

"Don't mind if I do."

Brandt closed his eyes. He let the sun's rays warm him. He shook off the heavy blanket that he'd wrapped around himself. The few days of rest had done him good. Findlay produced a very old-looking pocket watch from his tunic and began to wind it,

"This was my brother's. His name was Gregor. He was gassed at Wielje in the great war. They found him and five of his chums holding hands in a filthy little foxhole. The stretcher bearers remarked they looked like little boys who had lost their way and were waiting for someone to come." Brandt closed his eyes tight, trying to remember his mother.

"I've forgotten her face," he said.

"Your mother?"

"Yes, her face, I can't see her face," said Brandt.

"What they pulled out of your arm must be important," said Findlay.

They turned and saw Eva, Chainbridge, and a tall thin man with owl-like glasses step into the courtyard and shade their eyes.

Brandt looked up and around at the windows of the building. Too many opportunities to eavesdrop.

"Meant to ask – why the Russian uniform?" asked Brandt.

"The city is completely surrounded by them – throw f'king translation duties at the checkpoints in too," replied Findlay.

"Chainbridge speaks Russian," said Brandt.

"But not a convicted red," replied Findlay, "There'll be watchers and eyes on us now. My name would've made it to a Cheka list."

"You must've really screwed up to wind up here, Findlay."

"You have no idea, young man. No idea. But the

vodka is flowing like water here," he drained the dregs from the bottle, stood up and hurled it at the rubbish pile. It shattered spectacularly.

"Right, Chainbridge, me old mukka, what do you want?" he said.

"Brandt, Findlay, may I introduce Hopkins; we've been requested to accompany him."

Eva leaned in and kissed Brandt. The heat of her lips and scent of her hair as it fell about Brandt's face felt like a sudden electric shock. It sparked across his nervous system.

"Henry, we've decided we're going home. Home to Switzerland," said Eva.

"Our war is over. We need time together, you understand," said Brandt.

Henry Chainbridge studied them both for a moment; the rugged mountaineer and the charismatic beauty; their inexplicable chemistry and inate ability to survive,

"Kallerhoff's micro dot has yielded some surprising results. We've been summoned to Charlottenburg HQ, there's an American O.S.S., representative; a Mr. Keyburn," said Chainbridge.

"He's waiting. Not a patient man, I'd add," said Hopkins.

Brandt stood and finished the last of the biscuits,

"Best not let him wait then, should we?"

PART TWO

MEMENTO MORI

18

The Whip-Saw site, (500 miles north of the Orkney Islands.)

Edgar Halidane's Blohm & Voss BV 222 Wiking flying boat circled in a graceful sweeping arc before beginning its final approach. The pressurised cabin, luxurious carpets and leather upholstery deadened the roar of the six immense engines; Halidane hardly noticed his aged bourbon and ice sloshing around in the crystal tumbler. The weather had broken, and a surprising bolt of blue sky had turned the sea a deep, benevolent green.

He looked about for the island. Then a flock of wheeling gulls circling an area caught his eye.

"Watch this, Bellowes," he said.

The old man craned his neck from the deep leather seat in front of Halidane.

"I don't see anything."

"All will be revealed, my friend. Watch the gulls."

Bellowes´ eyes were tired. The flight had felt like a plush eternity - from the Kent coast, passing over Scotland's shores without stopping. In bunks below, a relief crew slept; Halidane was preparing the return journey to Switzerland, refuelling at Cherbourg. Olivia was an acting attendant now, dressed in a neat Halidane Corp blouse and pencil skirt. She seemed unaffected by the previous evening´s excesses. Bellowes lusted after and resented her youth.

Then the gulls scattered in all directions.

"Now, observe the ocean below them," said Halidane. Bellowes watched the sea boil and froth. Then, as if it were a desert mirage, the island appeared. It was so gradual that to Bellowes it seemed as though it must have always been there; how was it possible he hadn't noticed it at first?

"Electromagnetic degaussers, my good Doctor. You're watching the Zeeman effect," said Halidane. "Powered by thirty generators embedded into the strata. A miracle of modern engineering."

"Incredible," said Bellowes.

The only other person Halidane had shown this to had leapt out of their seat. Perhaps Bellowes was too old to grasp the full import of what he was witnessing. That or he was overly familiar with the concept. Halidane lifted a telephone receiver built into the armrest of his padded Pullman seat.

"You may begin your approach," he said.

The Captain's voice sounded tinny with its confirmation.

Olivia strapped herself into the facing seat. Bellowes eyed her long, supple legs. He recalled the fresh coppery taste of her blood, and, despite himself, licked his lips slowly. Kaspar Bellowes dragged his yellow eyeballs back to the window.

The gulls reformed and wheeled above the concrete harbour.

"The island is virtually invisible; I have over a million tons of equipment that can alter the electrical fields around it. An expensive form of camouflage, but highly effective," said Halidane.

"The RAF?" pondered Bellowes.

"Hundreds of miles beyond their operational limits. We know every Royal Navy movement in the area as well. Perfectly isolated, my good doctor."

The Flying boat navigated into the harbour, ploughing the unkind tides. Then, with a roar of the huge engines, it decelerated before mooring at a metal jetty. On the opposite side of the harbour was the Kawasaki H8K four-engine flying boat; it rocked back and forth on the undertow from the North Sea.

"Arrived from the Gulf of Cadiz a few days ago. The U-boat should arrive by the end of the week with the payload," said Halidane.

An armed colour party of twenty SS stormtroopers stood to attention. Their commander, Obergruppenführer Kurt Dietrich Hoeberichts, clad in leather and black, stood pristine, rigid and funereal. Planted onto his shaved head was a hat of black Russian sable with the death's head skull of his regiment. A jewel encrusted Cossack Kindjal knife was fastened to his leather webbing. His eyes were heterochromatic; as unblinking as a reptile. He saluted smartly as his men presented arms.

"Welcome, Herr Halidane. I was sorry to hear of the air crash over the English Channel, this morning."

"Any survivors?" asked Halidane.

"Unfortunately, no."

"Thank you, Obergruppenführer. I'll ensure the next-of-kin are informed."

"Welcome to the last defensive zone, Herr Halidane," said Hoeberichts.

"The fightback begins soon, Commander," said Halidane.

Oliva stepped out from the seaplane and Hoeberichts ground his teeth. His men had been stationed here after retreating their way across Germany to the coast. They hadn't seen a woman in years.

"*Enchanté*, Fraulein," said Hoeberichts.

He clicked his heels and bowed over her hand.

"May I present tonight's offering; Olivia," said Halidane.

Olivia stared in terror at the armed SS soldiers.

Then she began to scream.

***

"It´s vodka infused with blood," said Halidane. He was immaculately attired in American tweed and a crisp white shirt.

He wore a dark patterned silk scarf around his neck to reduce the chafing of the starched collar.

"The roasted marrow is sublime," said Hoeberichts.

The general snorted the vodka from a thin crystal shot glass in the Russian fashion. His bald, shaved skull angled to a promontory of lines and scars; it reminded Halidane of a prairie moonrise. Hoeberichts' uniform was a blend of deep black, leather webbing and fur. His leather greatcoat was slung over a dining chair like a freshly killed beast. This was a commander who had authorised purges, presided over mutilations, death squads and gang rapes. Obergruppenführer Hoeberichts enjoyed his vocation.

"One of chef's specialities," said Halidane. "The flying boats come equipped with a first-rate galley. The crispbread is a unique French recipe."

He gulped down the frozen liquid and mediated on the coppery aftertaste. He placed down his talisman tin cup and nodded for a refill.

The dining hall where breakfast was being served was embedded deep into the rock. Like every other area of the Whip-Saw site, it was constructed with bolted plates of metal, softened by plush furnishings and drapes. A crystal chandelier lit the room brilliantly. Like Fawkeston Gyre in Devon, the room had latticed windows that rattled in the unfettered northern gales.

From their vantage point in the dining hall, Halidane and Hoeberichts could see the body lowered into a cage.

"Poor Olivia didn't survive the initiation," said Halidane.

He dabbed his mouth with a warm, pressed napkin. The hovering uniformed attendant ensured a fresh one replaced it.

"There was enough for the consecration," said Hoeberichts.

The cage was lowered by a crane into the sea. Within moments, the sea around the cage began to churn. Fins and tails broke the surface in tight concentric circles.

"The makos will deal with her," said Hoerberichts. "It´s how we disposed of the work gangs. The island's energy fields seem to invigorate them."

"The U-boat commanders tell me this area was a graveyard for allied shipping," said Halidane.

"Rich pickings for the wolves of the sea," said Hoeberichts.

"Like us, my dear Hoeberichts, just like us - wolves; blood is our poison, our weakness, our passion," replied Halidane.

"I once bred Czech Wolf hybrids; strange creatures, unlike attack or guard dogs they will circle, always circling, looking for a weakness, then strike without a sound. They served me well before and during the war."

He smeared more marrow onto a crispbread. He inhaled another blood vodka.

"My men need to leave here soon, Herr Halidane; it is not a suitable environment for a combat unit."

"Better than a Russian gulag, Obergruppenführer," countered Halidane.

"Reichsleiter Bormann was insistent," said Hoeberichts. "The test was successful. The next phase should start when the U-boat arrives."

"About that, Obergruppenführer Hoeberichts; I was unaware of this launch," said Halidane.

Hoeberichts pushed the dining chair back. Unsheathing his Kindjal knife, he ran the wicked blade across his nails. In his cell beneath the dining room, his ceremonial knives had been cleaned and mounted, purged of Olivia's blood.

"Herr Bellowes was quite insistent about the launch; he had indicated an auspicious date and time. It was a success."

From the folds of his tunic, Hoeberichts produced neatly folded mimeographs. Halidane snatched them from him. As he rifled through the pages, his knuckles turned white.

"Have you access to his astrological charts?" asked Halidane,

"Reichslieter Bormann commands the utmost loyalty, Herr Halidane. It cannot be bought; it cannot be traded. He is now the acting Führer. We move toward him as we once moved toward Führer Adolf Hitler ..."

He found himself grinning at the American's discomfort.

"What was Bellowes promised?" asked Halidane,

"You can ask him yourself, Herr Halidane."
The oak door, inlaid with holy cuneiforms and runes, was at that moment opened by an armed SS soldier. Bellowes shuffled in and flopped into a leather settee near the dining table. He wore a thickly woven dressing gown, his eyes still drowsy from sleep. The attendant poured vodka into a glass and handed it to him. From a small crystal phial with an ornate spout, he administered a single drop of blood.
Bellowes sipped, his hand fighting a small tremor.

"It is certainly pure. The blood?"

"Olivia's, my good doctor," said Halidane.

"Excellent, excellent. Was there enough left over?"

"For the execution of the final Nero directive, yes," replied Halidane.

Halidane rose and walked to the bar, it was a well-provisioned sop to the disgruntled officers manning the facility. He reached for the telephone and dialled. He nodded a couple of times and hung up.

"Gentlemen, it seems we have a potential problem; My connections have confirmed that the British Military Headquarters in Berlin has had a top member of the O.S.S. paying them a visit. They've now beefed up security. Why have we still got slip-ups, set-backs and problems?" asked Halidane

"I'll make arrangements to deal with this; a loyal follower," said Bellowes.

He took a slice of bread from the attendant's tray.

"Would you, there's a good fellow?" he said.

The attendant spread the marrow across the bread. Bellowes motioned for the telephone. The attendant brought it over on a silver tray.

"Can this be phone routed through another exchange?" he asked.

"Yes," replied Halidane.

The old Belgian dialled shakily. After several arduous minutes of shouting in Flemish, he hung up.

"Not just O.S.S., but another agency's involved," he said.

"Russians?" asked Halidane.

"Unknown."

"Switzerland?" asked Halidane.

"Under control," said Bellowes. An arc of cigarette ash spilled onto the plush carpet.

"Careful with the furniture my good doctor, careful," said Halidane.

He thought of the dustbowl, the long exodus of vehicles across the American plains. The unremitting misery. A life of dust and ash, a taste of hell.

"Tell Malleus to advance to the next stage," said Halidane. Bellowes, sensing one of Halidane's 'Black dog' tantrums about to be unleashed rose and munched idly on marrow. Extinguishing the cigarette into his shot glass, Bellowes gave a jaunty nod. He made eye contact with the SS General.

"OMGUS in Berlin are procuring land and properties. I've ensured Malleus buys up the necessaries, through the aegis of the Halidane Zürich offices," said Bellowes.

Hoeberichts rose from his chair, donned his greatcoat as if it were a suit of armour and placed the sable hat on his head.

"The first artillery shell we sent through was standard siege munition. The one we are preparing here will deliver a considerably larger payload. How many US divisions are we talking about?"

"One million men," said Bellowes. "Office of the US military government. German industry being ear-marked for llied and Soviet reparations. Once the dust clears, the red hordes will get the blame and we, the British, the French and our new US allies will drive Stalin back all the way to the shores of Japan."

He skulked off across the room and placed the vodka glass rim-down on the polished mahogany bar.

"Obergruppenführer," said Halidane.

The skeletal commander turned on his heel.

"Herr Halidane?"

"Your revolver please."

The SS general handed over his Luger.

"Bellowes?"

Kaspar Bellowes began to shuffle back towards them.

Halidane fired four times.
Bellowes pirouetted and slammed back into the carved cuneiform door. He crumpled into a kneeling position before slumping sideways onto the carpet.

"You went behind my back, you piece of shit," whispered Halidane into the old man's ear. "Consider this your inauspicious date..."

Halidane shot Bellowes in the head. He wiped the blood from his hands with a handkerchief.
He handed the Luger back.

"I can no longer tolerate any loose ends. Once phase two is complete, there's very little accommodation on the U-boat. As you would say, General, the Führer, Bormann, demands it. Get rid of the mess on the carpet. Now."

"Very good, Herr Halidane," said Hoeberichts.

Bellowes' death would have ramifications - serious ramifications. Killing the new Reich's seer would be noted.
Hoeberichts gave a roar down the corridor. Two soldiers entered and lifted Bellowes' corpse.
Halidane stood staring out at the harbour for a very long time. His mind pictured formulae revolving in the air above his head. In his mind's eye, he pulled down and arranged numbers and sequences in his head.
His eyes remained fixed in the middle distance, his mind calculating, eliminating and settling on the conclusion. They never registered the cage rising from the deep, hunks of flesh sliding idly into the ocean as it was hoisted onto the craggy dunes, in preparation for the sharks` next feast.
All the variables had been examined. The chamber in Russia would have destroyed several square miles of land.
Phase two would be a gloriously destructive success.

19

Berlin, en-route / Charlottenburg HQ

Eva stared out of the window of the embassy car. A street of piled up masonry would grow up into a row of buildings as the car turned then level out again into more piles of rubble. Entire city blocks had been demolished. In one part of the ruins an entire living room was revealed intact from the shorn walls, the tablecloth and settings undisturbed. Dressed in a Russian female signaler´s uniform, she pulled her forage cap down low over her forehead. Her hair was severely pinned up, Hopkins had forbidden her to wear make-up. Findlay had smeared cigarette ash under her eyelids with cinematic sweeps of his grimy thumbs; it gave her a hollowed-out look. Her change of clothes travelled in a battered suitcase in the car's boot. Hopkins cast sideways glances at her as if she was a new sub-species he had just encountered.

Chainbridge and Curran sat in silent synod. The azure skies and distant feathered clouds allowed the windows to be opened a crack. The soft breeze circulated the smells of aftershave, pomade, tobacco, leather briefcases and faintly mildewed clothes; *three old men*, thought Eva. Squeezed in on the back seat, she felt oppressed and uncomfortable.

Brandt and Findlay, also in Red Army fatigues, followed behind in a jeep, mainly due to Findlay's impressive reek from alcohol, cigarettes and a general aversion to soap.

"Another checkpoint," said the driver. Beneath his black beret his shaved head folded into rings of razor-burned muscle. Two Russian soldiers, heavily armed, flagged down the vehicles. Two more leaned against the remnants of a wall. They smoked lazily; their weapons hung from the shoulder for easy access. The Embassy driver rolled down the window and handed over the papers, creased and worn by countless hands. Spotting Eva, the Russians peered in. She focused on some distant spot in the cloudless sky. The soldiers stared at her like idle wolves. Her beauty, though muted, called to them like fresh blood on the snow. Glancing around the car, they calculated the cost of taking her as a prize. After a beat, they handed back the papers and strutted off towards the jeep.

"Will I wait, Mr. Hopkins, sir?" asked the driver.

"Yes," replied Hopkins.

They heard the click of the driver's revolver resting on his lap as the engine idled. He adjusted his rearview mirror, and everyone craned their necks to see through the back window.

Findlay was barking something loud in Russian, Brandt proffered cigarettes. A huge burst of laughter from the soldiers broke the tension. Findlay and Brandt made a pantomime of joining in with the bonhomie.

Chainbridge allowed himself a smile. Findlay, the old drunken sod, had a way about him, he could disarm you with a smile.

The two vehicles were waved on.

"More roadblocks than usual, sir," said the driver.

"They're looking for something?" said Chainbridge.

"Hard to say, sir," replied the driver.

Eva thought of the Berlin of champagne towers she´d inhabited six years earlier, as an adornment on the arm of a wealthy American and close friend of Hitler. She thought of her friend Ellen; her roommate and confidante, reduced to sweeping the streets with a yellow star sewn onto her thin coat. Eva had bundled her onto the U-Bahn, ensuring her safe passage out of Germany. She wondered if Ellen was dead or alive.

A cyclist in a black suit cruised past them, his long legs pumping him along as he smoked. Something about his shape, his assurance, caught Eva's attention. He glided off onto another street.

"How far to Charlottenburg?" asked Chainbridge.

"About fifteen minutes, sir," replied the driver.

He moved away from the checkpoint. The jeep kept up close behind.

Berliners were walking, cycling, boarding buses or descending into the U-Bahns; bright flecks of colour against the charred facades. The battered trams trundled along repaired tracks, jousting with the buses and occupation vehicles. They passed a huge framed photograph of Stalin, his uniform decorated with a myriad of medals and flanked by Soviet flags. The driver slowed down and turned into the British zone.

Arriving at Headquarters they were ushered through the reception area into the inner offices.

"I'm afraid the lady will have to remain here," said Hopkins.

"Why?" asked Eva.

"If we require anything further from you, we'll give you a shout," he replied.

"She's an essential part of the team, Hopkins. She needs to be involved at every meeting," said Brandt.

"You're in no position to make demands, sir," said Keyburn.

They turned to face him, a dapper man with unlimited power at his disposal.

"Henry Chainbridge, Miles Curran, I presume?" said Keyburn.

He didn't offer his hand but stood, arms folded.

His eyes glanced over Eva, but that was all.

"May I introduce Eva Molenaar and Alastaire Findlay," said Chainbridge. Findlay's unique odour flitted around them.

"Before we go any further, take those Russian uniforms and dump them in the trash," said Keyburn. "As for the lady, I've read her dossier; she's Polish. In my book that makes her a potential red. A potential spy. She stays here."

Eva took the suitcase handed to her by the driver and made towards the toilets. In her handbag, she felt the secure weight of her Beretta.

She changed into slacks and a crumpled blouse which she tucked into her belt with vigor. Combat boots were lobbed into the suitcase, replaced by comfortable pumps. Fishing around in the suitcase, she found her shoulder holster and slotted the Beretta into it. She pulled out a light tweed jacket and shrugged it on. Unpinning her hair, she let it fall to her shoulders. She undid some of the tangles with her fingers and stared into the mirror.

She washed her face and powdered it, bringing a bit of life back into her expression. Looking around the toilet with its grimy tiles and chipped mirrors, she decided she needed a cigarette and breath of air.
Leaning against the bullet-pocked wall of the HQ building, she pulled out her silver cigarette case. Tapping the cigarette three times before lighting up, she looked at it. It had been a gift from de Witte. She had wanted to throw it away many times but love – however mis-cued or awry – should always have a memento.
A truck load of American GI's waved and whistled to her as they passed, all smiling teeth, crumpled fatigues and tans. She gave a little wave back, then spotted the cyclist.
It was the same man. The same suit. She had the same sensation of him not fitting the picture in some way. He coasted behind the truck, looking up and down the building. His gaze landed on Eva, passing over her without a flicker. He pumped his legs methodically into the Berlin traffic.
A car pulled up outside the entrance. It was an American Cadillac, a metallic blue monster with glistening chromium. Two pennants flew the stars and stripes. Compared to the military vehicles and battered German traffic, it seemed to come from the future. A tall, handsome man emerged from the back, dressed in gold Navy livery and braiding. He strode past Eva, manhandling a large travel case with aluminum edges. The Cadillac swerved out with a screech, ignoring the startled honking of horns.
Eva stubbed out her cigarette and followed the man into the building.

***

"Has he been drinking?" asked Keyburn,

"Probably," replied Chainbridge,

"There are three things that ruin a man, in my opinion: alcohol, power and women," said Keyburn.

"He´s in the clear on two of those, then," said Chainbridge.

"If I may continue, gentlemen?" said Findlay.
He tapped the pointer solemnly against the canvas screen. His face was flushed as he patted his head to locate his glasses with

his free hand. The audience was sitting at a round table; Chainbridge, Brandt, Keyburn, Curran and Hopkins. The walls were dark paneled, crudely repaired in places where wood had splintered from the bombing. Comfortable chairs with high backs and soft upholstery had been procured.

"Young Brandt here shared a cell with Doctor Friedrich Kallerhoff – presumed deceased – who, according to these documents from the micro-dot, led a team of *computers* – mathematicians – who worked on theories outside of Nazi ideology but necessary for their war effort."

On the screen was a list of typed names, Findlay found his grip and tapped on the fifth name down.

"Edgar Halidane. Here, gentlemen it gets interesting," his Scottish burr was toned down, lending him some badly needed gravitas. "Thank you – next slide please."

The next slide was a long-typeset formula.

"This, gentlemen, is the Unified Field Theory. The *Theory of everything* as it is known. This group of mathematicians was trying, if you can believe it, to crack Einstein's theories. The second one – electro-magnetic fields – is the reason why we're here today."

"Edgar Aloys Halidane is a former American citizen, a flim-flam man and a huckster," said Keyburn. "A lot of vagrant scientists worked for the US military during the depression. Halidane was recruited in 1935 and kicked out of the naval service two years later. His ideas were considered too extreme, too fanciful."

"And he winds up on a secret Nazi list," said Chainbridge.

"In Berlin," said Keyburn.

"Isn't he an American matter, then?" said Chainbridge.

"Next slide, please," said Findlay.

The projectionist, the tall handsome man in the gold braided naval uniform, cranked the projector. At his feet, the projector case lay open.

"This formula – the theory, as it were – appears to have been solved by Edgar Halidane himself," said Findlay. He let this sentence hang. "He cracked a bloody Einstein theory."

"There was a team?" said Curran.

"Yes. But look at this. This next slide is a detailed letter to Adolf Hitler. In it, Edgar Halidane is pitching a programme – a scientific application for the military – utilising Unified Field Theory. You can see stamped here at the bottom, Hitler's signature and approval. Halidane is the only one on that list capable of cracking the theory."

"And Hitler's the only one mad enough to sign off on it," said Curran.

The next slide was a schematic – a hexagonal cut-away of a room.

"The same blueprint as the Swiss microfilm. The one MI6 passed on, incidentally. He calls it a *Halidane Chamber*."

"An American scientist, now a naturalised British citizen, working for the Nazis before the war. That doesn't make him a criminal," said Hopkins, "A lot of English and Americans thought Hitler was the cat's pyjamas before the war."

"This cat's pyjamas, Mr. Hopkins, is playing Russian roulette with the universe. What he proposes, and my German is a little rusty – Brandt and Chainbridge will agree – is that he's capable of folding time."

"The sentence translates as *Whip time and saw-pierce a hole in it,* said Brandt.

Keyburn snorted in derision.

"Man cannot manipulate God's work – nonsense."

Findlay removed his glasses with one hand and crooked the pointer under his arm. Fishing a handkerchief out of his pocket, he cleaned the glasses slowly. A tic danced under an uneven eye.

"The theory Halidane proposes is to fold a tiny pleat in time and make a tiny hole in the 'fabric'. Then pass something through it; like a needle stitching a hem. His results, calculations and conclusions, on paper, in theory, are sound. Our boy here has got Hitler to sign off on a series of Halidane chambers which act like U-Bahn or Metro stations around the planet."

"Transporting what?" asked Chainbridge.

He tried to ignore Keyburn and Hopkins' derisory grins.

"I've no bloody idea, Chainbridge. But I'll lay a-pound-t´-apenny, those co-ordinates I deciphered have a connection."

X I J O-T B X = 5 9 D w 5 7 M n + 2 D Z Z M w.

The letters blazed across the screen.

"'Tis my belief that Whip-Saw has a Halidane Chamber at these co-ordinates."

"Int.7. being handed the microfilm by MI6, Brandt's micro-dot, these co-ordinates; they all make a compelling argument," said Chainbridge. He looked around the table; the reactions swung from Keyburn's derision to Hopkins´ poker face. "It requires further investigation."

"Halidane Corp. has transferred a huge amount of capital into Switzerland. We are dealing with a very, very powerful, secretive organisation," said Curran. "Our enquiries in Switzerland are being met with a wall of silence."

"But no facts. Just numbers on that screen and theories," said Keyburn. "You are taking a leap, gentlemen. This is nothing but hooey,"

"Mr. Keyburn, I respectfully disagree," said Findlay. "I've met Halidane personally; he met Einstein. Halidane is on that intellectual level. Those numbers and theories you casually dismiss as bloody 'hooey' are capable of something bigger than your atomic bomb. If he can do what he claims, i.e., shift magnetic fields, manipulate matter and with it the very nature of the world we inhabit, and he's one calculation off – *just one f'king decimal point off* – he's capable of destroying the planet. Simple as that, Mr. Keyburn."

He let his voice ring around the room. Chainbridge thought about the wreck of a man he'd met a week earlier, now commanding the room like an old masterful stage actor.

"He may have been involved in the killing of two British agents in Switzerland," said Chainbridge. "For that alone, we need to find out what he's up to."

"O.S.S. will pass on this, gentlemen, said Keyburn. "It´s a waste of America's time."

"May I request you check to see if Halidane Corp., has

bought any real estate or filed any planning applications via government contracts," said Curran.
Hopkins toyed with a pen. His eyes studied closely the individuals around the table.

"I can't see Atlee signing off on this, I'm afraid. We take this to the PM and the Foreign Office; we'll be a laughingstock. In common with our friends in America, the priority is Russia. Agents die every day, Mr. Chainbridge. In addition, according to your report here, these agents died from natural causes."

"What do we know about Halidane?" asked Chainbridge. "His weaknesses, his Achilles heel?"

"He's a committed bachelor, but he´s rather fond of women – young women," said Curran. He gingerly folded open the manilla file as if he might catch something nasty from it.

"Had quite the reputation in Germany, it would seem. When they weren't subjecting women to death camp vivisections, Kallerhoff and Halidane had a little underage harem going."

"Ann Chambrel was assigned to him," said Chainbridge. "That cost her life. *Chopin* might be a more viable option."

"I don't approve of your proposal," said Keyburn. "Your girlie upstairs has gone by the names Sheridan, Miller and Henning. Filed as deceased by the Gestapo in 1941. She's popped up in Berlin, New York, Sienna, Paris and heaven knows where else?"

"All her information has proven accurate and has never once been compromised," replied Chainbridge.

He held the O.S.S. chief's gaze. Unlike the obsequious Hopkins, Chainbridge knew he was dealing with a small-town shop-keeper mindset.

"I agree with Mr Keyburn," said Curran.

He toyed with a pen. His lips made a slight pout as he spoke.

"She has risked her life for the Allied cause," said Chainbridge.

"She's a potential red," said Keyburn.
Brandt glowered at Keyburn, taking in the dapper suit, dainty bowtie and expensive shirt, then he reached for a glass of water.

He sipped it. The bottles were Italian, chilled. He thought of people lining up and drinking from rusted old metal standpipes in the city.

"How much of Berlin have you seen, Mr. Keyburn?" he asked.

"Enough to know we must stay here for a very long time, thanks to your boss, Adolf Hitler, sir."

"Captain Brandt fought with US troops during the final phase of the war. Under Churchill's orders he was assigned to assassinate Martin Bormann. That's why he was found shot on the street. Like Miss Molenaar, he deserves respect and a seat at the table," said Chainbridge.

"I'm here on President Truman's personal orders. That's all any of you need to know," replied Keyburn. He set his square jaw like a journeyman boxer. His pocket handkerchief matched the silver and blue-striped tie. His double-breasted suit gave him a geometric stance.

The first shot seemed like a car back-firing outside. It was only when Keyburn spun off his chair in a plume of blood that Brandt reacted. The handsome naval officer took deliberate aim at Findlay and fired twice. Findlay stumbled into the screen, collapsing it under his weight. Brandt lunged for the water bottle and lobbed it at the officer. It shattered spectacularly off his head, making him miss a shot. Brandt's chair snagged on the carpet beneath, slowing him fractionally. A bullet hit the table inches from his face. Chainbridge rolled under the table. Brandt forced his legs, pushing the chair over. Hopkins, still standing, presented an obvious target. The officer, recovering his balance, shot him twice in the back. Curran, who sat petrified in fear, was shot once in the throat and then in the forehead. Brandt kiltered over on the chair, landing on his back. He could hear the calm footfalls coming towards him. He tried to roll free. Two more shots rang out and the calculated stride stopped. Brandt and Chainbridge rose to see Eva standing over the officer.

"Glad you could join us," said Chainbridge.

"Nice timing," said Brandt.

He struggled to his feet and hoisted Chainbridge up.

"Next time include me in these things," said Eva.

The officer gave a groan and rolled onto his back. His arm rose weakly with the gun.

Eva pulled back the hammer of her Beretta.

"Don't," she whispered.

Brandt struck the officer once with a chair and kicked the gun away.

Military Police thundered into the room. One posted himself at the door blocking curious on-lookers from the offices. Two more reached down and hoisted up the stunned officer.

Keyburn was dead, his tidy hair blasted apart above the left ear. Curran´s head was thrust back, his dead stare directed to some shadow in the high ceiling. Hopkins was carried out, a thick trail of blood making a snake-like wake.

Chainbridge and Brandt rushed to Findlay. Brandt opened his jacket, then the tweed waistcoat. He´d been shot in the stomach and just above the heart. Blood was pooling from the exit wounds. His rheumy eyes were already turning the colour of cream. Bubbles of blood hung around the corners of his mouth.

"You have to stop Halidane. He hasn't a f'kin' clue..." he said.

Chainbridge took the man's hand. Findlay's legs kicked out like a swimmer treading water.

"Have you someone? Someone to go to?" asked Brandt.

"Yuri. My precious Yuri..." whispered Findlay.

"Go then, Findlay. There's nothing more you can do... Go," whispered Brandt.

Findlay gripped Chainbridge's lapels, dragging him over.

"F'ck you, Chainbridge," he said, smiling.

Findlay's head stuck the floor with a dead thud.

"Rest in peace, you twisted old Leninist," said Chainbridge.

There was a commotion. The officer was gagging. The two MPs struggled with him, one forcing his fist into the officer's mouth. The man slumped into their arms, his weight dragging them to the floor. The unmistakable scent of crushed almonds filled the air.

"Sorry, sir – cyanide," said one of them.

"Get him on the table. Now," said Chainbridge.

They cleared the table and threw the body on top. The man was stripped, his wallet and personal effects were stacked on a chair.

"There," said Chainbridge.

On the dead man's torso was a tattoo – a six-pointed star framed by a snake whose head and tail met at an inverted swastika. A key was etched into the centre of the star.

"I've never seen anything like it," said Chainbridge.

"In the same spot as a Waffen SS tattoo," said Brandt.

He let the words hang in the room.

"What a bloody mess," said Chainbridge.

Eva looked around the room. Cordite still filled the air. A hustle of bodies moved the dead men. With care, Findlay was lifted and carried out. It was then that the faint reek of chemicals drifted over. Following it, Eva stood over the projectionist's box. All the slides had melted, doused in acid. The projector too, was damaged beyond all repair.

"He had no intention of leaving this room," said Eva.

"We need to re-group and contact Bracken," said Chainbridge.

Keyburn was the last body out. A dead American in the British Military HQ for Berlin. Truman would muster all his forces now.

"We need to get out of Berlin," said Chainbridge.

"That can be arranged," said a voice.

Doctor Pannu stood at the doorway.

"I'm afraid you can do nothing here now, Doctor," said Chainbridge.

"I have a car. We must leave," said Pannu.

"Not the safe house; it´s compromised," said Chainbridge.

"Switzerland," said Brandt. He looked around the room and then put an arm around Eva. "Well, we were leaving anyway."

20

Plymouth, Southern England

The Marlborough had been sitting at a siding near the city, in view of the destroyers at anchor. Communications and dynamo cars had been attached, increasing the train's length to eighty-four feet. The locomotive hissed in readiness. In the comms carriage, the teletypes cracked into life, clacking and clipping onto the reams of paper. Churchill ambled toward them. Bracken looked up from the morning newspaper. The teletext operator tore off the sheet and handed it to the hulking dressing gown.

"Russian decrypts, Bracken," mumbled Churchill.

"Bletchley, no doubt. I have a secondary source there."

"Your secondary source, Mr. Bracken, is indicating that there's been an explosion in Siberia. There's been telegraphic messaging between Beria and Stalin all morning."

Bracken folded the paper and swilled the dregs of his tea.

"What sort of explosion?"

"A bloody big one. Lots of casualties. Seems the Politburo is convening an emergency meeting."

Churchill tore off the sheet and pored over it.

"Better let Atlee and the FO know," he said.

"Not just yet, Churchill. Chainbridge and Curran haven't responded."

The second machine, a German Siemens & Halske teleprinter, began transmitting with grinding rolls and clacks. Bracken looked over the Navy Officer assigned to the carriage, his Brylcreemed demeanor as black as the machine. He decrypted the message and handed it over.

"Winston, Charlottenburg has been compromised. Chainbridge has just confirmed. Keyburn, Findlay and Curran dead, Hopkins critical. Attacker dead."

"Damn and blast," muttered Churchill, "That's the end of our little adventure, then. The safe house?"

The teleprinter transmitted back.

"Intact. Assumed compromised, alternatives commenced. Chainbridge." read Bracken.

"We need to garner our scant resources. Mr. Bracken. I smell a most unsavoury situation, one that we should examine without the government knowing," said Churchill. He swilled his morning Brandy in deep contemplation.

Another clatter of typing began. The operator methodically swiped it from the drum and re-read it. He handed it over.

"Co-ordinates somewhere north of the Orkneys. Stop. Dispatch reconnaissance to locate/confirm. Stop. Code-name Whip-Saw," read Churchill.

He looked up at the operator.

"Get me the First Sea Lord," he said.

"Patching you through now, sir," replied the teletypist.

The machines between Plymouth and Whitehall began to clack ceaselessly.

21

The Orkney Islands: RAF Skeabrae / 895 Squadron

The early morning frost had begun to thaw, but it clung in stubborn patches to the outer Nissen huts, sheds and hangars. Squadron Leader Marty 'Mick' Miller took his leather helmet from the Spitfire's control console, trailing radio cables and an oxygen tube, and tugged it on over his neatly trimmed and pomaded hair. As he did so, squatting on his starboard wing, Station Group Captain Roswick Dowling leaned in.

"Interesting communiqué from RNFAA, Coastal Command, sir," said Miller. "*Look for anything untoward.*"

Once his helmet was fastened, he turned on the petrol feeds of his Mk-22 Spitfire and pressed the starter button. The engine gave a throaty roar and belched blue smoke into the dawn.

"Anything untoward. Out of the ordinary, Squadron

Leader," shouted Dowling, "Take the rookies out over the Iceland-Faroes Passage, give the machines a good work-out. Test the Hispanos."

Dowling had the thin features and earnest brown eyes of a greyhound. His moustache seemed too big for his face. An antique sailor's corn-pipe jutted out from its depths.

The sound of two other Spitfires igniting their Griffon engines thrummed along the runway. Pilots Bonnar and Coady, two newly minted 'sprogs' from flight school, had arrived on the ferry the week before.

"That explains the extra fuel tanks. U-Boats?" asked Miller. The folded map strapped to his thigh had a grid plotted out from the encrypted co-ordinates from Plymouth.

"Dönitz is still playing silly buggers with his fleets," said Dowling.

"Still taking their chances?"

"If nothing else, this mission will give you more flight time before you transfer to Egypt."

Miller ran his eyes across the console. Every gauge and needle danced in anticipation of take-off. He touched the battered photo of Shona, his sweetheart, a superstitious gesture. Her blue eyes stared intently from the picture. He thought of her nylon stockings held by lace suspenders and how she slowly unfastened them. Through the canopy, he watched the first rays of dawn inch across the sea.

"Maintain radio contact - we'll be patching you through a secure channel, Squadron Leader," said Dowling.

He jumped nimbly from the wing and stepped onto the grass verge, burying himself deeper into his greatcoat.

"Take them up to twenty thousand feet, run a few high-altitude manoeuvres and bring them home in the afternoon. Keep your eyes peeled," he shouted.

The airman handed Miller his Mae West life jacket and slid the canopy closed. Miller heard it lock into place.

"Bonnar, keep your elbow tight to your hip. It'll stabilise you when you engage the hydraulics. Let's not have a repeat of yesterday," said Miller.

"Roger wilco, Squadron Leader," replied Bonnar, managing to get a tincture of highland sarcasm into his reply.

Miller thought of the first time he flew into battle; bouncing mercilessly along the runway and skywards - into the teeth of a marauding group of Luftwaffe ME 109s.

The rays of sunlight had turned the horizon to a sliver of pink.

He thought of tracer fire.

"Follow me. Keep in V formation and stay alert. Thin air and cold can affect performance. If you feel ill, just shout, we'll drop to a lower altitude."

Bonnar and Coady crackled confirmations into Miller's headset.

Miller's thumb brushed across the trigger of the 20mm Hispano cannons and he watched the arc of the propeller as it carved the air. Giving the Spitfire more throttle, he began to roll away onto the airstrip. He thrilled to the smooth response of the machine to every command.

"Ready when you are, gentlemen," said Miller.

He gunned the engine.

Roswick Dowling and the air crews watched the trio of sleek fighters tear upwards into the salmon-pink clouds. Then, slowly, the men trudged across the glistening gorse toward the control tower.

The fishing vessels and trawlers along the islands of Rousay and Westray flowed beneath Miller as he turned the stick a fraction, setting a course North-North-West. The Spitfire responded nimbly to this touch.

Looking for something untoward, out of the ordinary, well outside of the machine's operational range.

With two rookies in tow.

***

The Marlborough was now a bustling hub. The blackboard with Findlay's writing was now accompanied by a huge grid map of the Orkney, Shetland and Faroe Islands. Bracken and Churchill had been joined by two senior Navy staff. Both men stood quietly in the shadows, arms folded, their sleeve braids woven in golden strands. They perched like hawks against the carriage wall.

"RAF Skeabrae is broadcasting now, sir," said the radio operator.

From hidden speakers around the carriage, the voices of Miller, Coady and Bonnar crackled out.

"They're just at the co-ordinates now?" asked Bracken.

"Yes sir," replied the radio operator. He incrementally adjusted the dial to minimise the hisses, shrieks and static blasts.

"Must be hitting bad weather," muttered one of the Naval men in the shadows.

"Weather conditions are very good according to the shipping news," replied Bracken. "Almost perfect, in fact."

There was a sudden blast of static, causing headphones to be dragged off or held away from ears.

It took a few moments for the noise to abate.

"Can you repeat that, Squadron Leader?" came a voice.

"Who's that?" asked Bracken.

"Group Captain, Roswick Dowling, Skeabrae," said the other Naval man.

They exchanged glances with Churchill.

"Gulls, Bonnar, did you say gulls?"

"Affirmative, Squadron Leader. Sea-gulls, port-side, eight o'clock, they're circling."

***

Miller banked the Spitfire toward the patch of sea where Bonnar had spotted the birds. A flock of gulls were making slow circles above the water. The vault of blue sky was devoid of cloud. Toward the horizon, the dots of The Faroes appeared.

"Could be a dead whale, or a school of fish," said Coady.

"Or a fishing vessel," said Bonnar.

Miller looked at the fuel gauge, time for the reserve tanks. He calculated fifteen minutes of circling the gridded area here before returning to Skeabrae.

Time enough.

"Well, it *is* something unusual and untoward," he said. "Switch to your reserve tanks and let's go have a look."

The Spitfires descended from the heavens and accelerated a few

hundred feet above the waves.
The gulls scattered briefly, then suddenly reconverged.
A sudden flash of light caught Miller's eyes as a scream filled his headset. Glancing up into his mirrors, he saw Coady's aircraft ignite into a ball of fire. The aircraft skewed upwards and began a gradual death dive into the sea.

"Flying boat!" shouted Bonnar.

Tracer fire slashed across Miller's canopy and the immense shape of a four-engined flying boat lumbered overhead. Miller held his breath and forced the throttle, ignoring the screech and crack of over-stressed metal. As his Spitfire climbed up and over, he could see Bonnar's plane tearing away at full speed. A more experienced flyer would have begun evasive manoeuvres. Bonnar was a fraction slower than the turret gunner on the flying boat. A trail of tracer fire latched onto his fuselage in a deadly swarm. Bonnar's Spitfire rolled wildly, the cockpit a mess of shattered perspex. It descended steeply. On impact, it cart-wheeled across the churning waves, sending splinters of wings, tail and fuselage in all directions. As with Coady's stricken aircraft, no parachute emerged.

Miller's gauges whirred wildly. Fuel, compass, altimeter and even his wristwatch were spinning in all directions. His headset was hissing at a painfully high pitch in his ears. For a few moments, he couldn't discern the sky from the sea. He regained control once he spied the sun. He levelled out and lined up flat along the horizon.

He spotted the Flying boat. It was a powerful Japanese one.
He brought the Spitfire around in a tight arc and glided into the Flying boat's slipstream.
He opened fire.
The hail of bullets missed the first time.
"RAF Skeabrae, I'm engaging the flying boat. It's an *Emily.* Repeat. Engaging."
All he could hear was his voice distant in the static. But no response. For a split-second, he thought he heard German voices in his ear.

"Well *Emily,* you're a long way from home," he muttered,

"what are you doing out here in the middle of nowhere?"
The flying boat lumbered to port and into Miller's gun sights. He opened fire, the Hispano tracers guiding the bullets to the flying boat's tail. Suddenly, the flying boat vanished. There in front of him one moment, gone the next.
Vanished into the ether.
It was then that Miller became aware of a red ring around his peripheral vision. A burning ring searing his retinas apart, boring into his skull. He was blinded instantly. He began to scream. His flight jacket, Mae West and leather cap ignited into flame. Grasping for the cockpit release, Miller's gloves began melting onto his hands, leaving greasy traces along the canopy.
His weapons and spare ninety-gallon fuel tank ignited, turning his plane into a spiralling crematorium.

***

Halidane and Hoeberichts watched from an observation platform as the three Spitfires were destroyed. The crew manning a long tube mounted on a pivoting tripod cheered. The tube was telescopic, three metres long with mirrors and lenses adjusted to take an electrical charge from the Whip-Saw generators and direct it at a target. The pulse was catastrophic if it found its mark.

"Your beloved Interferometer's a bit hit and miss, but we were lucky with the two downed aircraft," said Hoeberichts.
He scanned the sky searching for any more possible attacks. The flying boat re-appeared and banked slowly towards the harbor.

"We'll have the Royal Navy to deal with," he continued.

"We jammed their radio transmissions," replied Halidane. "They might send a spy ship out for them. Maybe a trawler or small fishing vessel, that will be all. We're perfectly safe here."

Hoeberichts grunted, then slowly lowered the binoculars.

"We should leave, now, Halidane, while we still have time," It sounded more like an order than a request.

***

"Repeat, I said, repeat," said Bracken.

Dowling's voice was becoming increasingly distorted.

"We think he said *Flying Boat,* followed by the word *Japanese.* We've lost all three signals. We're trying to re-connect with them, Portsmouth. Please bear with us."

Dowling's voice was again shredded through the sonic screeches.

"I thought I heard a woman's name, *Emma*? *Emily*?" said Bracken.

He stood up. He ran his fingers through his thick unkempt hair. His gaze drifted to the two silent Naval officers.

"A flying boat, that far out?"

"We've nothing in the area, apart from Miller, Bonnar and Coady," said one of them. His silver hair combed back gave him a lean, vulpine appearance.

Churchill stood, placed his thumbs in the pockets of his charcoal grey waistcoat and rolled his cigar from one side of his mouth to the other.

"A Japanese aircraft. We need to get a ship out there, gentlemen, a destroyer group."

The assembled men looked at each other for a moment. A throat was cleared.

"We will need to inform the Prime Minister, sir," said the other Navy man.

Bracken reached for a communiqué and lit a cigarette from the butt of the last one. The crystal ashtray was piling up.

"Well, it´s certainly unusual and untoward, Winston," he said. "Have RAF Skeabrae received any form of contact?"

The radio operator shook his head.

The static was reduced in volume to a white noise around the carriage.

Bracken glanced over at the Naval men.

"This is a sensitive situation for His Majesty's Government."

"Why?" replied the vulpine one's companion. He was almost bald, his remaining hair pomaded into thin strips. His voice had the gravitas of coal.

"We have an American citizen, now a naturalised British subject, in cahoots with unknown forces, possibly acting against the Allies," said Bracken.

"Then we must obfuscate and thwart at every opportunity, Bracken. A detachment of marines will be required," said Churchill. The septuagenarian war horse lumbered past Bracken and the Naval officers, leaving a wake of smoke, and saluted his way to the exit.

"I'll arrange a car to Whitehall, it's a government matter now," he said. He turned at the doorway.

"I'll be in America in the coming days. I'd like to speak to President Truman personally. Destroy every piece of paper and correspondence. You may have my train for the duration of the situation. Good hunting, gentlemen."

"We'll arrange a marine detachment," said the gaunt Naval officer. "The First Sea Lord will need to be appraised."

Chainbridge and his team were up to their necks now, thought Bracken.

Spying was a waiting game; he would have to wait for them to contact him.

Assuming they could get out of Germany alive.

22

Berlin / Charlottenburg HQ

De Witte caught the first waft of her perfume as she climbed into the back of the car. It took him back to a cold London afternoon, the boat train to Southampton, and Paris. It was nineteen thirty-eight, the edge of the world was tipping inexorably towards the abyss. A young courier from Poland on her first mission, Eva had an air of pain about her, tempered with a quick intelligence he found so alluring. His fingertips remembered her skin, her lips. His memory recalled her heated whispers and cries of pleasure. They had become mo re than fellow spies and colleagues; they were lovers, their tryst spiced with guilt and near-death escapes as the world began to tear itself apart.

A subtle shift in the air about her told him she hadn't expected to see him.

"Good to see you, old friend," said Chainbridge. "Eva and Captain Brandt, you already know."

He patted De Witte's shoulder.

"Portugal's weather agrees with you, I see," he continued.

"Brandt," said de Witte.

"De Witte. Berlin again, of all places."

"Doctor Pannu, Brandt and I rescued your good friend here from the Abwehr HQ," said Chainbridge.

"Doctor Pannu has been a valuable contact for me," said De Witte. "He was concerned for your well-being here."

"Whoever attacked us will expect us to run," said Eva. "I know someone who can get us out of Germany - discreetly."

"There's enough military outside now," said Brandt.

The plaintive wail of an ambulance forced vehicles aside, creating a gap. Pannu fired up the Buick Super's engine, marvelling at De Witte's connections to procure such a vehicle. He inched it out into the Strasse. The HQ was lit up by a dozen sets of headlamps. Soldiers, MPs and staff dashed about, backlit against its walls.

"He's probably dead, or his place bombed to rubble, Memsahib?" said Pannu.

"Not René Parez, Doctor Pannu," said Eva, "He's one of life's survivors. Doctor, can you drive us to Lake Konstanz?"

"If we can get out of the Russian cordon," he replied.

"Leave that to me, Doctor," replied De Witte. "My Russian's a little rusty, but I think I can get us through."

***

The casino flanked Lake Konstanz's shoreline. Expensive carved stone façades flashed by as Pannu followed Eva's directions. It was late, streetlamps flickered uneasily, and the distant lights of Switzerland glinted brightly along the far shore. Chainbridge had once operated out of a safe house on a street nearby. The late Douglas Gageby had put a stop to that.

Amid the lake's blackness, the austere pavements and the empty street, the well-lit *Casino Astral* shone like a precious stone. The

Astral's smartly attired doorman held out a pristine white gloved hand. Pannu brought the vehicle to a smooth halt.

"Good evening. Herr Parez received your cable. He's waiting for you."

He took the keys from the Sikh doctor, bowed politely and surveyed his companions with a cool glance.

"Welcome. Refreshments will be served. For the sake of discretion, you will be escorted through the kitchens. Please enjoy your visit."

"Best let me do the talking," said Eva.

René Juan Parez looked up from his enormous polished oak desk and lowered his silver monocle.

"Eva, my darling!"

He pounced from his plush leather chair.

"Welcome back, ma cherie! How long has it been? Six years, or seven?"

He was tall and broad with the aquiline profile of a Medici. His thick gold ring with inset diamond and Rolex pearl watch set off the sumptuous purple velvet décor. The paintings hanging from the walls were subtly lit and, Chainbridge noted to himself, utterly priceless.

"Nearly eight, Renée – what happened to your Berlin enterprises?"

"The Nazis – before the war, they were happy to consort with our open-minded girls. Then, once in power, they became a righteous bunch of murdering monks. Still, Konstanz has become a profitable little operation since the surrender. Lots of them suddenly seem keen to leave their beloved Germany."

He looked over at the hulking Sikh, the dapper blindman, the scholarly type taking an inordinate amount of interest in his collection and the tall, rugged quiet one measuring him up.

"Gentlemen, you all look like you need a few days rest?"

"We've been driving for forty-eight hours non-stop, René. We just need to get across the lake," replied Eva.

"Not a social visit then? You promised me, remember?"

"If you pour me a drink, will that make us even?" replied Eva.

René Parez bowed over her hand and kissed it gallantly.

"For you, my darling, anything. If I remember correctly, bourbon – neat?" he said.

"Four Roses, two fingers, ice," grinned Eva.

Parez strode around his desk, he lifted the ivory inlaid receiver and spoke into it in Swiss-German.

"The Americans and French are running this sector and, as a result, all my phones are bugged. The only parts they haven't been able to bug are the casino tables and my booths – to the best of my knowledge. I keep a pleasure craft moored in Zürich – it should be here in an hour. Drinks first, then freshen yourselves up and I'll have dinner served in my private booth."

Pressing a hidden button, a section of the wall rotated around, revealing an elaborately stocked bar.

"Four Roses for the lady, I'm guessing a twelve-year old whisky for the two erudite gentlemen, vodka for the strong silent type and a soda water for the Indian gentlemen. Am I right?"

"Quite right, thank you, Sahib," said Pannu.

He shrugged off his great coat and folded it before placing it on the arm of the luxurious settee.

"Weapons are not allowed, sir," said Parez.

He eyed the Sikh's Kirpan uneasily.

"No fear, Sahib, I am merely their protector," replied Pannu. "I'm sure you have protection of your own."

"I'd prefer all weapons on the table," replied Parez.

"We'd prefer to keep them," replied Brandt.

"We lost a few friends today, René," said Eva.

"Very well, we're all adults here," said Parez.

He poured the drinks with the assurance of a prophet.

"Eva, darling, can I tempt you to come back and be my hostess here at the Astral again? Same arrangement from the night's takings?"

"I'm flattered René, but the past is the past," replied Eva.

The immaculate and diligent host handed out the drinks in crystal-cut tumblers.

"A toast is in order then, my friends; a toast to the past."

Brandt downed the vodka, enjoying the smooth frozen sensation.

Watching Eva navigate the situation reminded him that she was more than just a brilliant spy. She could fashion herself to any man's desire, her victims unaware of the ruse until it was too late. He began to wonder if the past was all he had left of her. He placed the tumbler down.

"Thank you, Herr Parez," he said.

"No names, sir," replied Parez. "Now please feel free to make use of the facilities here."

Eva reached into the hidden pleat of her slacks. From it, she produced the small packet of diamonds.

"How much do we owe you, René?"

Parez poured the jewels from the packet onto the huge leather blotter on the desk. He pulled the antique banker´s lamp over, produced a black loupe from a drawer and inspected the diamonds, each one held firmly in black tweezers.

"Exqusiite, Eva, where did you get them?"

"A masquerade ball in London before the war."

Parez's swarthy looks creased into a smile.

"I'll take five of the best, leave you three, agreed?" he said.

"You can have two, you rascal," replied Eva.

"Three, ma cherie?"

"What a hard bargain you drive, René," replied Eva.

Brandt and Chainbridge exchanged a glance.

"This is all too easy, Herr Parez," said Brandt.

"I'm honouring my best hostess and her companions; it is my pleasure," said Parez. "Now, sir, I suggest you smarten up for dinner."

The booth was screened off from the tables. Another world of unparalleled luxury existed on the other side. High-ranking American officers were gaming recklessly alongside their French and English counterparts. On their arms, beautiful women in expensive dresses cooed and cheered them on. The decadent rush of liberation permeated the atmosphere.

***

"Edgar Halidane? Yes, he has a reputation," said Parez, carving the beef joint expertly. Ice buckets full of champagne and fine wines graced the delicate lace tablecloth.

"He has a certain appetite only the most expensive clubs could provide at the height of the Reich, *spigots*. Blood," he said.

"Did you provide such a service?"

"No ma cherie. But he had a friend, an old buzzard named Bellowes. He provided the girls – set up the rooms in the clubs. Utterly barbaric – may I offer you a slice, sir?"

A slab of meat hung from the fork, bloodied and firm.

"Just the vegetables, Sahib Parez, thank you," replied Pannu.

Chainbridge and De Witte leaned in. Despite themselves, they insisted on whispering.

"Can you tell us anything? Have you ever met him?" asked Chainbridge.

"No. He has a huge office in Zürich though, a global conglomerate. And, as a creature of habit, his other appetites need to be whetted."

Parez, the genial host, ensured every glass was filled. Curtains masked the revelry outside. Eva glanced over at Parez, their eyes locked for a moment. His affection for her was still strong, their affair, brief, but memorable.

He raised a knowing glass. She smiled.

"Sex?" asked Chainbridge.

"No. Orchids," replied Parez. "He's an avid collector, exporter and expert grower. He has a private hot-house in the Hotel Prestige au Lac,"

"There's our in, then," said Chainbridge.

He looked over at Eva.

"Orchids," he said.

"Orchids?" asked Parez.

"My good friend here is right; the key is to have the object approach the agent, not the other way around," said De Witte. "We'll get Halidane to come to Eva."

"Slight problem, gentlemen," said Parez, gazing levelly. "His weakness is young - very young - girls. Not beautiful, intelligent women."

"Leave that to me," replied Eva.

She took a light from Parez, her fingers lingering deliberately on his hand. Brandt chewed mechanically and swallowed another glass of champagne. He tried to suppress it, but the first clawing sensation of jealously began to take root.

"When will your boat arrive?" he asked.

"Soon, my friend, soon," replied Parez.

"I don't like boats."

"You could try walking along the train tracks or swimming, my friend."

"How can we trust you?"

"You can't, sir. But I should advise you; I don't care for either your tone or your inference."

Parez tipped Brandt a wink.

Brandt fought the urge to punch him.

Sensing this, Chainbridge spoke up.

"I run an antiquities shop in England. I have a copy of a book that we could use to entice Mr. Halidane. Could I impose on you to arrange for its safe arrival in Switzerland?"

Parez took the piece of paper from Chainbridge.

"I'll arrange it," he said, "for another diamond."

"Agreed, René," replied Eva.

Brandt poured himself a large tumbler of water. He gulped it down.

"It'll be dangerous for Eva. There are a lot of Nazis on the run. The rich ones, we accommodate, the desperate ones turn to Halidane and his agents when I refuse them. He's a very powerful man with powerful connections, both in Switzerland and internationally," said Parez.

"Your concern is noted, Herr Parez," said Brandt.

The curtain opened and a smartly dressed croupier whispered into Parez's ear.

"My launch has arrived. Whenever you are ready," said Parez.

He offered his arm to Eva, who rose smoothly and latched onto it. Parez allowed her to kiss his cheek; it burned across his smooth jaw.

"Thank you, René," she whispered.
"Be careful, ma cherie," he said.

23

Cabo Verde Islands, Atlantic Ocean

The U-boat codenamed 'Pinta' – photographed by Eva in the Gulf of Cadiz – surfaced at midnight. Waves lapped lazily along the hull as the cross-shaped transmitter was directed heavenwards. Panning his binoculars along the moon-lit horizon the captain picked up semaphore flashes from sister U-boat 'Nina'; they had surfaced without incident and contacted the re-supply vessel.

"Now we wait, Reichsleiter Borman," he whispered.

"How long, Drexler?" asked Bormann.

Like Drexler and his crew, Bormann stank of dried-on sweat, diesel and cigarettes. His beard was grey, and he was noticeably thinner. He watched the antenna array mounted on the conning tower with agitiation.

"When can we expect to receive a signal?"

Drexler rubbed the unkempt stubble around his face.

"Two minutes, sir."

The volcanic islands a mile to port jutted into the stars. Beyond them, six hundred miles away, was the coast of Africa. This would be the last piece of dry land they would see for fifty-five days. He instructed his chief of the boat, Roumbalt, to allow the crew on deck.

"Routine drills, run a rota, check the gun."

"Whip-Saw is transmitting now, sir," shouted up the radio operator from inside the vessel. Drexler jotted down the transmission and decoded it.

+++ RAF visited x 3 – all down. Expect RN.
Divert SM? ObRHoeb +++

Bormann pored over the strip.

"How long before U-Boat 'Santa Maria' arrives at the site?" he demanded.

"About three days; she cleared Scotland last night," replied Drexler.

"Has she enough fuel and supplies to divert?"

"If they re-supply her at Whip-Saw, then she can divert."

"Tell them to divert once re-supplied,"

Bormann wrote out his response to Hoeberichts – eyes only for him;

+++ RE-SUPPLY SM, EVACUATE +++
/ FENRIR MUST NOT FALL ++

"It'll be a long voyage for them, Reichsleiter," said Drexler.

"For all of us, Captain," said Bormann.

Captain Drexler glanced over at the squat, arrogant man. He´d been obliged to give up his cabin so this preening peacock could travel in comfort. It crossed his mind to contact the Nina, sail into the nearby port of Mindelo and surrender. Hand this fanatic over to the Portuguese.

His thoughts were broken by his chief, Roumbalt,

"Supply vessel, Captain."

The low silhouette of a freighter appeared. Semaphore flashes blinked out her identity.

"Very good, Chief Roumbalt. Herr Bormann wishes to

spend a few hours aboard, ensure this happens."
The submariners glanced over at Bormann, who was staring up towards the stars.

***

Habitually, Edgar Halidane changed his clothes three times a day. His suits were all expensively tailored, custom-made by Ted Marks. At Fawkeston Gyre, these suits would be cleaned and pressed by Mercier and hung up ready for the following week. At his offices in Zürich and the Hotel Prestige au Lac, wardrobes of identical suits were religiously maintained. His shirts were crisp, always white and accompanied by a silk scarf or tie. Whip-Saw's confines didn't afford such luxuries. The garrison was dour, the combat troops edgy and keen to get off the island. Halidane was now coming to the end of his week's sartorial rotation and keen to travel on to Switzerland.

Killing Bellowes had been liberating; over the years, Halidane had mined the old man's knowledge to the extent that he could now chart his own destiny.

What a pity about the egg.

Halidane's reflection in the full-length mirror glanced down at his breakfast – a fried egg on toast - procured and served by the galley on his flying boat. The egg was overdone. Inedible. He thought of the hot summer of nineteen thirty-five when a Texan senator fried an egg on the Capitol's steps in the glare of the newsreel cameras. Halidane swilled the cold dregs of his coffee in his tin cup. He wondered why his thirst could never be slaked, his body in a state of perpetual demand.

He turned from his antique full-length mirror to face Hoeberichts.

"Divert the U-boat *'Santa Maria'*?"

"Fresh instructions from Bormann."

"I didn´t receive them."

"We are to leave. The Fenrir shell is to divert."

"To where?"

Halidane again felt the gnawing sensation of his life's works and achievements slipping from his grasp.

"Highest level eyes-only communiqué. The new location is the Casa Rosa site, Argentina."

"Argentina - is he insane?"

"He has issued a Nero Directive – Whip-Saw is to be destroyed before the Royal Navy arrive. This site is indefensible against a sea-borne attack. I don't want my men dying needlessly on enemy territory."

Halidane blinked hard, trying to process this.

"I won't allow it."

"You don't have a choice, Herr Halidane."

Hoeberichts brushed Halidane's used suit off the leather settee and settled down on it, his highly polished boots on the arm rest.

"Reichsleiter Bormann wants to leave no trace. Now, Herr Halidane, you *can* launch the Fenrir from Argentina? You do remember the Führer agreed to fund this project only because of your boast to, what was it? – *'send a projectile anywhere across the globe.'* Your exact words, if I recall?"

"Yes, it *can* be done," replied Halidane.

"Excellent, Herr Halidane, then let us commence our work."

"Yes, let`s," whispered Halidane.

He tossed aside his breakfast. The silver plate clattered tinnily around the room.

"I insist on a proviso to this – I have an operational chamber in Switzerland, General. You and the Fenrir will travel with me. That's my order, not a suggestion, a fucking order. As an American citizen, it would be my duty to inform my country of the location of two German U-boats at anchor off the coast of West Africa with several high-ranking fugitives. Now, you *can* perform the rites and interpret Bellowes' calculations?"

Hoeberichts rose lithely and was two paces across the room toe-to-toe with Halidane. The general towered over Halidane, his breath fetid.

"Are you suggesting Argentina is too far away?"

"Switzerland is closer, and I want to witness the results. I wasn't afforded that luxury in Russia."

"It was a success,"

"And you know this how?"

"I have my contacts – I assure you the target was wiped

off the map."

"I don't need your assurances, General. I need to see results."

"All in good time, Herr Halidane,"

Halidane tried to make level eye contact,

"You will convey my caveat to Bormann, General. Just remember who won this war," grinned Halidane.

"And don´t forget who's holding the purse strings, Hoeberichts."

He side-stepped the cadaverous SS General and left his private quarters.

Halidane sought the pilot's lounge and whispered in the Captain´s ear, who immediately rose and took the first officer to search for the relief crew, leaving half-finished plates of food. Halidane passed through the observation lounge and watched the boiling seas; a huge storm was brewing on the horizon and time was of the essence. With cool efficiency, Halidane gathered up the most important canvas carriers from Bellowes' quarters. Checking each drawer, he found a creased pocket notebook covered in ancient leather alongside a loaded Webley revolver. He pocketed both. Returning to his empty quarters, he locked the door. Pulling aside the full-length mirror, he sought out a section of the plated wall. Locating the pressure switch, he pressed once. A hatch the size of a manhole popped open at his feet. A service ladder led to a narrow corridor ending with a wheel-lock metal door. Halidane knew every plate and bolt, his fingers sought the wheel-lock in the dim light and turned it rapidly. It whirred on hidden cogs. The chamber lit up intensely. Beneath his feet the generators vibrated. He walked over to the three man-sized levers. With an effort, he manipulated the levers into three extreme alignments. Through the layers of rock and metal plating, the generators began to accelerate. A deep and hollow roar began in the bowels of
Whip-Saw.

"How fast can you run, Hoeberichts?" he whispered.

The lights began to flicker overhead. The perfect carbon circle on the wall shook loose and was nothing but powder as the long

metallic fingers overhead began to glow deep red.
The first Hoeberichts knew of the problem was when he spied Halidane's flying boat releasing its moorings. Edging slowly away from the jetty, the behemoth aircraft turned a tight arc in the boom, gliding out of the harbor. Beyond it, the skies began to close in, the storm gathering intensity. He abandoned the observation deck and sprinted to the dining lounge.
The crew of the Japanese flying boat were eating, still dressed in their flight suits.
Hoeberichts shouted; "We need to get out of here ... now!"
The first explosion in the depths of the island knocked them all to the floor. Hoeberichts dusted himself down and the men scrambled to follow his lead. They made it to the jetty along with half of his men.

"Christ almighty," said Hoeberichts.

The Japanese flying boat had been hit by flying debris. It was listing sharply into the harbour.
It dawned on him, that the U-Boat was immaterial, the Fenrir shell was immaterial and that now he too was immaterial.
He stared impotently at the huge aircraft ascending into the clouds. Halidane was snipping threads with every mile he climbed.
The next explosion hurled men, equipment and metal skywards. The very rock beneath Hoeberichts´ boots was shaking loose. He looked down at the murky depths and dwelt on the Makos that would be drawn by the blood.
The Japanese flying boat tilted upwards as it sank.
The underground aviation fuel tanks erupted; the observation platform collapsed.
From the flying boat, Halidane instructed the pilot to circle a few miles out. The storm drove long fingers of rain across the cockpit. Leaning between the pilot and co-pilot, Halidane watched.

"The phase-shift is about to happen," he whispered.

The fires were still blazing on Whip-Saw when it disappeared. The ocean closed over and the storm hurled its fury where the small island had been. Satisfied that nothing remained, he turned to the radio operator.

"Anything?"
He shifted the dial through the atmospherics.
"The Royal Navy have just dispatched a destroyer group from Scapa Flow, Orkney Islands."
"They'll be sailing in circles for a week – the U-Boat?"
"We've sent new co-ordinates, we're waiting for a response, sir."
Halidane grunted and walked back to his seat. It'd be close to seventy-two hours before he reached Switzerland. He didn't need Bormann.
He had another plan in place.

24

Zürich

The pension had been scrupulously maintained. Brandt handed Mrs Hausmann, the proprietor, a bottle of Amaretto purloined from René Parez. Still sporting her severe and neatly pinned grey bun, she broke into the rarest of smiles. Her apple-cheeks glowed. She kissed Eva and Brandt on the cheek and, with a gentle sweep of her comfortable shoes, herded the two curious cats at her doorway back into her living room.
She handed Eva the key.
Mrs Hausmann had been diligent, the rooms were spotless. A small vase of fresh flowers from the market stood twinkling on the table. The rooms smelt clean, the beds laundered, an old familiar haven.
"I'll run a bath, Brandt," whispered Eva.
She ran a longing finger through his stubble; her touch tingled and burned, mapping lost connections.
Brandt felt his penis thicken and harden.
"Fix us a drink," said Eva.
In the still air, he caught her perfume, her subtle mark as she

walked into the bathroom. Brandt found a bottle in a corner press; it was dusty but drinkable. Imbibing brandy in the steamy warmth of the bathroom, Brandt felt heat seep into the marrow of his bones for the first time in years.

He watched Eva. Her russet tresses hung across her profile. He studied her long back, her hips, smooth long legs that her dressing gown revealed. She glanced over her shoulder, her grey, green eyes full of mischief, but for a moment, edged with a flash of doubt.

"Strip, Brandt," she said.

Brandt removed the borrowed threads, jumper, boots and socks. He loosened his trousers and let them fall around his ankles.

His body was a patchwork of marks, bruises and scars. Discoloured skin and weals gave him a mottled appearance. The ugly shoulder wound reminded Eva of the old plough horses she'd seen in the Polish countryside as a child. The prison scalping had given way to the beginnings of regrowth. His eyes still flashed the energy and intelligence that had drawn her to him all those years ago, hundreds of miles behind the Russian front.

Her bruised and bloodied warrior wasn't ready to die yet.

"Now you," he said.

He kicked the trousers to the corner of the bathroom.

Eva slid the dressing gown off. She was a little thinner, but her body was nearing its prime; full breasts with the small nipples, neat stomach and whispy pubis. Without her make-up and with her hair down, this was the real Eva – the delicate beauty with an inner core of iron.

"Get in," she said.

Brandt climbed into the bath. The warm water felt impossibly luxurious. He couldn´t help but think of the Soviet prison cells. The stench, the cold, the frozen piles of faeces; the last testament of men shuffling to their deaths. He closed his eyes as Eva took a cloth and bathed him, tutting and sighing at his injuries.

"You're lucky to be alive," she said.

His muscles, though reduced, were still firm. His arms glistened and his large strong hands rested on Eva´s thighs as she perched on the side of the bath. His eyes were closed and his tightly clipped hair moist with sweat and steam. He opened one eye and, taking her hips firmly, planted soft kisses across her soft, yielding belly. His tongue found the old familiar scar that ran lengthwise down her hip. She never told him how she got it, but he knew a knife wound when he saw one. She gave an intake of breath as he drew the tip along the skin.

As Eva stood, he could smell her arousal, he ran his tongue through her pubic hair and playfully worked its way to her sour-sweet sex.

Eva gripped his head and pulled his face into her hips. He drank from her and she came quickly.

"Keep going, Brandt. Don't stop,"

She cried out with pleasure, her belly seeming to flow out of her body and into Brandt's mouth. He looked up.

"Water should be cool enough for you now," he said.

She could see he was fully erect; thick and twitching for her. Kneeling down, she bent into the bath and took him in her hand.

"Three years without sex probably means there'll be a lot of you?" she grinned.

His manhood seemed to swell even more as she worked a rhythm. She took him in her mouth, working her tongue expertly around the edges of his exposed gland. It didn't take long. Brandt gave a throaty gasp and she pulled away. He sprayed a huge amount of seed.

He climbed out of the bath and she toweled him down slowly, his lean form angular through the cloth. She kissed him softly across his collar bone, running her tongue along the skin. He held her head in his hands and kissed her deeply, their tongues exploring and strong. His stubble was uneven, his teeth discoloured, his nose had been broken and roughly reset. She kissed every part of his face. He picked her up and carried her to their old bed, the wrought iron frame that had sheltered their dreams during their most desolate moments.

"I'm mad about you, Eva," whispered Brandt, "when I see you, everything vanishes."

She slid from his arms and stood tiptoe to kiss him deeply. Brandt kissed her eyelids gently, her mouth and traced her jawline with his tongue,

"You numb me, Eva."

"Enough talk, Brandt."

They fucked like Adam and Eve on the first day in Eden and slept like children for the rest of the afternoon, wrapped in each other's arms. As the afternoon became the early evening and church bells tolled, they dozed and whispered their hopes and dreams. And slept.

***

"Can Parez be trusted?"

A china saucer from the kitchen rested on Brandt´s chest. The cigarette they shared tasted slightly stale.

"No, Brandt, no-one can be trusted. The game is different now," replied Eva.

"Poor old Findlay, he didn't deserve to die like that."

"None of them did," said Brandt. "And it looks like our plan of disappearing to spend the rest of our lives together might be on the back burner now."

"I'm going to have a bath, Brandt. That's as far as I'm thinking right now."

She disappeared into the bathroom, leaving the door open. Brandt leaned back on the bed and dozed. Gnawing quietly away, like a facial tic, was the way Eva held René Parez's hand as she accepted a light.

Three years was a long time; long enough to have lived several lifetimes.

He touched his scarred tattoo – whatever his old cell mate, Kallerhoff had sewn in there, the strange looking schematics, was raking up a body count.

He eased himself out of the bed and stretched. Padding around the room, he opened, removed and stacked up the contents from the cache of loose floorboards; one bayonet, a modest stack of $200, two ingots of gold, one diamond and the banking details of his stipends – not enough to retire on.

"Put the radio on, Brandt," called Eva.
Brandt turned the dial through the wavelengths until he found a US big band show. The room was filled with brassy Jazz. An American crooner sang about *Personality*, the next schmoozed over a latin beat about the Atom Bomb.

"Let´s dance sometime this week," said Eva.
As she splashed, she hummed the chorus.

"Maybe we should lie low, Eva, keep moving?"
He found the coffee pot.

"I'm tired of moving around, Brandt. I say we stay here; make love all day, sleep and dance. I loved it when we danced in Buenos Aires."
Eva stared up at the old cracked ceiling as she soaked. She was one of the lucky ones; her man had been returned to her, more or less intact. Fathers, sons and husbands were gone, never to return; others mutilated, shattered or dispersed across foreign lands.
Women too had suffered and made sacrifices, invisible scars that could never heal. Like Brandt she felt a moment of guilt, enveloped in her warm bath.
Closing her eyes, she thought back about her journey to this point; her quest had been at times solitary, heat-breaking and bleak. It was pure luck she now had Brandt again. He moved around with a certainty that allowed her to drop her mask, her role, her façade. There had been other men; ships passing in the night when she believed Brandt to be dead. But they were stops along a journey he would never know about.
Brandt was whole. He was intact and he stared at her unflinching. Eva brought her knees up and rested her head on them – a momentary pang ran across her gut, the fear her womb could no longer hold their child. She felt that God, fate, the very universe was playing with her as a cat would toy with a terrified mouse. Despite their sacrifices they would always be outsiders – both without a country, both skirting the shadows because of it. Death was only a heartbeat away, the nature of their lives, their work, their connections made them targets. She thrilled at the thought.

Eva pulled the plug and watched the water swirl away. She thought of René Parez's offer. It was tempting; René was well-connected, rich, lucky and intelligent.

"Mrs. Hausmann's chickens have been busy," said Brandt, breaking her thoughts.

A fresh batch of eggs were neatly stacked in a bowl. He took one and held it up. He hadn't seen or tasted one in years. He broke the eggs into the bowl and mashed up the shells into fragments with a spoon. He ate the fragments of shell.

Eva was humming along with the radio as he whisked the eggs. She came out wrapped in towels. Without make-up, her face had the mien of an angel. He poured her a coffee, split the plain omelette and they ate in companionable silence.

"I've done an inventory, Eva. That's everything, I'm afraid."

"I have money too, and the diamonds."

"I had a gun?"

"I used it."

Brandt grinned.

"I hope you got what you wanted with it."

"I did. Good eggs, Brandt."

"You?"

"A Beretta, from the British, one full clip."

"We're going to need another gun,"

"This is Switzerland, Brandt."

It was time to contact Liebermann.

25

Zürich

Herr Liebermann looked up at the man who entered; a man who had disappeared off the face of the earth.

"Herr Brandt, thank you for your cable this morning. Welcome back," he said.

"It's been a while."

"Four years."

"Four years? That is a long time."

"A long time, Herr Brandt."

Liebermann was disarming yet officious, imbued with a starchy Swiss reticence.

"My stipend?"

"Alas, exhausted, Herr Brandt. As agreed, I was to assume you were dead?"

"I was, Herr Liebermann," said Brandt.

Liebermann reached for a hidden drawer and handed Brandt an envelope. Inside was a key – the key to a railway locker.

"There are a few provisions you might find useful. I was planning to remove them in a few months."

"I'll check what´s there. Thank you."

The shop itself, tucked away in a side-street in the city, seemed chock-full, yet with nothing to buy. In the corner, amid a jumble of chairs and lamps, a heavy black and red lacquered Chinese cabinet rose like the bow of a ship. The shelves were filled with every kind of geegaw and bric-a-brac; shiny, but of little value. Brandt suspected that Liebermann's clientele came here, like him, on other business.

"I need a gun," said Brandt.

"American, Russian, British or German?"

Brandt placed a diamond on the counter between a jar of boiled sweets and a fat cigar smouldering in a crystal ashtray.

Liebermann popped a sweet into his mouth, picked up the stone with tweezers and studied it using a jeweller´s loupe.

"It must be solid and reliable," said Brandt.

Liebermann rolled the sweet around his mouth. His deep brown eyes, slightly drooping, looked out through thick, fashionably framed lenses. He slid off his high chair and disappeared behind a black velvet curtain.

Brandt stepped deeper into the shop, out of sight from any curious passer-by.

Liebermann reappeared with a sack-cloth. He unrolled it on the counter and took a drag on his cigar.

"Browning 9mm. American standard issue. Compact, robust and easy to assemble. Ten round magazine, two extra supplied," said Liebermann.

Brandt took the gun. It felt good in his hand.

"Shoulder holster?"

"I´ll check."

Liebermann stood back and ran his eyes along the drawers and shelves of his counter. He located the correct holster and handed it over. He sucked in another sweet and studied Brandt. The man's clothes were old fashioned and several sizes too big for him, giving him a misshapen outline.

He stepped around the counter to hold Brandt´s jacket while he fastened the holster.

"Herr Brandt, the diamond is remarkably well cut; sadly I cannot say the same for your clothes. This diamond will more than cover your purchase; might I suggest we put the surplus towards a new wardrobe?"

He handed Brandt a business card.

"My cousin, Murray, is an excellent tailor. I'll phone him and arrange a fitting for you."

Brandt took the card. He donned the shoulder holster and slotted the gun home.

"That´s kind of you, Herr Liebermann,"

"All part of the service, Herr Brandt."

Brandt turned to go.

"One last thing Herr Brandt."

"Yes?"

"Be careful."

"I will."

"I hate to lose good customers. You know how it is."

Brandt smiled. He stopped in the doorway, glanced up and down the street, and stepped out into the light.

Liebermann placed the diamond in his safe and another boiled sweet into his mouth.

He detested cash.

That evening after acquiring a new suit, shirts, shoes and a haircut, Nicklaus Brandt took the tram to the Bahnhof Railway

station. At a kiosk in the main concourse he bought a newspaper and sat down on a bench. Once he was satisfied no-one was paying him any attention, he made his way to the rows of lockers, expecting to find his emptied and a new lock fitted. To his surprise, his key fitted. Inside the locker on the top shelf, was a leather-bound case containing a bundle of US dollars, a Swiss passport and a small amount of Swiss currency. On the lower shelf sat his mountaineering kit bag; ropes, crampons, pitons and at the bottom, two carefully wrapped packages of plastic explosive – enough to reduce the main concourse to rubble.
He hoisted the pack onto his back and walked out of the station, failing to notice the black Mercedes Benz parked outside amid the tumult of bicycles and buses.
It slowly inched out onto the strasse and followed him.

26

Zürich

On mornings like this, Hermann Malleus' leg ached dully.
A heavy pall of light rain covered the lake, dragging the temperature down. He allowed his weight to shift onto his walking stick; the handle fashioned in the form of a wolf, its long tail tapering down to a vicious point. He had suffered severe shrapnel wounds during the invasion of France, but he never acknowledged his weakness. He swam every morning at 5am at the local baths, his atrophied leg dragging like an anchor.
From his vantage point, he watched the Rolls Royce Wraith glide up toward the offices of Halidane Corp. It glistened like a Cambrian slug.

"He's here," murmured Malleus.

"Are you concerned, Herr Malleus?"

Malleus turned slowly around, the sharp creases of his suit realigning as he moved.

"No, Miss Wolfe. No, I am not."

Hannah sat deep in the leather chair. Her long shapely legs

ended in expensive, fashionable heels. Loitering behind her stood Pfeiffer and Kahn, sharply attired with muted ties and the demeanour of undertakers.

Spread out on Malleus' desk were the notebooks Hannah had taken from Jefferson Clarke. They had been carefully sifted through, analysed. Typed out and neatly underlined were the words, *Photon exchange*, *Electromagnetic interaction*, and *Einheitliche Feldtheorie*. Malleus had seen such documents before – an entire branch of the Wehrmacht had been dedicated to the fanciful, the improbable, the downright lunatic; Hitler´s increasingly desperate search for a deus ex machina to rescue victory from the jaws of defeat.

Malleus' telephone rang shrilly. He answered it.

"He's in the elevator."

The seconds dragged until the door opened and the pretty secretary ushered Halidane in.

If Hannah was disappointed, it didn't show.

Malleus stepped around the desk and propelled himself towards Halidane.

"Welcome, Herr Halidane. Please."

He gestured towards the leather settee which had had been specially procured at Halidane´s request. The American appeared freshly groomed. Removing his hat and tossing it across the room for Kahn to catch, he side-stepped Malleus and homed in on Hannah.

"Good morning, Miss ...?"

"Wolfe."

Hannah's English sounded guttural, raw.

"Miss Wolfe, a pleasure, a real pleasure. Now. What have we here?"

He paced on patent leather shoes towards the desk.

"Miss Wolfe removed these items after neutralising Jefferson Clarke – the man you traced and requested us to investigate," said Malleus.

"MI6. OSS. Red Orchestra?"

"Either or all, Herr Halidane, our leads have gone cold."

Halidane shook off his raincoat and from one of the pockets, produced his tin cup.

"Coffee. Black. Sugar."

He handed it to Hannah.

Her expensively manicured fingers gingerly hoisted the stained mug and held it at arms´ length.

"Pfeiffer, please oblige," she said.

Pfeiffer sullenly left the room in search of a coffee pot.

Halidane sifted through the notebooks, the typed-up sheets. Grabbing a handful, he slumped onto the settee.

"Miss Wolfe, did the unfortunate Mr Clarke have anything written out in the room itself, on a blackboard, for example?"

His German was fluent and without any trace of an American inflection.

"I wiped the board down," she replied.

"Excellent. So, these were the only notes?"

"Yes."

She began twisting a cigarette into an onyx holder and lit it. Halidane's nose twitched in a murine fashion. He lifted his head and looked around.

"I'll have one of those, thanks."

Hannah stepped over to him. Her impressive figure appeared permanently sewn into a black dress. She leaned in and opened her cigarette case. Halidane took the lot and puckered one up between his thin lips.

"Thanks, Miss Wolfe."

He placed one cigarette behind his ear and pocketed the rest. Pfeiffer returned with coffee. Halidane swirled the tin cup and slurped from it loudly.

"Mr. Clarke was certainly thorough, but this is old research. I really don't see..."

Halidane stopped dead. He folded out a sheet from the back of a notebook. It was already aged and creased. The corner of it was blackened, as if someone had set fire to it, then changed their mind. Across the page was tiny scrawl, almost illegible.

Halidane looked like he had seen a ghost.

"Einstein," he said.

He stood up. He held the sheet out.

"Einstein's notes, a scrap, no, not just a scrap, the goddamn Rosetta Stone. It took me close to a decade to solve this, a decade and here it is!"
Malleus glanced around at Hannah, Pfeiffer and Kahn. Halidane's complexion reflected his state of frenzy. Beads of sweat popped out of his skull and raced down his face. He fought to control himself. Then, shaking himself like a dog, he took a deep breath.

"If this scrap of paper falls into America's hands, our plan is over. Over, I tell ya! Malleus, your lighter."
He lit the scrap without hesitation, catching the ashes in his old tin cup. He drank them down with the coffee as if it were a chalice of transubstantiation.

"Destroy all the note-books. Destroy the transcripts. Destroy the typewriter ribbons. Hell, destroy the fucking typewriters - I want this done now. Immediately. Now."
Halidane flopped back onto the settee. Massaging the bridge of his nose with his thumb and forefinger, he squinted in pain.

"There's a complete change of plan, Malleus."

"Change of plan, Herr Halidane?"

"We won't be executing the Nero Directive from Whipsaw," replied Halidane.

"Why not?" asked Malleus.

"Because it doesn't exist anymore. Day after day, week after week, I've felt my legacy being prised slowly from my grasp. Hoeberichts is dead. Bellowes is dead. Do you understand?"
He glowered over at Malleus, Hannah, Pfeiffer and Kahn.

"We're going to launch from here, from this very city. And we are all going to witness it. I'm going to my suite now. I need to sleep."
Malleus dialled the secretary.

"Prepare Herr Halidane's suite. He'll be remaining here tonight."

"One other thing, Malleus."
Halidane reached into the inside pocket of his Ted Marks pinstripe suit. He pulled out a folded photograph and tossed it over.

"A number of people availed themselves of René Parez's hospitality the other night - including his private yacht. This

photograph was taken inside the casino."
Malleus unfolded the photograph. It was a middle-aged man, hawk-like profile, swept back hair – a scholarly type.

"Henry Chainbridge," said Halidane. "What´s a two-bit Limey antique dealer doing in René Parez's *exclusive* casino?"
Malleus handed the photograph to Hannah. She bored into the image.

"I met him, in Italy. He posed as a Swiss art dealer."
She remembered his disarming smile, his easy demeanour.

"And in Argentina, he was with a tall Irishman."

"He's a fucking spy then, sweetheart," said Halidane. "Find him, find his accomplices and deal with them. I'm tasking you and your two goons there to deal with this."
Halidane rose stiffly, draping his raincoat over his arm. Kahn handed him his hat.

"Malleus, if anything goes wrong now, I'm holding the four of you responsible. Do not fail me."
With a faint waft of cologne and cigarettes, Halidane strode out to the lift that would whisk him to the inner sanctum of his organisation.
Hannah stared at the photograph. Wherever Henry Chainbridge went, that little bitch Eva Molenaar was never far behind. She remembered Lyon, the bank of the river as Eva was escaping. She remembered Eva's bullet whistling past her ear.
She had a score to settle.

***

Halidane sat squat-legged in his suite like a wizened sadhu. His face was a grease paint mask of white with a reversed swastika painted deep red in the middle of his high forehead. He was dressed in a scarlet silk robe with a large cowl adorned and patterned in ancient black cuneiform. Circling him were twelve lit candles marking the points of an ebony Sonnenrad, inlaid into the floor. The doors to his suite were double-locked, his clothes neatly piled after his ablutions. He was naked beneath the robe, except for a simple loin cloth. He breathed in the candle smoke and unrolled the contents of the canvas bags purloined from Bellowes' quarters. The Navamansh, the maps and the incantations were spread out before him. Edgar Halidane began to chant.

The candles began to gutter, and the room somehow became denser, darker, closing in on itself. Halidane worked himself into a trance, rocking back and forth on his bare heels. His eyes opened and gazed on the charts. They came to life - or was it a trick of the candle-light - all the lines and co-ordinates aligned. The stars mapped in the heavens spun and gyrated. Halidane rocked harder, swinging like a metronome. In his mind's eye, lines of formulae blended with the moving Navamansh – then a blinding moment of clarity occurred. One so intense, Halidane froze on his heels.

All twelve candles went out.

He had his auspicious date, time and location in the heavens. Halidane sat squat until the dawn light crept through his leaden drapes and the sounds of the city began to drift in. He showered and ordered coffee and bagels from reception. He shaved from his tin cup.

Suddenly he felt the need of replenishment, and his thoughts turned instantly to the Hotel Prestige au Lac.

Malleus´pretty secretary also sprang to mind, and the buxom Hannah Wolfe.

There was a discreet knock at the door.

"Enter," he said.

The pretty secretary carried in a tray. Halidane rinsed out his tin cup and gestured her to pour.

"What pretty flowers, Herr Halidane," she said, admiring the plants standing on a long table.

"They are Cypripedium formosanum, *Lady Slipper orchids*; my favourite of the genera," replied Halidane.

"They are very beautiful," replied the girl.

She was petite but well proportioned. Her waist was narrow. In Chicago, a girl like her would have been called dainty. She filled his cup, her hand shaking slightly. He gently placed his hands around hers to steady it.

"Very easy to grow from seed ... there's no need to fear me, Miss ...?"

"Hoffman, Herr Halidane, Birgit Hoffman."

"Well, Birgit, that is a lovely name, for a lovely girl. Thank you."

Birgit blushed deeply and turned neatly on her heels.

"If you need anything else, Herr Halidane?" she said.

"I'll be sure to call you."

He watched her as she left, imagining the taste of her blood.

27

Zürich

He had the care-worn look and slightly disconnected aura of the civil servant; Dressed in a plain charcoal grey suit, a beige raincoat draped over his left arm and a frayed felt hat in his free hand, it was as if he had been unexpectedly dropped onto the café´s sunny terrace.

"I thought we weren't to be raising any suspicions, sahib?" whispered Pannu.

"Must be Holmpatrick, Dr. Pannu," murmured Chainbridge.

The care-worn man craned his neck around the diners. He reminded Chainbridge of a pigeon hunting scraps. His gaze finally fell on their table. He worked his way through the diners like a floundering swimmer.

"Is this seat taken?"

Before Chainbridge could respond, the man tossed hat and coat at a passing waiter and flopped down into the vacant seat.

"Holmpatrick, Bern Office," he said.

He snapped his fingers loudly for service. A waiter arrived and glanced at Chainbridge, who gave the slightest of nods; indulge the man. Holmpatrick ordered a coffee and produced a coin pouch. He methodically counted out the centimes and stacked them on the table.

"The Office has received notice that you are in Switzerland – why?"

"Edgar Halidane," replied Chainbridge.

"The FO alerted us a day ago, they were unaware of any sanctioned operations in this jurisdiction."

"Two of your operatives died," said Chainbridge.

"Natural causes – that´s official."

"What's official for Charlottenburg?" said Chainbridge.

"Gas explosion," said Holmpatrick.

"Micro-dot? Findlay's research?" asked Chainbridge.

Holmpatrick leaned forward, the façade of disconnection slipped.

"Official Secrets, Chainbridge; you know the rules."

The coffee arrived and Holmpatrick casually tossed the stack of coins onto the tray. Chainbridge motioned for two more coffees. Holmpatrick didn´t stint on the cream. He held up a sugar cube as if it were a nugget of gold between his neatly manicured fingers before stirring it in.

"This is a luxury in England," he said.

"I've just left there, I know," replied Chainbridge.

"I have no desire to return, I like it here."

The civil servant stared at Pannu, taking in the imposing turban, beard and bulk of the man.

"The good doctor here is required back in Berlin; his regiment is about to chalk him up as AWOL."

"Int.7., requested he assist, so he was released to us," said Chainbridge.

"Int.7., is under close scrutiny now, Chainbridge. There's quite a bit of explaining to do."

"Explaining?" asked Chainbridge.

The lunchtime crowd had pushed away plates to make room for desserts and coffees. Holmpatrick eyed the trays of confections.

"The situation is now very, very delicate," he said.

"It always is," replied Chainbridge.

He turned to stare at Pannu.

"You best return, and thank you," he said.

"No, sahib. We both know it´s very dangerous. I think it´s best I stay."

He gave Chainbridge a curious look. Holmpatrick checked his purse.

"Allow me, Holmpatrick – what would you like?"

Menus were shuffled and cut like a deck of cards by the waiter. Holmpatrick selected a meringue brûlée. When it arrived, he carved it with a surgeon´s precision.

"The game has changed, Chainbridge. His Majesty's Government, along with the Americans, are negotiating with the Swiss. The negotiations are at a very sensitive juncture. Edgar Halidane is part of the American delegation."

For once, Chainbridge was at a loss for words.

Holmpatrick afforded himself a smile. His canines were badly stained, his thin lips revealed diseased gums.

"Negotiating what, exactly?" asked Chainbridge.

"Trade, safe haven. Reich assets; gold bullion, art works, plunder in Swiss bank accounts – if we are to rebuild Germany, they are going to have to pay for it – not just with reparations. The Halidane Corporation has considerable resources; it is overseeing the technological aspects of the negotiations."

"Both Miles Curran and Brendan Bracken felt Halidane was acting as a front for Bormann," said Chainbridge.

"Look, Chainbridge. It´s as simple as this; you're to stand down. The FO have been directly in touch with Mr. Bracken. Whatever he has you doing, you are to stop it immediately."

Holmpatrick chased a few crumbs around his plate and ran a tongue along his spoon like a greedy houseboy.

"I'm sure Ann Chambrel's family will understand," said Chainbridge.

"Natural causes," emphasised Holmpatrick.

"Gageby, Findlay, Keyburn?"

"Natural causes and injuries sustained in an unfortunate gas explosion."

"Hopkins?"

"He too, died as a result of the gas explosion," said Holmpatrick. He started to rise, reaching for his hat.

"May I ask one question?" said Chainbridge.

Distant interest washed down Holmpatrick's face. He'd catch the train, ride home on a tram. Be behind his anonymous desk in two days´ time, marking his life to the tick of the diplomatic clock.

"Findlay's code breaking, did it reveal anything?"

"Nothing."

"At all?"

"RAF Skeabrae reported a flying accident – rookies on a training run."

"Serious?"

"They've dispatched a destroyer group to the Iceland – Faroes Passage; possible U-Boat activity. If you call that serious, then yes."

"Training accident?"

"They may have lost three Spitfires. I emphasise the word *may,* Chainbridge."

He donned his raincoat.

"England is bankrupt. The Americans are calling the shots now. We owe them billions, the last thing we need is a bunch of amateurs acting out some vaudeville routine and stepping on their toes. Halidane's company is close to the Truman administration. Science, big science, Chainbridge, is now the order of the day; Halidane *is* the new order. Doctor, you are to return to Berlin by Wednesday next week at the latest. Chainbridge, good day."

They watched him stride onto the thoroughfare, spot his tram and trot across the road.

"That is that, sahib. I must leave. Will you be safe?"

"You've risked enough, doctor. I can't have you cashiered unnecessarily."

Pannu leaned back to address the diner beside them.

"Did you get all that, sahib?"

De Witte turned around at the sound of the voice.

"I did, yes, thank you. Henry, may I borrow the good doctor for the day?"

Chainbridge grinned.

"You may. Can I ask why?"

"No. Like the good doctor said, it´s too dangerous. And Henry..."

"Yes, Peter?"

"Your government just completely disowned you ..."

"I know."

Doctor Pannu rose and guided de Witte gently through the terrace.

Chainbridge glanced around before entering the café proper. In a back room behind the kitchen, photographs, maps, newspaper cuttings and encoded cables from Brendan Bracken's Int.7., offices in London were spread across a wide table. Clangs, booms and shouts from the army of chefs and waiters drifted in through the door, along with strains of a piano.

The owner, Mario, hadn´t been expecting Chainbridge, De Witte and the immense demon in the turban. Nevertheless, he swiftly arranged accommodation, food and contacts.

"Just like the old days, Henry - still hunting Nazis?" he asked.

"I didn't plan to, but here we are," replied Chainbridge.

"Plenty here, Henry," replied Mario.

"De Witte has a scent; once he gets that way, he won't stop," said Chainbridge.

"He brought that with him, thought you'd like it."

Chainbridge studied the pile of photographs – on top was a single image of Halidane himself; a grainy mosaic of dots morphing into the man´s bland everyman expression. White writing announced; *1942 – London*.

"This was sent in too, by a mutual acquaintance," said Mario.

He handed Chainbridge a parcel, neatly wrapped in wax paper. Inside was a very, very old book. The spine looked fragile, the leaves sere; in the flyleaf in aged typeset appeared the title; *The Natural History of Carolina, Florida and the Bahama Islands.*

"A book, Henry?"

"A book, Mario, yes, but it´s not just any old book, it's a 1748 edition – we're going to use it as bait."

"Bait?"

"For Halidane; we're going to use it to catch Halidane."

"Halidane is very dangerous man, Henry. He has hired

killers acting for him. Even a crook like René Parez won't deal with him."

"Why?"

"Did you see any bomb damage in Konstanz? No so much as a roof tile missing. The allies never bombed the city."

"Because of the railway and its proximity to the Swiss border?"

"Not so much as a scratch, Henry. Think on that. Halidane has hired trains to move equipment for a project into Switzerland – customs have been turning a blind eye."

Chainbridge decided to change tack.

"You've swapped that crumpled apron of yours for evening wear I see?"

"The war is over, Henry and everyone wants to forget. Expensive food, good wine and cocktails are the best remedies."

Mario´s maître d knocked on the door and looked in. Chainbridge stepped back. Suddenly he wished he had a gun.

"It´s OK, he's my brother," said Mario.

They whispered intently.

"Halidane arrived yesterday. He's holed up in his offices along the lake front."

"Can you direct us there?" asked Chainbridge.

"Not now. Everywhere is closed. I know his favourite café though – Cafe Sprüngli, he always has a table reserved. Our cousin is the maître d there."

Mario's brother then added another whisper.

"I'll have to go out front. Lock up when you finish and turn the lights off; the last thing I need is the police sniffing around."

He stepped out into the cacophony of service.

Chainbridge contemplated the delicate volume in his hands. They were on their own now. Would the next step go down as a bold gambit or pure suicide?

He went back to his maps and located the Cafe Sprüngli.

This visit called for Eva.

28

U.S.S.R. / last recorded location - 68° 18m N, 161° 38m E

The first of the dog sled teams had to stop at the rim of the blast site. The tundra had been reduced to a churned morass. A weak moon fought its way through the heavy, high-rolling clouds, making further exploration treacherous.

The huskies rolled in the layers of snow to cool off, a romping mass of energetic, yapping fur. They edged cautiously along the rim, snuffling the soil before generously urinating on it. The temperature would soon drop to minus twenty. Teepees were erected, fires lit, thick black bread and reindeer meat was shared out, along with steaming mugs of berry tea and coffee.

The furthest collective farms bordering Anyuysk had reported immense tremors followed by a thick, cloying dust. Moscow had aircraft on the way. Heavy trucks and halftracks were ploughing their way to the rendezvous, due to arrive in the next day or so, terrain allowing.

As the advance party bedded down for the night, bottles of vodka were handed around while an accordion wailed out a dirge. The dogs huddled in canvas kennels alongside their sleds, turning their heads away from the cruel arctic winds and the hard, toxic-smelling earth.

Moscow had also requested soil samples. The team of volunteers planned to tramp through the detritus for any signs of life. Panniers fitted to the sleds were already filled with chunks of twisted metal, and in one, a human leg, still with a boot on it.

It was the middle of the afternoon the next day when the team spotted the tail section of an aircraft jutting up out of the mud-and-rock moonscape. It pointed skywards like an accusing finger. The fuselage had been stripped of its skin, revealing ribs of steel. The wings lay torn a hundred yards away, along with pieces of the engine block. The cockpit was never found. A long-range radio transmitter was hoisted from a sled and the co-ordinates called in.

It was then that the distinct bark of one of the dogs - a deaf male who responded only to hand gestures - made everyone look up. He bounded across the ground, furiously sniffing around the far side of the wreck.

After a beat the husky´s uneven, throaty barks filled the air. As the men approached, he kept running up and dashing back to a spot just beyond the tail section of the plane. There, protected from the wind by a hunk of fuselage, lay a man. He was still strapped into his seat. He had a pulse, but barely.

Shouts and whistles brought more volunteers running.

The man's face was blackened and swollen. His clothes were torn to shreds, but his sturdy Cossack boots and prim leather gloves were still intact.

The deaf husky was thrown a piece of reindeer meat which he munched on in solitary bliss.

Gently, the man was released from his seat and rolled limp onto the soil. He was carried gingerly toward the biggest sled and laid carefully onto it. He was bundled up and a shot of vodka poured into his cracked and bloodied mouth. It spilled listlessly out, pooling around the week-old stubble on his cheeks and chin. More vodka was splashed onto a vicious gash putrefying along his scalp.

An eyelid flickered below matted, singed brows.

"Well, at least the wolves didn't get him," said one of the volunteers.

"Would have been better for him if they had."

In the distance, the drone of an aircraft filled the air. The vehicles would not be far behind.

"Get an airstrip cleared! Light some flares to guide the transport in."

"No papers or ID. Who is this guy?"

"He´s important enough to have the whole bloody nation looking for him. At least a commissar; the likes of us could never afford boots like that." The lead volunteer rubbed the head of his deaf dog, who was now a candidate for the Order of Lenin. Unaware of his imminent fame, the dog panted sloppily, his bony hips and back legs wagging along with his tail.

No further bodies or signs of life were detected.
The dogs were re-hitched and the sleds bounced out towards the incoming aircraft.

29

The Cafe Sprüngli, Zürich

Edgar Halidane walked to the café along the Bahnhofstrasse, taking in the spring morning. At a kiosk he purchased *Tagblatt der Stadt Zürich* and a packet of cigarettes. From the door of the confiserie he was escorted to a reserved table overlooking the street. As he ordered a mini pastry maracibo and double espresso, he spotted her.
A neat, slim beauty with russet hair in a page-boy bob. A mauve pillbox hat sat on the table beside her coffee cup. His eyes took their time looking her over.
An orchid was fastened to her grey jacket at a bohemian tilt; a lucious slipper orchid. She held the delicate china cup in long tapering hands, a pianist's hands, he thought to himself.
Unfolding the newspaper, Halidane angled it so he could watch her across the edges.
The woman, who appeared to be alone, was leafing through a very old leather-bound book. She looked up momentarily, as if to get the cheque. Noticing him, she looked over, smiled and shrugged slightly as if to say; *what's a girl to do?*
Halidane glanced around the café. It was bustling with shoppers laden down with haute couture shopping bags. Immaculately attired old ladies sat in chattering quartets enjoying the sweetened fare. Halidane went back to the paper, but the columns of print were now no more than a blur. He had to talk

to her.
If Edgar Halidane had learned one thing from spending five years as a vagrant on the streets of Chicago, it was to never miss an opportunity. Any opportunity.
He summoned a waiter.
"Looks promising; he's giving instructions to the waiter," said Chainbridge.
He was sitting a few tables back. De Witte sat behind him, facing away.
"Is he looking at anyone else?" he asked.
"No. Just Eva."
Eva carefully turned the pages of *The Natural History of Carolina, Florida and the Bahama Islands.* The book was exquisite, a real work of art. A fresh cup of coffee appeared at her table.
"From the gentleman there, miss," said the waiter. "He has paid your bill also."
Eva looked over at Halidane, who gave a jaunty wave. With a smooth gesture, he proposed joining her. Feigning surprise and pushing her hat aside, she motioned to the empty chair in front of her.
"She's in," murmured Chainbridge.
"Her back story is less than watertight, let's see what happens," said de Witte.
Chainbridge scanned the café. Halidane wouldn't go unobserved for long. If he was as important as Holmpatrick had indicated, O.S.S. and MI6 were sure to be hovering around.
"It's a narrow time-frame, de Witte. A very narrow time-frame," he said.
For Edgar Halidane too, time was of the essence; he slid out from behind his reserved table and hovered over Eva. With an oily smile, he perched on the vacant seat.
"A beautiful flower," he said.
"Cypripedium formosanum," replied Eva.
Halidane was temporarily wrong-footed, he´d intended to impress her with the latin nomenclature. Also, he couldn´t place her. The accent sounded German but infused with English cadences.

"A s-slipper orchid ...," he stammered.
Her grey eyes flecked with green under intelligent brows gazed intensely.

"I think a woman should wear a flower in her hair, don't you?"
She unclipped the orchid and placed it behind her ear. Her eyes twinkled mischievously.

"What are you reading?" he asked.
Eva turned the book gently around. He noted the absence of rings on her fingers. Her perfectly manicured nails were a deep vermillion.

"It's an original, an early work on botany. Are you American?"

"It's beautiful - yes, I'm American."

"I like Americans – so forward."
She eyed the battered tin cup that was so at odds with the exquisite china of the café.

"That's an interesting cup."

"A reminder of harder times," he replied.

"There have been plenty of those to go around."

"To come out swingin' is all that matters."
Eva allowed a laugh to drift out toward him. She leaned in closer. Her blouse parted, offering Halidane a tantalising glimpse of cleavage. Her underwear was red silk trimmed with black French lace, purchased at a high-fashion boutique. She could feel him mentally undressing her.

"It's a passion of mine," said Eva. "I love orchids."

"Then it´s a passion we share; I grow them."

"Have you a favourite?"

"The one you are wearing – you could plant one of the seeds and it would grow anywhere. You?"

"Cattleya."

"The virgin Hawaiian, a good choice."

"True beauty should always remain pure," said Eva.
She noticed a flicker across his eyes. She extended a wrist.

"You like the scent?"
Halidane took her hand and inhaled the air around her inner arm.

Her fragrance was subtle, blending with the flower. Her delicate bones and neat, pale veins added to her allure. He breathed deeply. He thought of her blood.

He had to stop for a moment. He released her, trying to compose himself. An unwelcome swelling had started in his groin. As a distraction, he picked up the book and studied it.

"It seems orchids are not the only passion we share. I also love rare books. This one must have cost a fortune, Miss ...?"

"Lindemann."

Eva offered her hand.

"Call me Ingrid."

Halidane took her hand and shook it formally.

"You can call me Edgar."

"Just Edgar?"

"For now. This book, how did you come by it?"

"At auction – at the Galerie Fischer."

"Never heard of it."

Halidane turned the book over in his hands. The faded cover was edged with intricate leaves, a motif continued with a central diamond.

"Lucerne," said Eva.

She weighed Halidane up as he fingered the book. His hair, though thinning, was set in an off-hand way to accentuate rather than hide his pate. His white shirt was crisp and new, as was the tailored suit. A garish red tie with yellow diamonds jarred against the sober slate grey and brilliant white. He was both fastidious and slovenly; his shoes were expensive and shiny, yet the laces were old and frayed. A fresh flower pinned to his lapel had the look of an after-thought. In his gaze Eva sensed the urge for instant gratification; for him she was an object, nothing more.

"Lucerne. Never been. MDCCXLVIII – what date is that?"

"1748," said Eva. "Roman numerals."

"Just testing – numbers are my bread and butter."

He handed the book back.

"Are you in the city for long?"

"For a while, yes. And you, Edgar?"

"For a while too. Are you alone?"

"Yes."

"What do you do?"

"I'll tell you over another coffee; my treat this time?"

She reached into her purse. The jacket and blouse moulded to her form.

"No, Ingrid. Unfortunately, I must leave, but perhaps we could meet again?"

"I'd like that."

"Where?"

"Here, tomorrow, same time?"

"I'll ensure we're not disturbed."

Eva smiled. Halidane failed to notice it didn't extend to her eyes. As a final hook, Eva crinkled her nose like a little girl.

"I'd like that, Edgar. A single woman in the city often attracts the wrong kind of attention."

"Well we wouldn't want that, now would we?"

Through the café window Halidane watched his Rolls Royce Wraith glide up to the kerb.

"My chauffeur is here, Ingrid. Until tomorrow?"

"Until tomorrow."

He pulled on his trilby and left.

Chainbridge and de Witte were playing chess on a wooden travel board as Eva made to go. She tapped her finger three times on the pillbox hat before pinning it in place.

The hook was in.

Outside the café, Halidane was met by Mercier, dressed in a single-breasted suit and black leather gloves. His steely eyes flickered momentarily at the sight of his employer. He opened the passenger door.

From the comfort of the car´s rear seat, Halidane looked back through the windows of the café. Ingrid Lindemann was gone.

"All set, Mercier?"

"Yes, sir," replied Mercier.

He inched the Rolls out onto the road and accelerated briskly. Halidane sniffed the tips of his fingers and inhaled the brief wisp of Ingrid.

"Good flight?"

"Yes, sir. Sorry to hear about Mr. Bellowes, sir"

"The island suffered a dreadful explosion. No survivors, I´m afraid."

Halidane eased back into the plush leather. From a hidden drawer, he produced a bottle of whiskey. He poured a generous measure into his old tin cup.

"My suite at the hotel?"

"Booked, sir, the whole floor, sir."

Halidane leaned back and spired his fingers.

Mercier stared ahead, allowing the silence to drift. It was broken only by the occasional slurping noises Halidane tended to make when enjoying a drink.

"I want you to make a background check, Mercier. Ingrid Lindemann and the Galerie Fischer; results of a recent auction."

"Very good, sir," replied Mercier.

30

Plymouth

The Marlborough's communications carriage was clacking out teletype codes collated by its only full-time cipher girl, Cissy Beacon. She´d arrived a day earlier from Plymouth Naval Reserve on an incongruous-looking bicycle, seemingly assembled from various makes and models. She started at six in the morning and worked through the first night.

Her dossier said she lived alone.

Her manner was brisk, her decryption rates efficient. She typed up the codes and placed them neatly in manila folders stamped *Eyes-only.* After rapping them into line five times exactly on her desk, she handed them to Bracken in the main carriage.

With the boxy shape of an outdoors woman, Cissy looked like she´d be more at home in wellington boots than fashionable heels.
Bracken was breezily ignoring urgent cables from Whitehall, hoping Churchill could continue to provide an effective barrier for at least another 72 hours.
He needed time to build a case for allowing Int. 7 to press for more resources.

"Thank you, Miss Beacon," he said.

The pristine dining table with its clean linen and glistening crystal was another world to Cissy. She was a *Bletchleyette*; a denizen of the netherworld of the Official Secrets Act, a dedicated worker.

"Those German Lorenz's are a real handful," she said.

Bracken appeared either absorbed or disinterested.

"A polyalphabetic cipher, those old machines can be a right cow, you know?"

"The Abwehr, or what's left of them, are still predictable," he replied.

Cissy´s asthmatic harrumphs and gasps drifted in over the next round of intelligence whirring and clattering in.
Bracken poured a generous shot of cognac into his morning coffee, took a cigarette from his case and lit it absently. A modestly stocked dining car kept a steady stream of tea, coffee and sandwiches rolling in. A clean bed was prepared every evening. Cissy was content to roll out her own bedding and sleep near the endless chatter of machinery.
Once the Spitfires had been confirmed as missing and a warship group dispatched, the Marlborough was cleared of Navy personnel. The warship and her corvette support group discovered a solitary German U-boat drifting a few miles south of the search grid; an area on Findlay's decrypt where three aircraft were reported missing. The U-boat was boarded by armed marines. The technically advanced vessel had been abandoned, with no crew and almost completely out of fuel. She was now being towed to Scapa Flow for a Royal Navy refit.
This only added to the fog of loose information.
Bracken slowly exhaled as he read through the last of Cissy's

de-crypts. It originated somewhere in Switzerland – a background request about a young female, about twenty-five years of age named Ingrid Lindemann who had recently been in Lucerne, Switzerland. Eva. Halidane and his cohorts were interested. Bracken hummed a John McCormack air as he flicked through the remaining intercepted de-crypts.

"Miss Beacon?" he said through the adjoining door.
Cissy strode into the carriage as if she were hiking the hills of Dartmoor.

"Mr. Bracken?"

"How's your German?"

"Excellent, Mr. Bracken."
Cissy had the faint twang of a black country accent. With her low hairline pinned up harshly into a bun above her unkempt eyebrows, Bracken imagined an ancestry of piracy or highway robbery. A wide gap between her front teeth over thin, pinched lips cemented the thought in his head.

"Swiss German?"

"It'll pass muster, Mr. Bracken."

"Splendid. Pull up a chair please. You and I are going to create an agent's back story. I want you to respond to this Swiss enquiry."

"Very good, sir."

"We haven't much time, Miss Beacon."

"Best press on, then hadn't we, Mr. Bracken?"

"Indeed, Miss Beacon."
Bracken began making phone calls to his ministry in London, while Cissy penciled out his instructions in code.

31

Zürich

Brandt and Pannu sat on a bench along the Mythenquai lake front. The Sunday morning bells rolled lazily above their heads as they leafed through the newspapers they pretended to be reading. A few people were taking constitutionals along the promenade. The boat club bustled with life as the rowers prepared their boats. Across the lake, the sunlight and dappled waters lapped at the huge flying boat they were observing while studiously avoiding eye contact with one another.

"Halidane's?" asked Brandt.

"Yes," said Pannu. "Registered here under the aegis of the American airforce, according to sahib de Witte."

Pannu´s cobalt turban and smart, modest suit conveyed solidity. The outline of his kirpan strapped to his side added to the low-key menace.

Brandt's new shoes were pinching his toes, he massaged his feet through the brown leather. Bending down, he made a show of tying the laces. A shave, a quick haircut and a new hat had revitalised him. From his well-cut beige suit, he produced a small pair of opera glasses and trained them on the aircraft. It was protected by two motor launches. Standing sentinel were lean-looking men in thick, heavy donkey jackets and flat caps. Two men per boat, with a second man panning around high-powered binoculars.

"VIP treatment," said Brandt.

Once the binoculars were off their side of the lake Brandt slid the ornate glasses over to Pannu, who scanned the lake in one slow sweep.

The flying boat was moored to a temporary jetty. Other men appeared and moved boxes on trolleys from a hatch that led into the bowels of the plane.

"That's a lot of activity," said Pannu.

"A lot of men," agreed Brandt.
A few boats flitted along the lake. A large pleasure cruiser chugged along, but for the most part, the city was still asleep in their beds. Brandt folded up his paper.

"Sahib," murmured Pannu.

Brandt followed his gaze. A huge metal crate appeared at the side of the plane. Gradually it was eased onto the jetty. It swayed under the weight. A truck appeared lakeside, reversing to the edge of the jetty. With a few shouts wafting over the waters, the crate was manhandled onto the truck.

"Fifteen, twenty men?"

"Twenty-five, sahib."

Brandt looked at his battered pilot's watch. It was 8am. He was due back at the pension. Chainbridge and de Witte would be arriving later that morning.

"Doctor, I think you'd better join us."

"I'll follow in a few moments, sahib."

Brandt rolled up his paper and dipped his hat lower, affording himself one further glance at the aircraft, nearly the size of a warship. He had rescued Eva from something similar off the coast of Finland; an aircraft ferrying the body of Lenin out of Russia. Eva had been reunited with de Witte, and Lenin with the Russian people. Brandt´s country now lay burning across the lake.

He stopped to light a cigarette.

Big as the flying boat was, it would only take a few pieces of plastic explosive to sink it. As he walked, Brandt considered how to get aboard. Deep in thought, he paid no heed to the man on the bicycle who began pedaling slowly along the pathway a few yards away from him to cross the thoroughfare, blending with the trams and buses.

32

Zürich

Herman Malleus pushed off from the bar, turning and adjusting his stroke, clawing the water. Above him, armed with a long aluminium pole, walked his instructor, Martin, shouting above the din of the pool. Children's screams ricocheted around the glass, tile and metal. Malleus´ progress through the learning lane was dictated by Martin's shouts and the metronome in his head. Turning his head, he took a gasp for breath; his lungs felt as if they wanted to burst out of his chest; he could see Martin's toned calves and strong, smooth feet pushing through his blue galoshes. His own legs propelled him awkwardly, the withered muscles on the right making him veer off along the lane before the aluminium pole nudged him back into the centre.

Yes, he was a casualty of war alright, but his tank crew had been less fortunate - they´d been killed instantly by the same French landmine.

Now came the tricky bit. As he approached the end wall of the pool, one length completed, he heard Martin shout;

"Turn ... now!"

Malleus attempted the mushroom float, turning, but the timing was all wrong; his feet collided with the metal bar, then came the pain, a momentary red flash across Malleus's vision.

"Christ, Jesus," he spluttered, the water pouring into his nostrils and swirling freely down his throat.

His composure broken, he scrambled to the safety of the support bar.

"Tread water!" shouted Martin.

He was grinning good naturedly.

Malleus tried but the leg was dragging him down like a twisted kite. He reached the bar and rested his head on the cold metal. Sharp, stinging tears mixed with the water. He felt helpless, he was wracked with sobs. He couldn't bring himself to look at his instructor´s perfect features.

"It's OK, Herr Malleus. You did well," said Martin.

A strong hand was lowered toward him. Malleus grabbed it and climbed up towards security.

"Thank you, Martin."

Malleus felt a little unsteady, like a tricycle with a broken wheel. He limped his way to the changing rooms where men of all sizes and ages were towelling themselves down. Complete specimens – no mutilated war veterans here. He waddled to the massage area and allowed himself to be pummeled in oil; his skin both thrilling to and reviling the strong ministrations of the masseur.

He closed his eyes and allowed himself to drift. The masseur was gentle with the twisted flesh of his leg, easing the tortured musculature.

"Don't hold back," said Malleus.

"If you insist, Herr Malleus."

The fingers became more probing, more incisive, more penetrating. Malleus clenched his teeth.

He took a long sauna, then dressed in a jumper and well-cut chinos.

Waiting for him at the reception area of the club was Hannah Wolfe, her ample curves pinched into a narrow waist.

"We're expected," she said.

"By...?"

"Herr Halidane; he has a car waiting for us."

Glancing through the double doors, Malleus glimpsed the malevolent outline of Kahn and Pfeiffer sitting in the back of a Rolls Royce - Halidane's Rolls Royce.

The receptionist handed him his jacket, hat and cane; he and Hannah clacked out different tempos as they strode out towards the waiting car.

Malleus thought of Martin, a strong but gentle fellow; someone who could accept his tears and place a strong hand on his shoulder. Then he looked at Hannah Wolfe; toxic and corrupted to her core. A strange rotten fruit covered in a shiny shell. She brought nothing but death and destruction in her wake.

"Let's find out what Herr Halidane wants then, shall we,

Hannah?"

33

Halidane Corp. Headquarters

Halidane was waiting for them in Malleus' office. He was sitting in the high-backed chair with his feet up on the table, paring his fingernails with a penknife. A leather-bound case lay across his lap. Behind him, surveying the impressive view of the lake, stood Mercier. The butler and valet of Fawkeston Gyre was malevolent like a crow, hovering behind his master's shoulder.

"Good news folks, a little soirée has been arranged. And, as a bonus, we'll have a few sweet 'n sinful dolls to enjoy."

Mercier allowed himself a smile. Malleus noticed Halidane's spigot pimp was completely unmoved by Hannah Wolfe's impressive cool beauty.

"Now," continued Halidane, tossing his battered cup to Kahn.

"Two sugars, cream, thanks – we have further information on this ... Chainbridge character."

Halidane motioned for Pfeiffer, Hannah and Malleus to come closer. He opened the leather case and produced a series of black and white photographs, some still tacky from development.

"Henry Chainbridge, Secret Service, retired. Last known operation: Tehran 1943. Ties to O.S.S., the defunct Russian intelligence services and STAVKA."

With a croupier's toss he served up another image.

"Peter de Witte." He glanced up at Hannah.

She noticed a tic under Halidane's left eyelid.

"Mr. de Witte made young Hannah here a widow. Killed her husband. Just imagine that; being done in by a blind man? Hannah escorted de Witte to Berlin, where he was rescued by Chainbridge, and ..."

The third photo showed a slightly haggard looking man of about forty with cold grey eyes.

"... Captain Nicklaus Brandt."

Hannah felt a blinding hatred growing in her gut. She held up the image.

"I shot him in Lyon. I saw him die," she said.

"Guess again, Miss Wolfe. He turned up in Berlin. Along with... Myles Curran, MI6, Bertram Hopkins, Liaison British Military Section and a certain Alastaire Findlay. These last were dealt with by Mr Bellowes' contacts. MI6 are saying it was a gas explosion."

Findlay's photograph was a mortuary portrait. His eyes rolled back into his head and his mouth gaped open.

"Findlay was jailed in England for being a Russian agent. But more importantly. MORE FUCKING IMPORTANTLY...!"

Halidane wiped the spittle from his chin with the back of his sleeve.

"Findlay was a *code-breaker*. A real unvarnished total-fucking-genius. The real deal."

Kahn appeared with the coffee and placed the battered tin cup reverently at Halidane's elbow. Halidane swung his legs off the desk and dragged the chair forward. He was inferior in stature to Malleus and seemed suddenly adolescent by comparison.

"The RAF show up at Whip-saw and, lo and behold, Mr Chainbridge materialises here with de Witte and this man, Brandt, in tow. Call me paranoid, but it would appear I have a tail. How did this happen, Malleus?"

"This department's focus was land procurement in Berlin. This objective has since been achieved. Unless we receive a direct order to pursue other interests, we stick to the agreed plan and its corresponding time frame."

"Fuck you and your fucking time frame! The issue is not your fucking time frame, it is your fucking incompetence!"

With an effort, Halidane composed himself. He then placed a single photograph on the table. It was a pretty woman with a page-boy haircut.

"Ingrid Lindeman. Twenty-five, a former nun released from her vows. Now working as a piano teacher for a private Jewish family. That's her back story from our contacts abroad – do I need to worry?"

"Yes," said Hannah.

"Why?"

"Because her real name is Eva Molenaar. She´s a spy for British Intelligence."

"Don't tell me – you killed her too?"

"Argentina, 1943."

"Another resurrection – Alleluia!"

"She was thrown to the sharks."

"Well, she must've walked on water, then."

Halidane turned the photograph back around. It was Ingrid's eyes that drew him to her, grey with flecks of green, the way they twinkled had a touch of Irish about them.

"You can´t be sure it´s the same girl."

"I am."

Malleus thought for a second and reached into a drawer. From it, he produced a battered looking leather-bound book, it smelled faintly of petroleum, smoke and water.

"We were hunting a female spy from Poland. Her true identity was confirmed to us by two girls – descendants of a degenerate Polish intellectual, Henk Molenaar. They were very ... forthcoming. Unfortunately, the poor little things didn´t survive the interrogation."

Malleus leafed through the pages. Lines of photographs were struck through with red lines– enemies of the Reich who had been eliminated.

"Her Allied codename was *Chopin*."

Malleus served up another photograph of Eva; the classic head shot of a film starlet.

"She posed as an actress for the late Donald Kincaid, an American friend of Nazi Germany – here it is Eva Molenaar, deceased 1941, Finland."

"It´s her," said Hannah.

Halidane placed the photograph beside the head shot.

"I ran into her in Italy in '42 and again in Buenos Aires a year later," said Hannah.

"And you killed her both times? Perhaps you should have codenamed her *The Cat* – she´s certainly not short of lives. You´ve made a mistake; those Polak broads look the same, after all. If you lived near Ashland Avenue, you'd know what I mean," said Halidane. He looked around at the puzzled faces.

"Chicago – two million of them live there."

"It´s no mistake, Herr Halidane," said Hannah. "She has a habit of latching onto powerful men."

She thought of their last face-to-face encounter – Eva had loosened two of her teeth before being dragged to the side rail of a luxury yacht, clubbed with a crystal ashtray and thrown overboard.

"Is she a virgin?" asked Halidane.

"Hardly," exclaimed Hannah.

"I got the feeling this girl is, you get a sense, a scent, a feeling - she seems pure."

Hannah gave a snort.

"Are you laughing at me? Laughing at me!"

Halidane's features contorted into a mask of rage. He hurled his trusty tin cup at Hannah, who side-stepped deftly. The cup bounced off a painting, smearing the expensive canvas in oily coffee.

Hannah narrowed her eyes. Once an instructor at SS-Junkerschule Bad Tölz Academy humiliated her in front of a group of junior cadets. He encouraged them to laugh at her country ways, her big build and her uncouth manners. The instructor was found one night in a field, emasculated.

His replacement molded her into the killer she would become. Her fellow cadets grew strangely respectful and kept their distance.

"Get me my cup, doll," said Halidane.

The tension was palpable. To defuse the situation Malleus limped over and retrieved the cup. If Hannah took matters into her own hands the whole operation could teeter over the brink.

"I'll arrange a refill," he said.

Halidane's complexion calmed.

"No need, Malleus," he said.

Halidane spat into his cup and ran a sleeve over the rim. Mercier gathered up the photographs and dossiers. Halidane then placed a piece of paper in the middle of the table with an address typed on it.

"Take care of this," he said, "No witnesses. Everything dies – understand? Like Miss Chambrel, we send a message – a warning to Chainbridge and his goons – he'll understand."

Halidane hopped out of the chair and Mercier handed him a jacket.

"Tomorrow afternoon, I sit down with the Brits, the Frogs, the chocolate clockmakers and the Krauts. While we make whoopee over the financial settlement, you will ensure the party goes ahead without a hitch. Capiche?"

He patted Hannah's pert backside as he passed.

"No hard feelings, doll?"

"No hard feelings, Herr Halidane," she muttered, through gritted teeth.

"See ya at the Prestige au Lac," he said.

He was determined to pursue Ingrid. He thought Hannah was a bit ditzy, a bit dumb; her blood would have been poisoned and corrupted by hundreds of men.

She was just jealous that's all. It gave him a sense of reassurance and power.

It made him feel like a man.

34

Plymouth

The incessant machine-gun tapping of the teletype machine in the carriage woke her. It was 2am. The typing halted suddenly. After two beats, it began hammering away again, in sequence. Cissy's hearing automatically homed in, every nerve in her body suddenly alert.

Cecily loved deciphering cryptic clues; her winning entry in a local paper´s crossword competition had brought her to the attention of the Bletchley recruiters in the first place. Once there she dealt almost exclusively with cryptarithms.

She reached for her pad, sharpened her pencil to a fine point and set to work. In less than a minute, she was through the door and knocking on Bracken's cabin, rapping her knuckles in a quick tattoo.

Bracken appeared, dazed and peeling his glasses onto his ears. His dressing gown was already fastened in a rigid knot.

"It's only me, Mr Bracken. A decrypt – same location, same Lorenz machine – Switzerland."

Bracken blanched at the communiqué.

"Christ. Is this the exact message?"

"Exactly, Mr Bracken. It's a confirmation – confirmation of a delivery."

Cissy Beacon coughed dryly.

"Delivery of what?" he asked.

"It's a U-boat code – southern Atlantic is my guess. One gets to identify these machines over time, like a piano tuner detects a flat. I call this Lorenz *Gruyére* – it's a bit smelly – transmitting out of Switzerland. Delivery of something into Switzerland, not leaving Switzerland is my assumption, sir."

She rocked on her heels expecting some recognition, a thank you.

None was forthcoming.

Bracken glanced at the other de-crypt – notification of a high-level meeting involving the Americans, British, French and Swiss banks. Halidane would be chairing the technical group.

"What are you up to, Halidane?" he muttered.

"This communication; is it to or from a U-boat?"

"To, sir."

"Has there been a response?"

"My experience is, they take an hour or so to respond. If he's a good U-boat Captain, he won't reply at all."

He guided her back to her carriage.

"Forward this to the FO. Encode it, let them know we are investigating Halidane. Tell them he's taken delivery of something and is using standard Enigma to an unknown vessel."

"Very good, Mr. Bracken. One other item here – what's a *code blue*?"

Bracken paused, his eyes staring off into middle distance.

"It´s an old Abwehr assassination code – spies to be eliminated..."

Bracken stopped – Chainbridge, de Witte, Eva.

"Cissy, get a warning to Chainbridge – tell him he and the team are potential targets. Add to it, as well as the usual precautions, something has been delivered to Halidane. If Eva can investigate, all the better."

Cissy Beacon nodded. As she did, her unruly mane of hair covered her features. She looked like a horse snuffling the air. A thick blanket with embroidered cats at play was wrapped around her, adding to her shapeless, feral demeanour.

"...Oh, and Cissy?"

"Yes, sir?"

"Well done."

"Thank you, sir."

From the doorway, punctuated by dry gun-shot coughs, Cissy Beacon hummed an old show tune; a Flanagan and Allen toe-tapper.

35

Eva pulled back the sheets and stared at Brandt's sleeping form. The moonlight sent a bolt of white through the curtains and across the room, landing on his rucksack and glinting off the blasting caps and three alarm clocks lined neatly on the dinner table.

His breathing was deep. Beneath the reddish grey lashes, his eyelids twitched in dreams. Eva let her gaze drift along his chest, lined and hard. Past ribs that had been broken on the shores of Norway, along his strong arms to his hands; strong hands that had mapped her body assuredly and cupped her breasts with their heat. His hips were narrow, his legs, sinewed and scarred from his mountain climbing exploits.

Eva kissed his chin, shaved expertly by a barber, picking up faint traces of cologne and oil. She rested her head on his shoulder. He stirred slightly. Eva was wide awake, her eyes flitted around the room and back to Brandt. An unworded sense of unease gripped her. She told herself she was being foolish. She prodded and nudged Brandt into a more comfortable position. He gave a huge sigh and settled into the mattress. Eva listened to his heart; it beat strongly.

Of course, there had been others. Ramsay, her trainer in Scotland after she had returned from France, the urbane René Parez and – like the Spanish matador whose name she never knew – a few ships in the night. She was about to utter a litany of indiscretions like beads on a rosary when Brandt´s arm slid about her and pulled her close.

"Dreaming, Brandt?"

"I was on a mountain again, you were in the plane," he said.

"Plane?"

"It was how I got out of the Gulag. A girl died on a plane."

"Lovely."

"Stalin's son, Vasily. A psycho. I had to rescue him. He'd crashed a plane. The girl died. Every day for the past ten years, I thought each day would be my last. I still think that now, Eva.

One day at a time?"
They held each other and watched the dawn creep in, fading up the white of the moon to a brazen yellow of late spring sunshine. They made slow, tender love, showered and set about their tasks.
Eva stopped on the threshold of the door when a sudden pang, a warning stab, made her blink. She turned around.

"Brandt?"

He was pulling on a well-cut casual jacket. He looked over.

"Marry me?" she asked.

He smiled, a genuine lupine grin.

"I'd love to."

She ran back into his arms and kissed him deeply.

"Go break a heart, Eva," he said.

Eva took the tram, then side streets rather than making directly for the main thoroughfare. She glanced back occasionally, stopping once to look in a display window where she could use the glass as a mirror.
Zürich bustled with Monday morning workers. Bicycles, buses and luxury cars battled each other to the start of business. Nothing seemed untoward, but Eva felt on edge.
She was fashionably late by the time she approached Halidane at The Cafe Sprüngli. He stood up and waved.
She looked slowly around to see if a face looked out of place. Nothing. But no Chainbridge or de Witte either.
She was on her own.

36

Berlin

OMGUS (Office of Military Government US)

Ed McElhone was tossed the keys to the Dodge T214 by a mechanic.

"You sure you want to go it alone, sir? It's the fuckin' Wild West out there."

The mechanic, Sergeant Kelly, wrung an oily cloth around his hands. The stub of a well-chewed cigar jutted out through the stubble. He looked like a beer barrel topped off with a tiny woolen hat.

"We're all still allies here, Sergeant, thanks," said McElhone.

"You from Manhattan, sir?" asked Kelly

"West 39th Street, Sergeant," replied McElhone. "Abattoir Row."

"Fuckin' Hell's Kitchen? Well, you'll feel right at home here, sir."

Kelly tossed a Thompson machine gun onto the back seat.

"I always carry a little extra protection, sir. On the house."

"Thanks, sergeant?"

"Kelly, sir,"

"Thanks, Kelly,"

As McElhone started up the engine, a civilian contractor named Queloz climbed in beside him and buckled up. Edward McElhone was O.S.S., dispatched from New York on the orders of Truman. Queloz had been cleared by the OMGUS to return to civilian life after clearing Military Law No.8. A former Nazi, in other words.

"Here are the zones bought up by the Halidane Corporation," he said.

Queloz opened out a military map and used a battered red crayon to carve out the route.

"I know this one – through two big Soviet roadblocks. No

shortcut."

"Great," muttered McElhone.

Inside his khaki fatigues he had letters of free movement signed by Eisenhower. Stamped in glorious red were the words ***CEKPETHO / TOP SECRET*** – meaning only a Commissar or higher could refuse passage.

"Put this on ..." he said.

He tossed Queloz a US army helmet.

"... And say nothing."

Queloz stared imperiously down his long nose. Like his general demeanour it was elongated, sharp and bitter.

"I'm fluent in Russian, sir."

"No need for ´sir´ Queloz; everyone calls me *Mac."*

"Okay, M-ac."

The word sounded guttural and coarse. Queloz had supposedly been de-Nazified, but he was still a long way from rehabilitation. McElhone revved up and drove out of the OMGUS compound. Military trucks lined up alongside jeeps and American cars with fluttering stars and stripes pennants, lined up as if on parade. Two armed sentries waved them on through the reinforced steel gates.

McElhone had been summoned to Washington from Newark, NJ, three days earlier to, of all things, a poker game. President Truman invited him to play a few hands in an ante room of the White House. Sitting around the table were joint chiefs, head of the OSS, Harry Hopkins and a few off-duty bodyguards. After several hours and numerous bottles of bourbon, McElhone and Hopkins were mandated to check out intelligence recently received from Churchill.

"I don't like Atlee, I don't trust Atlee," said Truman. "British intelligence leaks like a sieve these days."

His blue eyes, magnified by strong lenses, were covered by a green eye shade, giving the president an amphibian appearance. His sleeves were pinned up with cuffs. He looked like a croupier at Halloween. He loved the role of dealer, shouting instructions like a Kansas City barkeep.

"Winston wouldn't contact me on a whim, but it's a

go-look-see only. Roosevelt liked you, recommended you – I've read your file," he said.

"I worked with FDR and his team in Tehran, that's all, sir," said McElhone.

"The file says you did more than that, son."

McElhone ended up counting his meagre winnings on a rickety non-stop flight to Berlin. Not even growing up in Hell´s Kitchen prepared him for the devastation.

From Berlin Templehof, he was driven to section G-5 USFET, one office away from Eisenhower and the top brass wrestling with a shattered civilian population.

"Food & Agriculture section?"

"They're waiting for you," said the uniformed attaché, without looking up from his desk.

Inside was a broad man with a florid bow tie and matching complexion, alongside the funereal Queloz.

"Time is precious, McElhone," said the man in the bow tie. His snow-white hair had been pomaded into a complex swirl. Queloz looked like he'd just been dredged from a lake.

"Walt Keyburn is dead. Died on the Brits´ watch at their military HQ. We're having problems retrieving his body, but there's another pay grade above us to deal with that."

He pulled over the shutters and lit a desk lamp.

"Herr Queloz here is a scientist. To be exact, a physicist. Before being cleared for civilian duty here he was part of the Wehrmacht's Vengeance Weapon program. He was, briefly, a colleague of Edgar Halidane. Herr Queloz and his family will be transferring Stateside in the next week or so."

McElhone had read the dossier.

"Halidane's now up in lights in Washington?"

"Mr Halidane has been procuring zones around Berlin under the aegis of the Quartermaster General. He's rich, powerful and appointed by a senate committee to oversee the dismantling of Germany's technical capabilities. It´s probably nothing, but we've been asked to assist – without drawing undue attention."

"Henry Chainbridge?" asked McElhone. A teletyped sheet was clipped to a photograph of Chainbridge.

"You know him?"

"Old MI6, I met him in Tehran in '43."

If Chainbridge was involved something was brewing. Peter de Witte and Eva Molenaar wouldn't be far behind.

"Did this intelligence come in from another department – Int.7., maybe?"

"So that's why Truman picked you. Yes."

McElhone ground the gears. The Dodge growled along. Queloz had an irritating habit of using hand gestures rather than words to indicate directions; any excuse for a stiff-arm salute, thought McElhone.

The Soviet roadblocks waved them through. After an hour they came to a wire-fenced zone. Double tiers of razor wire encompassed a block of buildings. A sign in English, French, Russian and German read *Danger! Keep Out!*

The buildings had been damaged, but not flattened. They now boasted a crisscross of new scaffolding along their facades.

"You sure this is it?" asked McElhone.

"I'm sure."

"You worked here?"

"The basement level was refitted. Halidane had a facility here before it was shut down."

"When was that?"

"Nineteen forty-one."

McElhone hoisted himself out and Queloz followed a foot behind. He stood with his eyes closed simply smelling the air. He spied a flower and picked it up.

"An early spring, Mac, yes?" said Queloz.

"If you say so. I arrived yesterday, Queloz."

"You can call me Thierry."

"I´ll stick with Queloz, thanks."

"As you wish, Mac."

The sky was an azure blue to the heavens without a cloud in sight. The sunlight glinted on some of the building´s new windows. A roadway leading away from the fences looked recently paved. The razor wire glinted ferociously. McElhone walked along the edge of the wire. He suspected the second row

of fencing was electrified. There was no signage.
The site looked abandoned.

"If we're moving troops and civil servants in, you'd think it'd be an around-the-clock operation?"

"You would, Mac," said Queloz.

Queloz was staring down at the battered gorse and grass, turning in tight concentric circles. He reminded McElhone of an eager gun dog. McElhone glanced around. There was just the Dodge and a few battered looking buildings. The place was off the beaten track, it looked like an old industrial facility – it was a miracle it hadn't been levelled by bombing. He'd been a beat cop for twenty years in New York before being transferred to the secret service. To this old detective something didn't smell right.

It was then he spotted the dogs. Big, slavering, well-fed dogs on the far side of the fence. They congregated close to where Queloz was kicking away. The animals didn't bark, didn't make any sound, just stared. They were Belgian Malinois, five of them, tan fur with black muzzles and twitching ears. McElhone went back to the Dodge. He checked his own gun, a Colt, and slung the Thompson over his shoulder.

He turned back. Queloz was gone.

He started to walk toward the clump of grass he had last been standing on. The pack of Malinois skulked along with him.

Quleoz's head appeared through the grass.

"Found it, Mac," he said.

They descended a long service ladder leading to a concrete tunnel.

"Halidane's offices were here."

Despite the sunlight filtering through the hole above the ladder, they whispered like thieves.

McElhone thought of the dogs. Facilities like this had a secret flap that would allow them freedom to roam. All they would need is a command.

"What kind of facility?" he said.

"Classified, but something involving transport – a jump gate."

"We're slap bang in the middle of Berlin – what kind of

jump gate?"
They came to a large wheel lock door. Even between the two of them, they couldn't turn it.

"Locked from the inside, Mac."

"The cement smells fresh, the service ladder isn't rusty and this door looks freshly minted. Well, it's a dead end. For now."

"How could the Reds allow this on their turf?" asked Queloz.

"Pay a guy enough to look away, he will."

"To look away from what, Mac?"
McElhone looked around. Lines of lights lit the corridor. He looked back at the door. Stamped just above the wheel lock was the Halidane Corp. logo; the world surrounded by lightning bolts.

"No idea, Queloz. Let's get out of here."
At the top of the ladder stood five guards shouldering machine guns. All five were struggling with dogs on tight leashes. Just behind them stood a man in black uniform. Black beret, shiny black boots and a machine pistol levelled at McElhone and Queloz.

"You're trespassing, gentlemen. May I see some identification please?"
His accent was cultured, clipped. English officer class.
McElhone tossed his ID over. The dogs began deep throaty barking. They pitched and jumped, lurching violently against their leashes. They bared their teeth in wicked smiles.

"Welcome to Berlin, Mr McElhone of the O.S.S. You've clearly taken a wrong turn."
He tossed the badge back.

"Clearly," replied McElhone. "My guide here lied through his teeth when he said he was fluent in Russian. It won't happen again."

"I'd suggest you hire a more capable individual, sir," said the man.

"He's French, what can I say?"
On cue, Queloz gave a gallic shrug.

"He needed to take a shit, fell down a hole," said McElhone.

"This is a construction site, sir, there are lots of holes." His pencil-thin moustache twitched with a smile. He pursed his lips at an angle.

McElhone figured they could take down two dogs, two men, possibly three –before they'd be ripped apart.

The man whistled a low-pitched tone.

The dogs all went on their bellies and panted happily. Their handlers remained stony-faced and expressionless.

"Do you need to be directed back, sir?" asked the man.

"No thanks, sir, we´ll manage. Keep the home fires burning, eh?"

"We will indeed, sir. Good day."

For once Queloz dropped the master race act. He was silent on the drive back to the compound. McElhone found the carpool sergeant.

"You were right, sergeant, this place makes Hell's Kitchen look like a walk in the park. Thanks for the Thompson.

"Keep it, sir. You can never have enough guns in this city."

"Agreed."

As McElhone typed up his report, his mind constantly drifted back to the dogs. He slept uneasily that night. The clear blue sky troubled him for no apparent reason.

The man with the bow tie read through McElhone's report.

"Could be electrical equipment, a power station?" he said.

"Could be anything. Private security, though not ours or the Russians´– heavily armed," replied McElhone.

"Halidane is paranoid by nature – *Jump Gate*?"

"That's what Queloz said. Big door, wheel lock like a bank vault."

The man in the bow tie looked up. His nose was covered in burst blood vessels. He was the kind who needed a shot of something to get the day going.

"Bank vault suggests money, valuables?"

"Yes, it does sir. May I ask if we know the whereabouts of Henry Chainbridge?"

"No."

"Halidane?"

"That I do know, McElhone. Switzerland – a conference. He's bought up the entire floor of a hotel – The Prestige au Lac. Out of his own pocket, thank God; I´m guessing the American taxpayer might object to bankrolling an orgy after sacrificing their kids for their war effort."

McElhone sensed Chainbridge would know something more.

"Mind if I go over there?"

The man in the bow tie leaned back and his chair groaned under his bulk.

"Son, this is the USA, we can go anywhere now."

37

The Cafe Sprüngli, Zürich

Eva watched Halidane swirl coffee in his battered tin mug. From time to time he would glance at the passers-by on the street below. Parked on the far side was his Rolls Royce Wraith. Leaning against it stood a man reading a paper. To Eva, he was the kind of man you'd see loitering on a street corner in Berlin in the thirties; a thug for hire. He was pretending to read a newspaper. At the count of three, he'd turn a page and look around from under the peak of his shiny chauffeur's hat.

"I have a confession, Edgar."

Startled to hear his first name uttered, he looked at her.

Eva had an orchid over her ear, pushing her hair back, it accentuated her long cheek bones that tilted to her full lips. She reminded him of a starlet, one of those women who'd flit into a scene in a B-movie and steal the thunder from the leading lady.

"Confession?"

"I lied."

"About?"

"I didn't buy that book at auction, I stole it. From an antiques store in Lucerne."

Halidane paused.

"Stole it?"

"Stole it. You see, Edgar, I'm a refugee. A nun. Or rather, a former nun – I'm sorry, I'm really not making sense."

Eva paused dramatically and dabbed a tear from her eye.

"Bormann crushed the churches in Germany, we practiced our faith in secret, then the Russians arrived. I had to flee."

Halidane had the photograph of Eva with him. He´d studied it on the drive over. It sat creased and folded tight on the inside of his freshly pressed suit.

"A Mackerel snapper?" he said

"A – what?"

"A Catholic, you know, fish on a Friday – a *mack-erel* snapper?"

He thought of the Chicago soup kitchens in sub-zero temperatures, the fat, warm religious and all their insincere piety.

"Yes, I'm a Catholic, but lapsed. I was released from my vows."

The waiter arrived with fresh coffee and pastries. As Eva leaned in, she made sure her loose blouse fell open. Halidane eyed her full breasts in black lace.

"They match," she said.

"Match?"

"My underwear. After many years in robes and habits, I love the feel of expensive, well-made lace."

"Oh."

"Just teasing. But it´s true, I do find expensive underwear incredibly liberating."

"Did you steal that too?"

"No. It´s my one indulgence."

"Men? Boyfriend?"

"No. Never."

Eva bit into a soufflé and allowed a smear of cream hang on her lips. Halidane reached over with a napkin and dabbed it off.

"Edgar, you spoil me, too many cakes!"

"*Any* man?"

"Edgar, if you're asking me if I'm a virgin, then yes, I am. It´s common for a woman of my age, unmarried."

Before Halidane could speak Eva said.

"Twenty-five."

A smile danced briefly around his mouth. Eva noticed the collar of his shirt was a little too big. His neck was mottled in red, it appeared flaky in places. The only interest he'd shown this morning was when she´d said she was pure.

"Any kin?" he asked.

"No. My family were in Hamburg when the RAF bombed it. They died."

"Too bad. Listen, I must be somewhere in an hour. Can I see you tomorrow? Have you an address?"

Eva stared steadily into his eyes. She took his hand and held it.

"A lady must have her secrets, Edgar."

She took his fingers and kissed the tips. Halidane's nervous system went into overdrive. A bolt of heat shot across his loins.

"Tomorrow it is then, Ingrid," he said.

Eva rose and allowed him one more sweep of her chest. She pulled on her coat and pecked him lightly on the cheek. Then she was down the stairs and out of the café.

Halidane took out the photograph and unfolded it. Watching Eva look up and down the street, he studied it again. She skipped across the street and waited for a tram. Mercier was already in the Rolls Royce.

For a moment, Halidane thought he'd seen Eva look up to his window and give a little wave. Despite himself, he waved back. The tram arrived and Ingrid Lindemann was gone.

He refused to believe this girl was the one in the photo.

"Sweet and sinful," he murmured.

***

"The manifest and customs forms state it's an 'Antique tan stove for a Victorian greenhouse'," said de Witte.

He produced documents from a leather satchel and handed them round. Mario and his brother had adapted the old storeroom above the Café with temporary walls and a couple of camp beds. Despite his protestations, the brothers took it in turns to help de

Witte navigate the narrow staircase through to the kitchens. With space at a premium Dr Pannu found a Sikh gurdwara – a modest place of worship – and had been living quietly with a family from the congregation.

An old door on top of two upended crates acted as Chainbridge and de Witte's dining table and planning board. Dossiers and intelligence stood stacked in the light of the naked lightbulb overhead.

Brandt, Pannu and Chainbridge passed the details around.

"I still have a few contacts at Lloyds in London, and they confirmed that this was dismantled and shipped from Halidane's estate in England."

"A tan stove, even though he's a genius with electrical power?" asked Chainbridge.

"You would think, Henry. But he's a collector of orchids, a fanatical one by all accounts, and he's a bit of an iron-and-steam man. Thinks the Victorians had it right. He owns a private collection of American rolling stock too. Loves trains."

The schematic of the tan stove meant tunneling deep under a greenhouse and extending out.

"Shipped to where?" asked Chainbridge.

"The Hotel Presige au Lac," said de Witte. "Our boy Halidane built a nineteenth century hot house at the rear of the hotel. He's booked an entire floor for a party."

"How do you know all this, sahib?" asked Pannu.

"My apologies, Doctor. When I gave you the slip, I got a taxi to the hotel. At reception, I acted somewhat befuddled and confused."

The blind man allowed himself a grin.

"Please don't do that again, sahib," rumbled Pannu.

Chainbridge reached into the pile and pulled from it a creased and bloody matchbook.

"The hotel Prestige au Lac. Anna Chambrel had this on her when she was killed. Holmpatrick in Bern sent it here. It was like pulling teeth. Incidentally, he keeps telling me to leave Switzerland."

"Apparently Herr Halidane is famous for his orgies. This

hotel is his playground," said de Witte. "The concierge was quite chatty while I was waiting in reception for a taxi. A hefty tip certainly helped."

Brandt studied the schematic.

"Something this size would need more than one crate; but that's all myself and Dr Pannu saw."

"They could have been offloading all day or night," said Chainbridge.

"Just an update, then," offered Brandt. "I have enough plastic explosive to hole the plane. But it´s well protected and visible from every angle. Is there any way I can get aboard?"

"I doubt it," said Chainbridge. "If he's here on behalf of the Americans, they'll protect it. So, all we know is that Halidane has shipped something; maybe it´s the chamber from the micro-dot we pulled out of you?"

"We'll take a look at his greenhouse then," said Brandt. "It´s probably easier to blow up that than the flying boat. I'll pick up the necessaries."

"I'll come with you, sahib," said Pannu.

"You know you're now chalked up as AWOL?" said de Witte.

"I'll be on the first train tomorrow," he grinned.

"I'm going back to the hotel," said de Witte.

The men stared at him.

"If Eva has done her work, she'll be a guest there. I'll give them the helpless blind man act again. I'll book a room, behave like an eccentric – they'll love me."

"Hiding in plain sight, Peter?" smiled Chainbridge. "Isn´t that a little dangerous?"

"It´s either that or stay here and be deafened by your snoring, Chanibridge. I´ll take my chances."

They laughed as Mario arrived with coffee and bread.

38

Brandt and Pannu took a circuitous route to the pension. They sat at opposite ends of the tram, alternating seats on each short journey. The afternoon was hot, and Brandt was annoyed that he had a heavy sports jacket on. Taking it off would reveal his Browning in its shoulder holster. Pannu seemed unfazed by the rising temperatures and read a battered looking paperback.
Two streets from the pension they alighted and walked several yards apart to Mrs. Hausman´s door.
It was open.
The old landlady never left her door open. Brandt held up a hand and Pannu stopped.
Brandt pulled out his Browning, glanced up and down the street. A black Mercedes Benz was parked a few feet from the door. It was unoccupied.
Brandt eased the door open with his shoe and stepped inside the house. Pannu unsheathed his kirpan and let it hang loose in his hand.
They found the first cat lying on its side. It was dead. Blood pooled around it and smears and splashes showed it had jumped around in a frenzy before expiring.
All Brandt could think of was Eva.

"Careful, sahib," whispered Pannu.

Mrs. Hausmann's door was ajar. Pannu inched it open while Brandt levelled the Browning. All the shades were pulled down. They found a second cat, beheaded. Then they found Mrs. Hausmann.
Brandt had fought in battles, hand-to-hand combat. Intimate killing had come with his training. But nothing matched the brutality of this old lady's end.

"Dear God," whispered Pannu.

Brandt was already out of the room, dashing up to the pension. At the doorway he paused. Pannu was at his shoulder, silent as a

shadow.
Brandt tried the handle. The door opened. He stepped into the room.
He saw two flashes of light and felt a sudden, unexpected heightening of his senses. He squeezed the Browning in reflex. The gun pitched in his hand.
He heard a scream of agony.
Brandt felt a burning wetness around his chest. He slipped to his knees and slid onto the floor. He could hear distant muffled sounds vibrating up from the ground. He heard his own laboured breathing ebb and flow. He was paralyzed. The last thing he saw before losing consciousness was a tall blonde woman.
Pannu set off across the room, slashing the kirpan. Two men were with the blonde. One had been hit by Brandt. He was falling slowly back clutching his stomach, crying out in pain. The other man produced two wicked spring-loaded knives from inside his coat sleeves. But Pannu had a longer reach. He sliced the man's throat open. A spray of blood rushed upwards. The man, clutching his throat, lurched toward the bathroom, exposing his back. Pannu ran him through with his sword, just above the lower ribs. The blade stuck, affording Hannah Wolfe time to take steady aim. The two men fell struggling over each other into the bathroom.
Hannah fired five times at close range into Pannu's broad back. The material around the entry wounds ignited, filling the room with the smell of singed material.
Satisfied that Pannu was dead, Hannah dragged Brandt away from the doorway and left him prone near her feet. He was bleeding heavily. She took his pistol and tossed it to Kahn.

"Get help. Shoot anything that isn't our organisation."

She lit a cigarette. Her hand was steady.

"I'm dying," Kahn said.

"Be a man. Get help. Now!"

He staggered through the door.
Hannah loaded a fresh clip into her gun.
Half an hour passed and then Eva Molenaar appeared silently at the doorway. The blood had drained from her features. She was

dressed in a long coat, a stylish broad brimmed hat and a small matching handbag.

"Take off your coat. Slowly," said Hannah Wolfe.

"I should've killed you in Italy."

"Life is full of regrets, ma cherie. I thought we'd killed you in Argentina and then you pop up in Lyon."

"Didn't get me that time, either."

"So I can see. You shouldn't have come here – wasn´t downstairs warning enough?"

"That poor old lady didn't deserve to die like that."

"She told me what I needed to know, eventually..."

Hannah levelled her gun steadily at Eva. Eva glanced around the room. The cognac bottle on the counter could be a useful club. Her other purse, containing a lipstick with the lid hollowed out for cyanide pills was in the bathroom. Her Beretta was under the floorboards where Hannah was standing. She spied on the dresser her vintage hand-held mirror; heavy and metallic – it had potential.

Brandt wasn't moving. Eva fought the urge to glance down, to look at him. The room smelled of cordite. Eva could feel hysteria rising through her chest. She fought the sudden gasp building in her throat.

Hannah Wolfe cocked the gun. Her hand was steady. Her gaze equally so.

"Let's drop the pretence, shall we, Eva. We'll soon have company."

"Anyone I know?"

"I´m afraid not, Eva. They'll have a few questions for you: you may find their manners a little ... distasteful. Your lover is dying by the way."

Her cold blue eyes were unwavering, steady. They were calculating, enjoying the moment.

"I'd give this fool another five or ten minutes. Let him go, Eva, he's not worth it, are any of them?" she smirked.

Eva held up her hands.

"He means nothing to me. I only used this place as a bolt-hole."

She saw a slight flicker across Hannah's eyes. A momentary cloud of doubt.

"If I'm going to die, how about a last cigarette?" said Eva.

Eva reached into her overcoat, slowly she produced a cigarette case.

Hannah's eyes flicked to Eva's cigarette case; it was slim and anonymous.

"You're the one with the gun, ma cherie?" said Eva.

Hannah Wolfe nodded.

"There´s coffee in the pot in there – if we're expecting company, let´s at least make ourselves comfortable."

"He's bleeding out and you want a coffee? Help yourself."

In Brandt's knapsack was an army medical kit. It had gauze, bandages and phials of morphine.

Eva casually tossed over the cigarette case. Without breaking eye contact Hannah picked it up and flipped it open. She drew a cigarette out with her lips and tossed the case back. With cool assurance, she produced a lighter and lit it. The lighter followed across the room. Hannah's eyes never once broke contact.

Eva picked up the case and lighter and lit one too. She casually threw the lighter back. Hannah's lightening reflexes caught it.

"May I?" asked Eva, nodding to the hob.

A small flame flickered under the pot in the kitchen.

"If you do anything, I'll put one in his brain, then I'll deal with you," said Hannah.

Fighting the tremors raging through her, Eva got to the hob. In a single movement, she grabbed the coffee pot and threw it at Hannah. It struck a glancing blow and Hannah squeezed off a reflex shot. The bullet showered Eva's hair with plaster. Dashing to the dresser, Eva hurled the long-handled mirror; it shattered across Hannah's forehead. Eva hunted desperately for something else to throw before Hannah steadied her aim. She was bleeding from a gash on her forehead, blood blinding her. She had to use a hand to wipe the blood away from her vision. Eva lunged at her, trying to wrestle the pistol free. Another shot rang out. Eva slapped Hannah, who lashed back with her free hand, leaving a smear of her blood across Eva's cheek. They both gripped the gun tightly. The two women fell among the mirror's shards. Hannah was wriggling free, the woman's strength surprising. Their gasps, punches and slaps filled the room. Eva managed to wrangle the gun free. With her free hand, Hannah Wolfe jabbed a splinter of the mirror deep into Eva's shoulder. With a hiss, Eva tried to elbow Hannah's nose. The gun spilled from her grasp; her hands greasy with blood.

The younger woman's writhing was working; in seconds she would be out from under Eva and within reach of the gun. Blood from their wounds made everything slippery. Eva's hand sought everything and anything. Scrabbling desperately, her fingers found a tapering shard of mirror. Before Hannah Wolfe was across the floor, Eva swung the shaft of glass high and brought it down onto the crown of Hannah's skull. The mirror drove in with a ferocious crack. Hannah's scream was choked with blood. She gasped her last onto Eva's blouse.

Eva pushed her aside and scrambled to Brandt.

So much blood.

Rolling him over she cradled his ashen face, tears mingled with the blood falling onto his face.

He was cold.

"Brandt," she whispered, "Oh, Brandt, No. no..."

She dashed to the bathroom. She stopped.

In the bath lay a man with a very high forehead, bad skin and a vicious line across his throat, a gaping, bloody hole. One leg dangled over the edge of the bath, the other was folded under him, covered in blood. Prone on the tiles, the tiles where Eva had washed and pleasured Brandt, lay Pannu.

Trembling, she felt for a pulse. Nothing. A faint gurgling gasp came from the man in the bath. Eva closed her eyes to his desperate, flickering glances. She walked back into the room and took Hannah's gun. It was a Makarov 9mm. Russian issue; not standard, modified for a smaller hand – a woman's hand. Hannah's eyes stared up at the ceiling, dead and somewhat surprised. Eva shot her through the forehead to be sure.

"Au revoir, ma cherie. No hard feelings."

She went back into the bathroom and put a bullet in the man's

high forehead.
She pulled towels from the presses. She filled the basin with cold water and soaked them. Rummaging in the knapsack she found the medical kit. She dashed back and rolled Brandt out. Two bullet holes were gouged brutally around his heart. His chest was doused in arterial blood. He was cold. She pressed the towels over them, pressed as hard as she could. But she couldn't stop the blood. She packed on the gauze and unrolled the bandages. Wracking with sobs, Eva tried to move the dead weight around. Brandt slid around limply. She tried her best.
Removing the morphine, Eva stared at the needles. There were two of them. Enough to kill a man.

"Brandt. Brandt. Say something?" she whispered.

It was too late. He was gone. The darkness that consumed her made her think of joining him. Why not? She had nothing to live for now; three years of searching and now he lay dead at her feet.
Eva screamed. She screamed long and hard until the nodes in her throat cracked.
She took a deep breath.

"No... Brandt. Jesus, no..."

He was dead. She cradled his head and kissed his mouth tenderly one last time. She looked down at herself, she was covered in blood. She tried to wash her hands in the sink, but Brandt's blood clung to her. She went back to the bathroom. Stripping quickly, she pulled the long shard of glass from her shoulder. Using the remaining gauze and bandages she patched herself up. She scrubbed her face of running make-up, blood and tears. She found her lipstick and popped open the secret compartment – four cyanide pills lay cradled in cloth. She re-applied her lipstick. Eva smelled of blood, perfume and sweat.
She picked her way across the glass and blood to the bedroom. A jumper, trousers – she hadn't time to unfasten her stockings and suspenders. She clenched back the tears at the sight of the bed. Eva packed the knapsack with essentials; morphine, the two pistols, blasting caps and clocks. In the bathroom she found Pannu's kirpan and threw it across the room. It landed beside the

knapsack. Hannah's body lay prone over the boards where Eva's Beretta lay hidden.

She was running out of time. Donning her greatcoat, she placed the kirpan inside it and found her hat.

She looked around the room one more time. It smelled like a midday butcher's shop, the very air cloying with blood.

Eva went to the window and glanced out through the curtains. The street was a hive of activity, the people below going about their daily chores seemingly unaware of the violent slaughter in the small, discreet pension above their heads. Then she saw the man. He staggered out of a phonebooth, clutching his stomach and waving a white handkerchief in the air. Blood was oozing out over his fingers. A second black Mercedes Benz pulled up alongside the first one. The wounded man collapsed into the arms of the first passenger who alighted. They looked up at the window.

Eva closed the curtains. The authorities couldn't discover this. She walked to the table. Opening the knapsack, she pulled a stick of explosive. In less than a minute, she had a timer and blasting caps primed on a piece of plastic explosive. She set the alarm clock for five minutes. For a moment, she thought of holding the bomb close to her. She looked back at Brandt. She rolled him on his side and placed the bomb underneath him.

"I'm sorry, Brandt. I love you."

She kissed his cheek and allowed a tear to fall.

"See you on the other side, Brandt."

Eva turned on the gas under the hob and opened the oven. The street outside seemed suddenly quiet. Pressing her ear against the pension door, Eva listened for a sound. Satisfied the corridor was empty, she slipped out.

Her shoulder was throbbing, and she put her hand into the greatcoat's pocket in case any droplets of blood fell. Pulling her hat low, with the knapsack on her shoulder like a fashionable bag, Eva took the steps two at a time.

At the doorway, she eased the latch and looked up and down the street. It was late afternoon and the sun was dipping toward the alps. The injured man was being tended to in the back seat of the newly arrived Mercedes. Curious on-lookers stopped to stare. Taking her cue, Eva strode across the street. Several buildings down, she spied a shop. Pausing in front of it, in the window´s reflection, she watched four men in black hats, black suits and raincoats climb out of the Mercedes and dash into the building. Eva was at the end of the street when the bomb under Brandt detonated.

She had to get to Chainbridge.

39

Plymouth

"It's the smelly one, sir, the *Gruyere*. It´s started again," said Cissy Beacon.

Bracken lumbered over to Cissy´s desk. A delicate china teacup and ornate strainer perched above newspapers and periodicals. They´d switched to sleeping all day and working through the early hours. Cissy, thriving in her new-found role, eschewed the shower facilities on the train in favour of dipping 'au naturale' in the Plymouth Sound to the "Trills of the dawn chorus".

"Did the U-boat ever respond to the previous messages?"

"No, sir. He's a good captain, a cool customer. *Smelly* here is sending an odd one. Seems there's been a security breach?"

Bracken afforded himself a grin. This was what he needed – Chainbridge was up to something and had smoked out a response. A warning. Obfuscate and thwart at every opportunity. They paused. The machines remained inactive, silent.

"This requires more tea, sir," said Cissy.

Bracken was about to go back to the dining car when a new

sound started. Cissy sat close and made a hushing sound. Her eyes were squeezed tight.

"I'm going to call this one '*Ahab*', she said.

"Why?"

"From *Moby Dick,* sir; because our clever U-boat captain is a very, very long way from home. You see, the signal is sporadic. His batteries are low, so he's not getting the strength of signal." She removed a pad from a pile of jotters and began deciphering as she spoke.

"*Ahab* is telling *Gruyere* something – it's a repeat signal. Long. *Smelly* has to respond with a confirmation."

Cissy hummed quietly as she worked. As suggested, Bracken came back with a pot of fresh tea.

"I'll do the straining, thank you, sir," she said.

The machines clacked and whirred, fueled by electrical impulses and atmospherics. The Marlborough had the very latest technology and Bracken knew he would have to forward everything on to the FO. MI6 in Bern would need alerting.

He stopped. After a beat, while Cissy scrawled, he logged a call to Plymouth Naval HQ.

He requested a solid brazier, a can of petrol and kindling. Just in case.

"Here you are, Mr Bracken," said Cissy.

Bracken looked at the decrypt;

ADQKHM * MDQN = CDMQHQ / 52D31
M00SN-13D23M21SE

"Is this all of it?" he asked.

"Yes, sir – repeated three times in full a five-minute break and then repeated three more times in full. It was the last one from the U-boat. Wherever he is, he's most likely out of power."

"You know this how, Cissy?"

"I was on the Convoy watch, sir. North Atlantic route."

Bracken went into the dining carriage and hunted along the chalk board still marked with Findlay's ingenious scrawl.

"Cissy."

Cissy strode in and craned her neck wildly as if looking for a book on a high shelf.

"We had a gentleman with us a few days ago – he was able to crack a code pretty quickly – Ah!"

Pinned behind a map of the Orkneys was a slip of paper. Stained and watermarked with tea was the Whip-saw code.

"The last part is probably co-ordinates. Fancy a stab at the first part?"

"Leave it with me, sir," she said.

"He mentioned Caesar somewhere in his notes."

"Caesar code, got it, sir!"

"...And Cissy?"

"Sir?"

"As quickly as possible please?"

"Yes sir."

Bracken jotted down "*ADQKHM * MDQN = CDMQHQ / 52D31M00SN-13D23M21SE.*"

He stared at the clock. It was three-thirty in the morning. Bracken got down to work. In the other room, Cissy coughed dryly and repeated out loud the code as if it were a mantra. Before long, she was singing out the letters as she worked.

40

Eva gulped down the vodka. It coursed through her bloodstream like icy venom.

"Brandt, Pannu," she said.

"Christ," whispered Chainbridge.

Mario had closed the restaurant for the evening, pulled the shutters down and turned off all the lights. He tended bar, setting the shots up one after the other.

"Gone," she whispered.

The tears had stopped. The grieving would come later – after the reckoning with Halidane.

"There was a lady, a lovely lady who owned the pension – she'd make such a fuss of Brandt. They killed her too. They showed her no mercy. Knives."

Mario poured another. Eva tossed the lemon out of it and downed it in one.

"Pannu killed one of them. I killed the other – she's – she was, a Nazi agent – Hannah Wolfe."

"Wolfe? I met in her in Italy – Count Orsini's companion," said Chainbridge.

"A real piece of work," said Eva.

"Her handler was rumoured to be Hermann Malleus. A wily old fox. In which case he may well be in the city."

"Halidane is working with the Reich?"

"Seems that way, Eva. Should we mention the possibility of a Nazi cell here on neutral soil to the authorities?"

"The Kantonspolizei are indifferent at best, unless you're a refugee," said Mario. "Right now, they're investigating a serious explosion. I keep a radio-transmitter here to track their broadcasts, so we know when a raid is coming. This explosion, this lady here wouldn't have had a hand in it?"

"I couldn't leave Brandt like that, just couldn't. I left the gas on and set a bomb. God knows what they'd have done to him," said Eva.

"Two Mercedes cars, six men in total. If you got the lot – including Hannah – it's a good day's haul," said Chainbridge.

He reached out and held her hand.

"You hit Halidane hard. He'll also think a possible female agent is dead and you can move freely. Revenge for Ann Chambrel, Curran, Gageby and Findlay."

"You hated Gageby, Henry."

Eva felt another huge sob welling. She drowned it in vodka.

"I did, but he didn't deserve to die," said Chainbridge.

He produced a garish cigarette case.

"You still have that awful thing, Henry."

Eva afforded herself a slight smile.

"My doctor won't approve," he said.

It was gold, with a bright red star and Russian cyrillic letters surrounding it. Chainbridge opened it and handed it around. The three of them smoked silently. The sounds of the city drifted in.

"A man that powerful will have informants in the police force, Henry," said Mario.

"The party is two days from tonight. Thankfully Swiss bureaucracy will thwart even a man as wealthy as Halidane. De Witte has a suite two floors below."

Eva winced and touched her shoulder.

"I need a bath," she said.

"Top of the stairs, first on the right. Leave everything out, I'll burn it tonight. Where will you get more clothes?"

"Renée Parez, he knows my size," said Eva.

"I'll leave you out a shirt. I think there's slacks around and a nightshirt – all clean. Use my bed; it´s clean too."

She took the vodka bottle with her.

"Eva?"

"Henry."

"Are you up to meeting Halidane tomorrow?"

"Yes, Henry, I am."

She shut the world behind her and stripped. She tossed the blood-stained clothes out onto the landing. The warm water enveloped her. Mario's tub was a big, deep cocoon. She washed around the wound inflicted by Hannah, then poured a hefty measure of vodka over it. At the party she would have to wear lace to cover it. On the inside sleeve, under a bandage, she'd pin the morphine phials. The cyanide would be in her lipstick. She closed her eyes and rested her head. As she soaked in the bath, she felt Brandt's blood washing away. There would be no funeral, no place of pilgrimage, no grave.

She drank and cried.

Brandt.

She dried herself, bundling herself up in towels. The smell of clean towels. That's when she realised everything was gone.

A wave of darkness, a cloying pall of black swept over her.

Outside Henry Chainbridge stood with dry clothes.

"I heard a scream."

"I'm sorry, Henry."

"Let me help you."

Henry crooked an arm and guided her to the bed. He averted his eyes as she climbed into an old, heavy night shirt. Henry pulled up a chair, sat down and kept vigil by her side. He sat with her, holding her hand and gently brushing her hair back, soothing her. Eva slipped into a sleep as dark and lonely as Brandt's.

She dreamt of fire and blood.

41

Plymouth

After hours working non-stop on the code, Bracken was desperate for sleep. Cissy had gone off for her dawn dip and was cycling back in a hurry. He watched her heave her unwieldy bike pell-mell towards *The Marlborough*, head bent, legs ploughing methodically. Her vast mane of hair dangled like an unhinged electrical storm. She sported a heavy duffle coat and battered wellingtons.

"Please tell me you're dressed under that, Cissy," said Bracken.

"The human body is a marvel, sir. Nothing to be ashamed of. I always ignored the nuns anyway, ha!

"So there I am paddling, d'you know-that-sort-of way, when it comes to me."

He looked at her blankly.

"The code."

Cissy coughed roughly for a few moments before catching her breath.

"*Smelly* has to respond. Why? Because he has something *Ahab* wants – he wants it so badly, he keeps asking for it, you know? So *Ahab* is losing his cool, showing his hand. Stamping his wooden leg, so to speak.

"The second part of the message is made up of co-ordinates – 52 degrees 31 minutes 00 seconds North, 13 degrees 23 minutes, 23 seconds. And *E* is?"

Bracken looked at the sheets of paper in his hand, then at Cissy.

"You have me at a loss, Cissy."

"*Berlin*, Mr Bracken! The second part of the code is Berlin. We were deciphering codes right up to the surrender, don´t forget. It was either these co-ordinates or 'Bear'– the symbol of Berlin. But I digress. I looked at Mr Findlay's – rather lovely – handwriting, I looked at his notes. The code *ADQKHM * MDQN = EDMQHQ* is a sliding code, and assuming it's the letter to the right ..."

Bracken quickly scrawled out; ***BERLIN * NERO = FENRIR***

"A Nero directive," he said.

"A what, sir?"

"One of Hitler's 'scorched earth' directives; areas lost to the enemy must be made uninhabitable. 'Even the cities must burn,' to quote Goebbels."

"Isn't that good, sir? The Germans started the bloody war."

"No, Cissy, it´s not good at all. Now there are close to two million British, French and American troops in Berlin, trying to keep the Russians from over-running the place."

´ "Aren't they our allies, sir?"

Bracken sat back and ran his fingers through his hair. His skin had taken on a bloodless pallor.

"What on earth is Fenrir?" he said.

"Library opens at ten this morning, I'll take a trundle down there."

"Before you do that, Cissy, I need to start sending a few dispatches."

"Will do, just need to get dressed, sir."

Bracken was guessing *Smelly* was in fact Halidane who had access to a weapon codenamed *Fenrir*. If *Ahab* was the U-boat, who aboard would be able to give that order?

"Who´s is the wooden leg?" he murmured.

"Beg pardon, sir?"

"Nothing, Cissy."

Hitler? Bormann? Eichmann? None of these men had yet been found. 'Even the cities must burn ...'

"No time, Cissy, start transmitting – standard code to MI6. Send one coded dispatch to Whitehall, another to the Bern desk, Charlottenburg HQ Berlin, and one to this device."

"Who's this, sir?"

"Henry Chainbridge. Flag it as urgent."

"Henry Chainbridge, sir?"

"Yes, Cissy. Time is of the essence; he may well have encountered *Smelly*."

42

The Cafe Sprüngli, Zürich

Edgar Halidane checked his silver Dunhill watch for the umpteenth time. He began to think she wasn't going to show. He ordered another coffee, insisting the waiter pour from a pot. He would never allow his tin mug to be taken away for fear of it never returning.

Reaching for a toothpick from a small crystal dispenser, he worried a piece of grime from under a thumbnail.

The waiter loitered.

"Let's give the lady a few minutes more," said Halidane.

The waiter moved back a discreet distance.

According to Berlin, the OSS had been found nosing around the target site but hadn't requested that it be opened. They had been escorted off the site without incident. Despite this news, Halidane appeared unconcerned.

Mercier sat outside in the Rolls Royce, keeping watch. Malleus had argued for an armed escort, but Halidane never doubted Mercier´s readiness, and he had plenty of firepower at his disposal.

Halidane took a napkin and produced an elegant fountain pen; a rich tortoiseshell of ambers, reds and gold, with a silver nib. He etched out formulae, numbers and equations, filling the white space with dense lines and numbers.
The Fenrir would have to be consecrated below the greenhouse. After that, Halidane would send the shell into Berlin. He would transmit the details to Berlin. The maths would be challenging, to say the least. If Kaspar Bellowes crossed his mind, it didn't show. The men guarding the Berlin site were also expendable.
Halidane´s auspicious date was now seventy-two hours away. He closed his eyes, practising the rites and incantations in his head. He´d studied Hoeberichts closely at Whip-saw while working on Olivia, impervious to her pleas. Halidane would stain the weapon in the same fashion – this time in Ingrid Lindemann's blood.

"Miss me?" said a voice.

Halidane looked up and gave a gasp. Eva was dressed up in a stunning stone-coloured tweed trouser suit; the jacket tailored neatly into her waist. Her blouse was angled in a steep V and a deep blue silk scarf somehow managed to both mask and accentuate her cleavage at the same time. A broad-brimmed hat finished off her appearance. She held her stylish sunglasses with the poise of a ballerina. Eva looked intense, her lips a deep blood red. In the spring light coming through the windows, her skin had the luminosity of a rare pearl. Her flawless skin had only the slightest blush and her long lashes framed those grey-green eyes that held the gaze and never wavered.
Ingrid, the grown-up version of Anna Chambrel. They had met here until she'd exposed herself as a child and a spy. And not a virgin.

"Yes, Ingrid, I did," he said.

He stood and pulled the chair out for her.

"I bought you a present. I saw it and I thought of you."

Eva handed him a gold money clip, with an embossed horse-shoe motif.

"Bought it or purloined it, Ingrid?" he grinned.

It glowed in the sunlight as he held it up. It was deceptively heavy.

"Bought it, Edgar, really! I considered having it engraved." She unslung her bag. Inside it was Hannah's Makarov 9mm, fully loaded. Eva had to hand it to the girl, it was an easy piece to use. She pictured firing it into Halidane's face, shattering the jaw, his eyes wide with surprise.

"That looks interesting," she said, eyeing his notes.

"I'm a mathematician," he said. "I met Einstein once. Right here in this city, but you weren´t even born then."

"You're not that old! I find a meeting of minds more powerful than physical attraction, don´t you"

"You don't find me attractive?"

"Not in a conventional way, I will be honest, Edgar, but I'm drawn to your mind."

"They are calculations, Ingrid. Calculations, nothing more,"

"They look like musical notation. You know, Edgar, music and maths are closely intertwined. May I? Just for fun?"

She reached out to take the napkin. Halidane folded it up tightly and pulled it away.

"This would be beyond your understanding."

He didn't like Ingrid's sudden assurance. He didn't like her trying to take control.

"Use the clip, it´ll make you look like a rich man," grinned Eva.

She fought the urge to end Halidane there and then, but Chainbridge had been insistent. Don't kill him. Yet.

"I meant what I said about a meeting of minds. I know nothing of romance, love... sex."

She lifted her eyes and held his gaze. Edgar Halidane felt a rush of lust. The very air around her was electric. His body thrilled to her stockinged foot roving slowly up his leg.

Her demeanour was coy above the table, but beneath it her snaking toes were working a dangerous magic, like a fan dancer in the Chez Paree in Chicago.

"I have a suite, a private suite, Ingrid," he said.

"Mr Halidane, are you trying your luck?"

"I have my lucky clip. There's a party at The Hotel Prestige au Lac, along the lakefront. I'd love you to be my guest."

"That's a very exclusive hotel, Edgar."
Her voice was somehow deeper. It was a drone of bees in a lavender patch, somehow reassuring and tempting at the same time. It was full of promise.

"For a very exclusive girl."
Halidane reached into his jacket pocket and handed her a gilt-edged invitation. Eva opened it and read it.

"Tomorrow? Yes, Edgar I'd love to."
Mercier alighted from the Wraith.

"Duty calls, Ingrid."

"You must be a very important mathematician, Edgar."

"Economics, money, banking," he said.

"Sounds important."
He noticed her wince as she put on her hat and glasses.

"Tennis injury," she smiled. "Do you play?"

"No."

"I could teach you. Does the hotel have a tennis court?"

"No. I got rid of it,"

"Why, Edgar?"

"To make room for my greenhouse."

"They allowed you to do that?"

"Ingrid, I can do whatever I want," he said.

"You can show me that after the party?"

"I can guarantee it, Ingrid."
She pecked him on the cheek.

"I'll leave you to it then, Edgar. See you later, alligator."
Edgar felt her lips burn on his old cheek like a branding iron. He watched her leave. He pocketed the café's crystal tooth-pick holder and stuffed a few lumps of sugar into his pocket for muching on the drive. He pulled on a coat and strode out of the café.

Wrapped up in watching Eva's long legs, he collided with a man, knocking the walking cane out of his hand.

"Watch your fucking step, bub!"
The man raised his hands in apology and slowly picked up the cane. Raising his hat, he smiled.

Halidane climed into the Wraith.

"Stupid old fool," he muttered.
Mercier looked at Halidane through the rear-view mirror,
"We need to talk to Malleus. Then you can take me to the meeting."
Mercier nodded. The Wraith slipped out into the early morning traffic.
Safely around the corner, Chainbridge took out Halidane's gold money clip with the folded napkin inside. He ordered a paper from a nearby kiosk.
"Now what are you up to, Halidane?" he murmured.
He wrapped the clip up in the newspaper, then glanced carefully up and down the street before crossing over to catch the tram to Mario´s.

***

Eva took the tram to Bahnhof. She purchased a ticket to the mountain resort where Brandt kept an old disused shepherd's croft. As Eva boarded the Pullman, she fought the waves of nausea welling up. Her hand shook slightly as she took out a cigarette. She opened out Edgar Halidane's gilt-edged invitation. The font was cursive and florid.
'*Mr Edgar Halidane invites Miss Ingrid Lindemann as his private guest to attend a celebration at The Hotel Prestige au Lac, Thursday 25th April 1946. Formal wear. 8pm Sharp. RSVP.*'
The flowery script somehow made the invitation look cheap rather than elegant. At the bottom in tiny script Halidane had scrawled;
'A small blood test may be required – EH.'
A blood test? Eva pondered this. The Swiss countryside flowed by. She closed her eyes, enjoying the warmth and sunlight. She dozed for an hour, allowing the simple pleasure of travel to dull her pain.
At the small picturesque station, she waved down a taxi. They navigated a roadblock of cows meandering to their meadows and climbed a steep incline with grinding gears. Eva paid the driver and asked him to come back at first light.

"I'll need you to drive me to Zürich," she said, "I'll give you another $100 when we get there."

The old pot of lavender was still outside the crofter's door. The plants were bending towards the sun in a dense, fragrant cluster. Reaching under it, she found the key. Inside, a faint sheen of dust covered the floor. There were a few old pots and pans in the kitchen. The battered sofa where Eva had nursed Brandt's broken ribs after Norway was still covered in an old crocheted throw. Eva threw open the Windows, allowing the Alpine air in. She hoped that if Brandt's spirit was still loitering in purgatory, maybe it would find a little sanctuary here.

Eva found Brandt's mountaineering equipment and fed out the long lines of rope through her hands. He had been taken so suddenly from her it was almost as if he´d never been there in the first place. His boots, creased and battered, stood neatly side-by-side with crampons, an ice axe and a flare gun. In the bedroom, an old jumper of his hung from a peg. She put it on.

In a press in the kitchen, she found an old jar of instant coffee. Walking out, she started towards the old pump. The Alps swept out before her in dizzying hues of white, blue and grey. She cranked the old pump with her good arm and filled a small pail. She found an old portable stove and lit it. She took a light for her cigarette, bundled herself up in an old blanket and sat sipping coffee on a crude bench that Brandt had knocked together.

Eva suddenly felt grounded. This old cottage had given her roots; somewhere to run to. Even Chainbridge knew nothing of this place.

Smoking, Eva closed her eyes and imagined Brandt was there, his arms around her.

43

Zürich

It was just the two of them this morning. Malleus concentrated on his strokes, forcing every doubt, every fear, every pang of loss into the simple action of forward propulsion. When doubts wormed their way into his concentration, Martin nudged him gently back into lane with the long pole.

One phone call to a well-connected friend had confirmed the worst. A gas explosion. Hannah, Pfeiffer and Kahn dead. Their support team dead. The two Mercedes thrown across the street and flattened.

Malleus scrambled for the bar as it tilted wildly in his goggled vision. As water plunged into his nostrils and mouth, he heard Martin's echoing encouragement. Malleus grabbed the bar and caught his breath.

Hannah was gone. A firebrand but a ruthless and efficient agent, nevertheless. This hurt him deeply even though she had scorned his advances. Her private suite at The Hotel Storchen had been shut down, her personal effects destroyed. Her enormous private wealth had been transferred to Ausland Organisation Swiss bank accounts. It had been a busy night.

Questions would be asked. A simple warning to other agencies sniffing around Halidane Corp., had ended in a bloody fiasco with the Swiss authorities all over it like a rash.

Miraculously no passers-by had been injured, otherwise no amount of money could have kept the canton's prosecutors at bay.

Malleus pushed off the wall and swam another length.

He knew he was expendable. And without his angel of death, Herman Malleus was also vulnerable.

After eight more lengths his bad leg started dragging. Martin helped him out. Malleus then had a lengthy sauna.

Martin wasn't at his station. He wasn't in the massage room. Halidane and Mercier were waiting for Malleus in the changing rooms.

"I´ve instigated my own investigation, Malleus," said Halidane. "Seems this explosion was no accident."
Malleus´s wet towel dropped to the floor and although Halidane was unfazed, Mercier averted his eyes. Malleus limped over to his locker and started to pull a shirt on. His jacket was hanging just a little too high; his gun was inside it.

"One unidentified body, we think it´s a man. His injuries are consistent with a hand grenade."

"Herr Halidane, my people only carried small firearms and knives."

"The place is nothing but rubble now, Malleus," said Halidane.
He made a motion. Mercier glided out from behind his master and picked up the towel from the floor.

"I said to send a warning. Didn´t I say that? Didn´t I say that, Mercier?
Mercier nodded. Slowly, methodically, he wound the towel into a tight, wet rope.

"Instead, Mae -fucking-West and her goon squad turn a sleepy little Strasse into a fucking war zone ..."
Mercier stared into the middle distance, as if he was somehow separate from the proceedings. Halidane threw something to Malleus.

"Found on the body of the unidentified man."
Malleus held it up. It was an aviator´s watch, big and bulky with a cracked face. Blood had been wiped from the bezel and crystal.

"Well, actually, just his arm; there´s nothing left of the rest of him. One of yours wear this?"

"No, Herr Halidane."

"OK Malleus, I´ll give you a clue here; it´s British."
Mercier had taken two steps and was suddenly eye level with Malleus. In an instant, the towel was wrapped around his throat. With measured twists, Mercier began to tighten it. On the tiled floor, Malleus' bad leg gave out. He tried to grab the locker door, but Mercier hoisted him away from it.

"A bomb goes off and we find a British watch beside a Browning 9mm. Didn't I say 'no more mistakes'? Maybe I'm goin'

deaf, but I could've sworn you said OK?"
Malleus´ breathing was cut off, his bad leg sought purchase. Mercier kicked the other one out and Malleus' dead weight suddenly compounded the constriction. His fingers groped for the towel and his eyes began to bulge.

"Goodbye Malleus," said Halidane.

Mercier put his shoulders into the final twist.

44

Plymouth

Cissy Beacon carefully set down the code as the transmitter clicked out Chainbridge's message. Both the *Smelly* and *Ahab* ENIGMAs had fallen silent. The machine clicking away was an old Polish one that hadn't been used in years. Before it sprang to life, Cissy had devoured several periodicals and the newspaper. Three library books added to her cluttered pile. Jammed into the pages of a battered encyclopaedia – under the letter F – was a manila envelope. Apparently, *Fenrir* was a monstrous wolf from Norse mythology, a demon.

"Well, Hitler always called the Nordic regions his 'zone of destiny'," said Bracken.

"Mr Chainbridge has just transmitted these – says Halidane jotted them out."

"Formulae, maths symbols – any ideas, Cissy?"

If Findlay had been here, he'd have smacked his lips, called for whiskey and devoured this.

"Cryptarithmns are my speciality sir, d'you-know? I'm OK with numbers, but this is advanced calculus, sir."
Cissy's brash assurance had faltered for a second. But she was all he had.
"I'll give it a go, sir," she said.
Having lain dormant for over a week *The Marlborough* was now re-energised. The FO had stopped hounding Bracken to explain himself. Instead, the slow wheels of Whitehall, the Admiralty and MI6 were grinding into action.
He had Roswick Dowling at RAF Skaebrae in the Orkneys to thank. The destroyer battle group hadn't found an island. But they did find two bodies floating in the sea, two bodies dressed in Waffen SS Wiking Korps uniforms. A captured German U-boat and two bodies lying in a temporary morgue in Kirkwell was enough for the agencies to act.
Cissy was about to be relieved by Naval decryption officers. Bracken needed her one more time.
"Any luck, Cissy?"
From the communications carriage came a long, breathless sequence of coughs.
"I've only just bloody-well sat down Mr Bracken, please don't shout."
He heard her humming and faintly singing. For once, he wished she'd stop being so bloody cheerful all the time.
Bracken had the Berlin co-ordinates laid out on the table. Carefully, as if playing a game of patience, he laid out the pages; Chainbridge's notes, Findlay's notes, the last transcripts of the three Spitfires. Photographs transmitted to a machine the Americans had installed for Churchill produced an image of two dead SS soldiers drenched in the waters of the North Sea.
Over these he placed Cissy's transcriptions and notes. Across the table, a fortnight of communications made a mosaic of something very sinister indeed. A fortnight of murder and mayhem in the shadows. He was still waiting for the OSS and Charlottenburg to respond.
"The best I can do, Mr Bracken," said Cissy.
"What is it?"

"If you ask me, sir, it's a time, a specific time, followed by a series of degrees, minutes and seconds. But they're not ordinance or location details. I wrote them out and tossed them around."

"and...?"

"They seem to be a direction in degrees, minutes and seconds only – very unusual – no hours. From above, below and across at the same point, at the same time. Here."

Cissy's small, strong, unadorned finger drew a decreasing circle around the numbers and symbols.

"It looks like a mathematical target. A pin-point target."

"In Berlin?"

"Best guess, yes."

"Thank you, Cissy."

Outside Churchill's armoured train, a group of jeeps and trucks pulled up. Peaked white caps, naval braiding and heavily armed marines stepped out.

"It's out of our hands now, isn't it, Mr Bracken?"

"I'm afraid, so," he replied, "The cavalry has finally decided to get off its fat arse and arrive. Thank you, again, Cissy,"

"Thank you, Mr Bracken. It was a pleasure to be in the thick of it again, d'you-know?"

"The pleasure was all mine, Cissy, all mine."

45

Zürich

The Hotel Prestige au Lac was situated along the far end of Seefelquai, close to the Chinese Gardens, with a sweeping view of the lake. A former health resort, the hotel had been rebuilt and refurbished in Art Nouveau style, softening its former Kurhaus severity. The signage was muted, in contrast to the bold flags of America, France and England swaying on white poles alongside the Swiss Cross. Ornate cypress trees bordered the exquisitely manicured terraces and pebbled walkways, offering shade from the warm sun.

Peter de Witte felt its rays through his panama hat, across his hands and along his comfortable slacks. He had been blind for close to forty years. The images that flitted through his head, or the aural images he processed while people talked, always had a certain sepia tinge. Braille allowed information to travel through his nervous system and he was more attuned to the world as a series of multiple sensory dimensions than a collective image.

"The greenhouse held close to a thousand species of orchid. Since last month, it has been completely off-limits, ostensibly for maintenance and an overhaul of the underground heating system. Halidane has paid for the removal and upkeep of all the plants until the renovations are finished. He has private security – discreet, mind you – watching it at all times. Access to and from the greenhouse is through the walled gardens behind the hotel – a single doorway with rotating security rosters."

Henry Chainbridge looked around the hotel grounds. Light shimmered on the Zürichsee, turning the water silver. A pleasure boat drifted along, its sail fluttering and flapping with the vagaries of the breeze.

"Armed?"

"The concierge became very reticent when I asked him that, Henry."

"Safe to assume so then."

De Witte always pictured Chainbridge as a young man. They´d met a few times on the boat to Russia; as volunteers they were willing to do whatever it took to halt the Bolshevik revolution. Back then Chainbridge had thick black hair giving him a thin, crow-like aspect. Shocked by de Wittes injuries sustained during the rout at Murmansk, Chainbridge sat beside him on the homeward journey, chatting to him and changing his clotted bandages.

"the views of the lake are spectacular," said Chainbridge

"I'll take your word for it," replied de Witte, "though room service managed to find me a fine cognac a Martel XO. Helped me settle in,"

"Halidane's floor?"

"Third floor, completely sealed off. The elevator stops at the second floor. The door is sealed from the stair-well. Only a special pass can allow access. I don't know what the passes look like, so I couldn't lift one."

"When´s he due back?"

"Tonight, after the conference. The concierge is quite tickled that the Americans, French and British are getting nowhere with reparations – or access to Swiss bank accounts."

"That should put Halidane sufficiently on edge."

The two men considered this.

"Eva's missing," said Chainbridge.

"No, Henry, Eva's preparing – there´s a difference. Don't worry, my friend, she´ll show."

He raised a finger and with a smile, added:

"I received a gift this morning, I have an old friend in Portugal, a Jesuit. He sees me as a worthy opponent and a sinner worth saving."

"I think we're both beyond that."

Chainbridge was never one to judge. Of course, he knew all about Eva's relationship with de Witte. Together, they had been daring agents in pre-war Europe. But the advent of Brandt had changed everything.

Reaching down into his satchel, de Witte pulled out a travel chess set. He handed it to Chainbridge.

"Below the tray you'll find another drawer."

"Exquisite workmanship, a real antique."

"Old men and priests, Henry, who pays attention to the likes of us?"

He found the hidden drawer with his nail and popped it. A thin line of correspondence unrolled. Chainbridge glanced around. A few guests were checking out and loading their cars. Two newly-weds were taking a stroll along the pathway close to the shore.

"I'm a little rusty with braille, old man."

De Witte registered the faint degradation of age in Chainbridge's voice.

"Nazi cells all over Europe – Spain, Portugal, Sweden and Denmark – have reactivated. They´re on the move, Henry."

"There will always be a few who get through the net, Peter."

"Their communications have suddenly streamlined. Militarily, they're defeated, but the wealth, technology and plunder accumulated during the rampage is still unaccounted for. Halidane Corp. is a continual thread, Henry. The last part is interesting."

Chainbridge ran the braille through and stopped.

"Malleus, liquidated? That right?"

"Yes."

"The AO hierarchy won't like that."

"Last piece is from Bracken."

A German U-boat somewhere in the Southern Atlantic was directing Halidane. Chainbridge´s fingers paused on the last item.

"Nero directive?"

"Halidane has been instructed to fulfil Hitler's dying wishes."

Chainbridge took out his cigarette case and lit two Turkish blends. He handed one to de Witte, then set fire to the sere embossed strip of braille paper. It burned readily. Chainbridge tipped the ashes onto the ground and kicked them into the breeze.

"If Brandt were alive, we'd have some chance," said de Witte.

"Eva's equal to the task."

Chainbridge studied his friend. If de Witte was pleased Brandt was gone, it didn't show.

"His old comrades in arms?"

"Like those ashes, Peter, scattered across Europe. We have to assume they're dead."

"Then it´s just Eva?"

"Just Eva, Peter."

They smoked in silence.

The crunch of a waiter's shoes made them look around.

"I'm sorry to bother you, gentlemen, can I get you anything?"

"Tea, thank you," said de Witte.
And a small miracle, thought Chainbridge.

"Will the gentleman be staying for lunch? Chef has several excellent specialities I could recommend?"

"Thank you but no. The gentleman won't be here for long."

"Ah, the conference must have ended early," said the waiter.

Chainbridge followed his gaze.

A Rolls Royce Wraith with fluttering stars and stripes pennants drove sedately up the drive. Several other high-performance cars, festooned with flags, followed. Behind them cruised three black Mercedes Benz saloons. Even from their table on the southern terrace, Chainbridge could make out the forms of four men per car.

"Looks important," said Chainbridge,

"A private party, the guests are arriving. Gentlemen, if that will be all?"

Chainbridge watched the waiter stride back towards the hotel.

"Will you be safe here?"

"Absolutely, Henry – who's going to pay attention to an old blind man?"

The tea arrived in exquisite china and silver. Chainbridge and de Witte smoked and chatted. To the casual observer, they looked like two louche retirees enjoying the spring sunshine.

"I'd better hang around, just in case," said Chainbridge.

"I have Dr Pannu's kirpan with me, Henry."

"It should be returned to his people, Peter."

"It will be, Henry – when this is all over."

Chainbridge watched the bellhops and a bowing concierge welcome the newly arrived guests.

"The odds are against us, Peter."

"They always are, though, Henry. They always are."

46

It was all down to atomics or 'humantics' as Einstein liked to call it. Humantics, atomics, infinitesimal patterns. The IBM corporation developed a huge scanner with the intention of transporting information or even objects. But Edgar Halidane had been far more ambitious. His experiments during the Reich saw test subjects ripped apart. Believing that modern educated Europeans were more highly evolved, he switched to untermensch subjects. They too had been shredded by the forces he generated.

But he knew it was possible.

Sitting in the back seat of the Rolls, Halidane watched the hotel glide towards him. He closed his leather-bound folio of sketches and designs and absently tapped the old tin mug on his knee. Tin was the solution. This same tin mug had successfully departed the 'jump gate' in his underground chamber at Fawkeston Gyre, skipping across the planet and boomeranging back in seconds, using each separate chamber as a stepping-stone.

On the strength of this he´d had a special suit commissioned; a suit made entirely of tin. The *Fenrir* artillery shell sitting snug between the rails in his chamber below the Prestige au Lac had been completely re-clad in tin as well. It would carve through the earth's electro-magnetic fields like a bayonet through time.

"The girls have arrived, sir," said Mercier.

A long limousine pulled up and two women alighted; Birgit, the secretary from his reception area, and Ingrid Lindemann. They looked up at the hotel, each fashionably attired and shimmering in sunglasses.

"Excellent, Mercier. Did they give you any trouble?"

"No, sir."

Edgar Halidane was about to unleash Armageddon across the border and he was thrilling to the prospect. Birgit's blood would consecrate the artillery shell lying in the chamber below in the greenhouse. Ingrid's would consecrate his suit.

Halidane noticed Ingrid had a large bag, almost the size of a knapsack, over her shoulder. He assumed it contained a change of clothes. 'Too bad, she'll be dead by 9pm,' he thought.
The afternoon session with its fruitless and frustrating meetings had left no mark on Halidane. He sidled up to the women and kissed their hands;

"Good afternoon, ladies, so glad you made the rendezvous!"

Men in dark suits with tightly cropped hair and sunglasses emerged from each car. They dashed to the back doors. Eva noted the tell-tale bulge of a shoulder holster in more than one jacket. Looking around, the hotel and its grounds seemed surprisingly isolated, with the broad sweep of the lake and trees past the wide terraces.

"Where shall we put them, sir?" whispered Mercier.

Eva noticed his hands kept clenching and unclenching. He was like a coiled spring.

"Juice them up at the bar, let´s get settled in."

The conference delegates, six in all, were dressed in top hats and frock coats. Halidane sprang over to them with the energy of a politician; all 'hail-fellow-well-met.' Mercier strutted behind, like a well-fed vulture. They were ushered from their embassy vehicles to the small restaurant behind ornate crystal panels, their patent leather shoes soundless on the deep red carpet. Cocktails were prepared and laughter soon pealed out. Halidane had promised a feast for the eyes and the senses. But first he had to prepare.
He sent the concierge out to Eva and Birgit, insisting he take them to the ladies´ bar.
With Mercier at this elbow, Halidane rode up to the third floor in the elevator.

"We'll send for Birgit, Mercier. Start on her first," he said.

They were met by one of Halidane´s personal security team. He was lean and toned and twitching with anticipation.

"We'll make sure you have some sport with the ladies too, son," grinned Halidane.

The young man gave a salute and took his post at the elevator door.

They walked along the narrow corridor. A large dining table in one room was laid out with a series of name cards and the little paper flags of the respective nations. In the middle of the table stood two larger American flags. The preparations were somewhat different but no less thorough in the rooms which lay beyond the dining suite. Restraints, ties, chains and implements lay coiled and ready. Leather aprons and masks hung menacingly on pegs. The teeth of a cat-of-nine-tails glinted wickedly in the light beside a set of handcuffs. At the far end of the corridor was an ornate tiled bath and shower room. A surgical table stood centrally. To the left of it, a dentist's chair with wrist and ankle restraints was tilted horizontally. A tray of scalpels and tourniquets lay in surgical spirits. Mercier's sterile playground was ready for the first girl.

***

René Parez had a good eye, thought Eva, as she caught her reflection in a full-length mirror. The dress was a shimmering black sequined cocktail dress, nipped in at the waist. Beneath it, her underwear was expensive silk and lace. Knowing her intimately, Parez had bought well, enhancing her confidence and freedom of movement.

Birgit and Eva had been ushered into the smaller white-walled bar on the ground floor. Intricate metal light fixtures hung overhead. A narrow window allowed the early evening light in, launching hues of vermillion across the plain white ceiling. A dour young barman mixed drinks for the two of them.

Halidane had purchased privacy on a grand scale; it felt more like a country mansion than an exclusive hotel. There were hardly any guests. The expansive spaces exuded the atmosphere of a cloistered ruin.

Finishing off her first Martini, Birgit was already giggling loudly. Eva suspected there was more than just alcohol in the glass. Birgit motioned for another. Eva excused herself to go to the bathroom, hoisted up the knapsack and walked out in the reception area, pouring the contents of her glass into a potted plant. She had to either stow or hide the bag before it was

searched. Then she spied Chainbridge. He was perusing a stack of newspapers. Eva stood beside him momentarily.
She dropped the knapsack at his feet.
The laughter from the restaurant grew louder. Champagne corks popped like gunshots.

"Gun, flare gun, extra ammunition," she whispered.
Chainbridge slid the bag between his feet.

"Flare gun? OK. I've taken a wee stroll around. There´s only one way in and out," he murmured. "The elevator. The third floor is completely sealed off, no access by the stairs either."

"Henry, I know. It's a one-way trip."
They stepped apart from each other when Birgit's shrill voice filled the reception. She was skittish on her heels and laughing. Mercier, looming over her, guided her to the elevator.

"Eva, the names are all there. In that restaurant beyond. Whatever Halidane is up to now, we must have the names."

"He killed Brandt, Henry,"

"The greenhouse, Eva, think on that. The greenhouse is the reason why we're here. We need to get him to it. We need him to show us what he's up to."

"I'll think on it," she replied.
Eva's eyes glittered with hatred. He'd never seen such anger.

"There's only myself and Peter here, Eva," he whispered.

"All the cavalry, then," said Eva.
The elevator had reached the third floor.

"Goodbye, Henry," she said over her shoulder. "No funeral, OK?"

"No funeral, Eva."
Chainbridge hoisted the bag and stepped outside to the walled garden that led to the greenhouse. He decided he was going to start a fire. He stood and watched the sunset across the alps, taking a moment. The frozen peaks were a myriad of yellows, reds and purple. The lake was gradually turning from glittering silver to black. He took a deep breath and ambled towards the walled garden at the back of the hotel.
She pressed for the elevator. It descended slowly, aged gears and wheels clunked and groaned. Impatiently, she pressed the

button in quick jabs. The elevator stopped and hung behind the door for an interminable pause. Then, it started up again with its arthritic descent. The door opened.

She already had the cyanide out of her lipstick cap when it stopped at the third floor.

"Miss?"

Eva was applying her lipstick in the polished mirror wall of the elevator. She turned and smiled at the guard. He was young, British and suddenly sweating at the sight of her.

"Oh, please, I'm sorry, Edgar is expecting me."

She pretended to be drunk, bending over and struggling for her invitation from her tiny purse. She allowed him a generous view of her cleavage.

"Allow, me."

He stepped into the elevator. She was smiling helplessly.

"You're a handsome boy, my word, yes, you are," said Eva.

She leaned up to him to offer a drunken kiss. He responded. Eva used her tongue – to push two cyanide tablets into his mouth. A sudden uppercut to the jaw shattered the capsules.

He was dead within seconds.

Taking the young guard´s gun, Eva suddenly realized the Browning must have been Brandt´s – she recognised a deep score along the grip. If they had Brandt's gun, perhaps she´d find other items belonging to him.

Eva dragged the guard's body out of the elevator and into one of the bedrooms. Advancing along the corridor she spied the empty dining room with name cards laid out on the table but was stopped in her tracks by a scream, a shrill howl from the depths of a woman's soul.

Birgit.

Mercier appeared in a doorway at the far end of the corridor, dressed in a surgical gown smeared in blood. A scalpel glinted in his fist.

Eva fired repeatedly, hitting him in the chest, neck and face. As she walked toward him, she kept firing until he tilted backwards like a felled oak.

Eva stepped over the threshold into the bathroom. Birgit was strapped to a chair, tilted back at an extreme angle, her hair pulled over her shoulder. Her wrists were cut, her throat and abdomen a vision of gore.

Under each twitching hand, trays were filling with her blood. Her eyes stared dead at the doorway.

Edgar Aloys Halidane stood naked beside her. His flaccid penis twitched idly. A dimpled gut hung over his pubis. A crystal goblet was already half full of blood. Eva calculated she had four bullets left in the Browning.

He turned and knocked over a tray of Birgit's blood. He slipped and dropped the goblet.

Eva stepped around the blood. She took off her heavy coat and placed it over Birgit. From her bandaged arm, she produced a phial of morphine and jammed it into Halidane's neck.

Halidane took the hit and slumped to his knees. As the narcotic took hold everything began to move out of phase. He could hear Eva somewhere at the back of his mind.

"Get dressed, Edgar. I want to see your greenhouse," she whispered.

A wave of euphoria washed over him. It made him more agreeable.

"Now, Edgar,"

"Sure thing, doll."

In a small ante-room Eva spied black silk robes with deep red cuniform symbols hanging from pegs. She donned one, pulling the huge cowl over her head.

She found Halidane struggling into his pants. He was sliding around in a pool of blood, grinning to himself.

"Quickly, now," she said.

Eva darted back to the dining suite, sweeping the name cards into the pockets of her voluminous robe. When she got back Halidane was more-or-less dressed, though fixing his tie seemed beyond him. She helped him with it.

"I have a luscious new orchid waiting for you," she said.

"Ooh, I can't wait," he said.

"Show me," she whispered.

"My pleasure, doll," he smiled.

Parking Halidane in the doorway, Eva looked back at the tray of surgical spirits. She reached into the pocket of the coat and found her lighter. She struck it and threw it onto the tray. A good sized blaze started immediately.

***

A nail-clip moon hung low over the clouds, offering little illumination. The lights from the hotel spilled weakly over the walled garden as Chainbridge picked his way along. The walls along the hedgerows were higher than a man, adding to the gloom. He turned a corner and saw the first body on the stone walkway. It was a man dressed in black. Chainbridge rolled him over. He had been stabbed repeatedly in the chest and stomach. Further down, a second body lay sprawled in a clump of dried grasses. A leg jutted out awkwardly over the border. The faint light glinted on the hilt of Pannu's kirpan, which was sticking out of the man's neck. Then Chainbridge saw de Witte.

He peered around in the dark.

"Peter," he whispered.

Nothing.

Rummaging around in Eva's bag, Chainbridge´s fingers settled on the flare gun. It would have to do. He hoped it was loaded.

"Peter?"

No sound.

His joints groaned and popped as he went down on one knee. He took out his lighter and struck it. He held it up to de Witte's face. He shut his eyes and sighed.

Peter de Witte had been shot through the right temple at close range. Half of his skull on the left-hand side was missing. Blood and brain matter spewed from the open wound.

"Rest in peace, old friend," he whispered.

At least death had been instant, he thought. It didn't stop the welling up of tears. Chainbridge gave his eyes a wipe with his gnarled hand.

De Witte´s death spoke of at least one more armed guard nearby. Under his breath, Chainbridge cursed himself for not mapping out the walled garden while he´d had the chance. His

breathing laboured in his chest. He felt a momentary surge of panic.
Then he heard a click behind him.
Instinctively, Chainbridge fell sideways and fired the flare gun in the direction of the sound. The cartridge took off across the pathway and struck a man full square in the chest. More startled than injured, the bright red chemicals suddenly ignited his clothes. His submachine gun clattered to the ground as he tried to struggle out of the flaming material. The fire ran out of control and the screaming started.
Chainbridge finally found a pistol in the bag. He shot the burning man and caught another guard in the chest point blank as he came around the corner in response to the commotion.
Rising unsteadily, Chainbridge grabbed tufts of dried grass and tossed them onto the burning man.
He started shouting "Fire!"

***

All along the third-floor corridor, Eva braced herself for more security; there was none. She could smell smoke along the corridor, it was creeping out from under the door of Halidane´s makeshift operating theatre.
In the elevator, with a conspiratorial finger to his lips, Halidane produced from his inside pocket, a flat card with rectangular holes in it.

"It's my secret floor, Ingrid. Our little secret."

Eva thought of Halidane´s esteemed guests – how long could it be before he was missed and someone was sent to find him?

"The greenhouse, Edgar?"

He stared at her with pupils no larger than pin pricks. He idly scratched the puncture hole where Eva had injected him,

"Better, oh so much better, Ingrid..."

He opened a flap below the elevator´s buttons and slotted in the card. The elevator plummeted to a sub-basement.
Their footsteps echoed along the metal floors. The air smelt tired and the walls were greasy with condensation. The cowl offered little warmth. Dampness pervaded the atmosphere as they

descended to the lower basement. Eva´s gun was buried in Halidane's ribs.

The entire corridor was clad in buffed, smooth metal. Floor and ceiling lights cast a harsh sodium glare, guiding the way to a wheel-lock door. Tracing his fingers along the metal wall beside it, Halidane pressed his palm down firmly. The wheel-lock spun on hidden gears and silently opened.

It was a chamber more than a room. Hexagonal in shape, every bolted panel was perfectly symmetrical. Looking up and around, Eva saw a vaulted ceiling with enormous coils of copper wiring attached to long metal shafts suspended from the bolt-plated arches. Dials and gauges along a paneled workstation twitched and spun. Several enormous levers – like those found in a railway signals hut – rose from the floor at various angles.

"What are those?" she asked.

"Gears, Ingrid. Gears."

"And that, Edgar?"

It was an artillery shell. It shone burnished shark-like in the overhead lights. It was covered in dark brown daubs similar to the red cuneiform motifs on Eva´s silk robe. It was blood. Swastikas were carved crudely into the metal. It was over twelve feet long and it sat between two long metal rails.

"Rails, standard German gauge, Ingrid – are you ready? You don't have to be that pure," said Halidane. "Close range will suffice."

He was already at the levers, perhaps the narcotic's high was waning. He was starting to move with assurance again. The chamber was freezing.

"Impressive," she said.

She fingered another phial. Switching hands with her gun, she angled her arm to jab him again.

But Edgar Halidane had recovered. Spinning around, he delivered a blow across her jaw. Stunned, Eva staggered back and lost her footing. She fell close to the rails.

Halidane pushed the levers into acute angles.

The floor beneath her began to vibrate. The wheel-lock door began to close. It hissed as it sealed the chamber.

Eva looked around. It was the only door.

"You're about to become part of history, Ingrid," he said.

He turned. He had a Luger in his hand.

Eva didn't pause.

She ploughed the Browning´s four remaining bullets into his body in quick succession.

Halidane got off a wild shot that ricocheted around the room, then he collapsed into the levers, sprawling awkwardly. Knocking them out of synch caused the vibrations to accelerate.

The long metal tubes overhead began to glow. Fingers of energy leapt from point to point. They began to reach out toward the artillery shell. The floor began to get warm.

Eva got to her feet and went over to Halidane. She threw off the robe and forced the two remaining phials of morphine into his neck.

"That's for Brandt, you bastard" she whispered.

"Who?" he gasped.

Blood was flowing from his chest wounds and his skin had taken on a pasty pallor.

With all her weight Eva thrust a lever forward. Halidane howled as his ribs shattered. He flailed his arms and legs like a pinned bug.

The shell was starting to glow. Points of energy were glancing off it. The thousands of coils beneath the rails were beginning to glow.

"It´s too late," shouted Halidane over the static shrieks. "In less than a minute Berlin will be no more than ash. And us with it."

Eva looked around. There was a chair – a high backed chair of wood and metal. It offered little hope, but she dragged it over.

Halidane was laughing amid immense coughs of blood.

She jammed the chair midway along the shell's length, using the rail as a fulcrum. A sudden shift of the world beneath her feet knocked her over.

The shell was beginning to glow from end to end. Eva got to her feet and put everything she had into the chair. The shell shifted slightly. It inched slowly.

She was praying for momentum and tried to lever it further off the rails.

Suddenly, it spun across, knocking her over with its tail.

Halidane had gone quiet. His eyes widened in absolute terror.

Eva wasn't afraid. But instinctively she stepped slowly back. She pressed herself against the wall and inched toward the corner of the chamber. Her fingers sought out anything, a door, a lever, something that offered her a way out.

A white-hot hole was forming on the far wall, but it was flickering, twisting.

"See you in hell, you little bitch," shouted Halidane.

He let out a howl over the sonic shrieks and electrical bursts. A wolf-like howl.

His head slumped onto a lever.

The glow along the far wall was stretching out to mirror the length of the shell. The temperature was approaching a frightening, breath-sucking heat.

Her fingers found a catch. It was hip height against the wall. She pulled it. A hatch opened. It was a heavily armoured chute. She would fit with a squeeze.

She hoped.

Eva forced herself in. It tilted slowly into place. Eva kicked and wriggled, using her weight to close it.

It moved slowly. Too slowly. Squirming in on herself around and down, she pushed her shoulder into the metal wall. It moved another inch. Then a thud came from behind her. Looking back, through the narrowing gap of pulsing red and amber light, Halidane's fingers appeared.

No. No. No, she thought.

Like blinded worms, they inched and sought purchase along the metal rim, pulling the chute back toward the chamber. Eva threw herself further into the wall. Halidane gripped the rim harder. With a monument heave, screaming at the top of her lungs, the fulcrum finally swung, and the chute sealed, shearing off Halidane's digits. They fell onto her feet and legs like burning slugs.

Before she blacked out from the searing heat and exhaustion, she heard the very world beyond opening and catching fire.
The airless hatch felt like a tomb and smelled of blood.
And then became dark.

47

Chainbridge backed the Traction Avant slowly down the driveway. Finding a car key on one of de Witte's assailants, he´d spent an agonising ten minutes getting from the gardens to the line of delegate´s cars where he tried the key in each one until the Citroen fired up.
Guests from the hotel gathered in groups pointing to the blaze on the top floor. A deafening shriek of glass and metal made everyone dive for cover. The greenhouse had collapsed. A tapering finger of flame shot toward the heavens, followed by a deep rumbling. Chainbridge stopped the car.
The passenger door opened.

"Small world, Henry," said a voice.

Chainbridge squeezed his eyes shut and gave a heartfelt sigh. Raising both hands he turned to face his executioner.

"McElhone?"

The American OSS man dressed in evening attire, flashed the identity badge inside his jacket pocket.

"Word is that the Russian Embassy in Bern just dispatched two Zil limos full of NKGB from their consulate in Zürich. One of Beria's top guys is running the show; just flew in from Moscow. They'll be here before the fire tenders and Kantonspolizei."

"I'm waiting for Eva," replied Chainbridge.

"Henry, I'm instructed to get you in one piece to Konstanz. Right now. If the Russians find you here, you're finished – drive."

"Five minutes, Ed?"
McElhone looked at his watch. The hands were spinning wildly.
"We'll have to guess what five minutes looks like."
The entire top floor of the Hotel Prestige au Lac was now a raging inferno.
"That her handiwork over there?"
"Yes."
"She's some gal, Henry!"
Chainbridge reversed to the front gate, turned off the headlights but left the engine running.
"What brings you here?" he asked.
"Edgar Halidane, Henry. We think he's screwing us as well as the Germans."
They felt, rather than heard, the knocking on the back window. It was Eva.
Chainbridge leapt out and opened the door for her. McElhone took the driver´s seat.
"You OK?"
Eva looked bedraggled and reeked like an industrial smelter.
"Yes."
"Halidane?"
"Dead."
She opened her hand, in her palm was Halidane's ring finger.
"Let's go, so," said Chainbridge.
He rolled the window down and tossed out the severed digit. The ring with the engraved grinning SS Totenkopf framed in swastikas was pocketed.
"I'll drive," said McElhone. "Eva."
He grinned at her in the rear-view mirror.
"Agent McElhone. Long way from home?"
"Here on the orders of President Truman."
McElhone floored the accelerator and swept the car in a tight circle out of the hotel grounds.
"If we can get to the Konstanz Bridge, we have a chance - you'll be in the American sector. Any idea what Halidane was up to?"
"I didn't stick around long enough to find out," said Eva.

"If the Russians are showing their hand in a neutral jurisdiction, you're a wanted woman," said McElhone.
The Citroën bucked and bounced along the lakeside road. A fleet of police cars, official limousines, fire engines and ambulances tore past them heading towards the blazing hotel.
McElhone slowed down to avoid attracting attention. Once the taillights disappeared in the mirror, he accelerated.
The city lights appeared as the roadway merged with the main thoroughfare. Chainbridge was lost in his thoughts. De Witte lay in the ruins of the hotel. He felt a pang of survivor guilt.
"Shit," muttered McElhone.
In the mirror appeared three heavy black cars.
"Russian Zils. Goddamn NKGB!"
They were catching up fast. McElhone swung the wheel and the vehicle pitched and bumped down one side street after another. The Russian cars split up to patrol the area.
"I know a short-cut," said Chainbridge. "Pull over."
A thunder cloud had drifted in over the city. It pulsed with lightening, then the deluge began. Droplets pounded off the roof and bonnet of the Citroën as they switched drivers. Chainbridge set off at a sedate speed through the backstreets before turning onto the main road to Winterthur. It was just as they passed that town, forty minutes later, that the Russian Zils reappeared. Chainbridge tapped the clutch twice and hit the accelerator. The Citroën slipped and skidded, then found its grip. They were minutes from the town of Kreuzlingen and beyond, Konstanz´s Old Rhine Bridge.
As soon as the Zils got within range the gunfire began.
Eva felt around the car's back seat.
"Either of you have a gun?"
"No."
A bullet clipped the back window and knocked out a tail light. Chainbridge yanked on the wheel to shift the target. McElhone and Eva scrambled for grip as another pulse of rain slammed into the windscreen.
"There it is, Henry, the bridge, up ahead."

On the far side was a US army detachment. Chainbridge flashed his headlights and sounded the horn.
The Russian marksman in the first car wiped the rain from his face. The vehicle in front was weaving wildly and making a dreadful din. The bridge was coming up fast.
He took a breath and exhaled as he squeezed the trigger.
The machine pistol barked into life and the bullets struck the two back tyres, blowing them out.
A trail of sparks arced up behind the crippled Citroën. The next burst of gunfire shattered the back window.
Chainbridge braked hard and the car spun wildly around. It crashed into a fence and slid backwards for several hundred yards.
The three Russian cars slowed down and came to a halt.

48

Old Rhine Bridge; Zurich

Before the Russian cars screeched to a halt, Eva leapt from the Citroën and sprinted in her stockinged feet. Shattered glass fell from her hair like sprinkled light. Her long legs propelled her pell-mell to the bridge and she expected to be cut down by machine gun fire at any moment. Her breathing was raw, tearing at her lungs. She heard shouts in Russian then Chainbridge shouting something back, also in Russian.
Eva reached the side of the bridge and vaulted onto the side rail. Despite the rain she managed to get her footing on the slippery ledge. She looked over her shoulder at Chainbridge one last time.
"Eva," he mouthed.
She didn't seem to recognise him; a decision had been reached. Chainbridge thought of the moment she walked into his shop in London. A girl with a newspaper under arm, barely out of school. With one smooth movement that hung for a moment in time, Eva slipped off the bridge into the waters of Lake Konstanz below.

Valery Yvetchenko, Commissar first rank of the NKGB, stepped out of the first Zil limousine. With a casual gesture, he motioned for one of his detail to follow him to the bridge.

The soldier strafed the waters with his machine gun. The pops of the bullets caught on the breeze. Yvetchenko leaned forward, spying something. Producing his side-arm he carefully aimed and fired. This prompted the other men of the detail to unsling their weapons. The soldiers fired in controlled bursts, directed by Yvetchenko's pistol.

He shouted for a torch.

Chainbridge began to drag himself on leaden feet towards them. A soldier turned and levelled his weapon at him. Chainbridge stopped. He raised his hands as if, somehow, this alone would save him.

Commissar Yvetchenko raised his arm and the firing stopped. A soldier passed him a powerful torch. Yvetchenko panned it over the side in broad sweeps. With a satisfied grunt, he tossed it back to the soldier. He turned and faced Chainbridge. He inspired true fear.

"She made her choice, Yvetchenko," said Chainbridge.

Yvetchenko's wire framed glasses glinted in the Citroën´s headlights.

"I completely concur with her decision. She was a collaborator. A foreign spy."

Yvetchenko´s English was guttural and slowly annunciated.

The armed detail filed in behind him. Chainbridge looked past them. More cars were coming. More Russians, probably out of Bern.

"So ... this is how it ends?" asked Chainbridge.

"I'm afraid so, sir."

"You may lower your weapons, I pose no threat," said Chainbridge.

"Just you and her?"

"Yes."

The Citroën's engine was still ticking over. Smoke rose from the back and the whole vehicle appeared somewhat deflated in the pouring rain.

Yvetchenko holstered his pistol. The rain was falling heavier now, worming its way down inside collars of coats, shirts and uniforms. Droplets swirled in the headlights.

Slowly, Chainbridge unbuttoned his overcoat.

"May I?"

Yvetchenko nodded.

Chainbridge reached with one hand into the folds of the coat, his other hand still raised. He produced the cigarette case, emblazoned with the red star.

As Chainbridge lowered his hands, Yvetchenko barked at his men. They walked back to their vehicles with the louche assurance of untouchability.

"One for luck, comrade?" shouted Chainbridge. His voice bounced on the breeze against the metal of the bridge. He tossed the cigarette case. Yvetchenko caught it awkwardly with a gloved hand. He opened it and walked into the no-man's land between them.

They stood facing each other. An old man in a heavy overcoat and a pitbull in a soviet uniform, one of the new masters of Europe. Yvetchenko proffered the cigarette case and Chainbridge took out two. They shared a light and smoked.

"Thank you, comrade," said Chainbridge.

He was buying time; time to run, or – the thought only now occurring to him – time to kill Yvetchenko. Either way, the odds weren't in his favour. Any commotion risked McElhone being discovered and shipped off to a detention centre in Moscow as if he had never existed.

"You can keep the case," said Chainbridge.

"It was a gift?"

"Times have changed."

"I agree, times have changed."

Chainbridge fought the urge to run to the bridge, leap into the water and hope for the best. The bridge itself vibrated as the first of the vehicles reversed into the darkness.

"I hope you're not offended?"

"Offended?"

"The cigarette case."

"No, Henry. No. Thank you."
Yvetchenko finished his cigarette and stubbed it out methodically with his boot.

"Perhaps we should both quit, comrade?" said Chainbridge.

"Perhaps," replied Yvetchenko. He turned the cigarette case over in his free hand.

"Unfortunately, this option isn't available to me, comrade."
Chainbridge offered his hand.

"As of today, I have officially retired. May I wish you the very best of luck?"
Yvetchenko pulled his glasses off his head and stared at his adversary. The old Soviet dog removed a glove and took his hand. Chainbridge noticed raw scars across the fingers and knuckles, still far from being healed. His face was puffy in places from crude stitching. The commissar looked like he´d been assembled using parts of various men.

"Farewell, Henry. Enjoy your retirement."
He turned and walked back to his shiny black limousine. The driver hopped out and stood to attention at the passenger door. The staff car reversed slowly back and was swallowed by the night.
A sudden squall drenched Chainbridge. He seemed rooted to the spot. He pressed his hat down firmly on his head and glanced at where Eva had leapt from the bridge. Findlay, Hopkins, Keyburn, Curran, Pannu, de Witte, Brandt and Eva. All dead. He took one last drag on his cigarette and crushed it with his shoe. It lay twisted alongside Yvetchenko's.
Oblivious to the rain, Chanbridge walked back towards the Citroën.

"Hey Ed, it´s me, it´s clear."
McElhone crawled out from the rear footwell. He pulled the collar of his rain coat up and stood beside Chainbridge.

"You OK?" he asked.

"Yes, yes, I am, thank you."

"Eva?"

"Gone."

"Gone?"

"She threw herself off the bridge."

"Jesus Christ, Henry. I'm sorry. I had to keep my head down. If I´d been spotted ..."

"She made her choice, McElhone. I think it was the right one."

"The reds would've tortured her."

They stood side-by-side in the rain. It seemed impossible but the rain fell harder still, drenching every pore, every layer of material.

"Let's get going, Henry."

"To Berlin?"

"Yes, Berlin. I've a place you can stay."

"The car's pretty well beaten up, McElhone."

"Then I'll guess we'll have to walk, Henry. And hope there isn't a late-night train."

Henry Chainbridge, MI6, Int.7., (retired) and Edward Patrick McElhone, OSS, trudged along the sleepers of the rain-lashed bridge to Konstanz.

And on to Berlin.

THE END.

Eva's wartime series:

Get Lenin

Zinnman

A Finger of Night

Hollow Point

Eagles Hunt Wolves

Eva Molenaar – Born 1917 / died 1946. No known next of kin.
"*Niech Spoczywa w Pokoju* "

Author Bio

Robert Craven has been writing short stories and novels since 1992.

His Eva series: Get Lenin, Zinnman, A Finger of Night and Hollow Point have received rave reviews and garnered four and five-star reviews on both Amazon and Kobo platforms.

His Sebastian Holt novel 'The Road of a Thousand Tigers' released in 2018 went to No.#1 on Kobo downloads during the summer of 2019 in Canada, Australia and New Zealand.

A former touring musician, he also regularly reviews CDs for Independent Irish Review Ireland.

Robert is a member of the Irish Writer's Union, and lives in Dublin.

Printed in Great Britain
by Amazon

55336555R00154